A Witchly Influence

A Witchly Influence

a novel by
STEPHANIE GREY

Livonia, Michigan

Editor: Grace Nehls

Published by BHC Press

Library of Congress Control Number: 2020934351

ISBN: 978-1-64397-139-1 (Hardcover)
ISBN: 978-1-64397-140-7 (Softcover)
ISBN: 978-1-64397-141-4 (Ebook)

For information, write:
BHC Press
885 Penniman #5505
Plymouth, MI 48170

Visit the publisher:
www.bhcpress.com

Also by Stephanie Grey

The Immortal Prudence Blackwood

For my mother, Diana,
for being a wonderful woman
whose love and support for
my passion in life never wavered.
You are truly inspirational, Mom.

Always.

A Witchly Influence

Chapter One

T he courtroom was smaller than I had imagined, and much colder. It was in an older building and had high ceilings with beautifully carved crown molding. The floor had been replaced over time with cheap linoleum worn thin after thousands of feet had crossed it over the years. The judge sat high and mighty in his chair, the leather polished to a gloss so shiny it was almost comical.

I took a seat in the audience section and the chair squeaked loudly. I cleared my throat and the seat quieted immediately. The seats were burgundy and made out of some rough fabric that was meant to be durable, but really took away from the original architecture of the building. Another chill passed through me and I looked upward. Warm air began to flow over me and I smiled, shrugging off my coat and putting my gloves into my purse. I ran a quick hand over my pale blonde hair to smooth the static that threatened it.

A small gate separated the audience from the actual participants. It reminded me of a perfect little fence you'd see in front of a row of perfect little houses, though this was stained a rich brown and not whitewashed.

Today there were four people facing the judge: a couple and their lawyers. One of the lawyers was average height, a little plump, and had curls that were so filled with gel that they looked glisteningly wet. He unbuttoned his dove gray suit and leaned forward on his table. "My client wants everything," he said easily.

The other lawyer, a scrawny man wearing pinstripes, shot up from his chair. "Absolutely not!" he protested. "The assets are meant to be split equally."

The first lawyer snickered. "In the case of infidelity, that is out of the question," he argued.

"That has yet to be proven."

"There has to be a DNA test on the child when it is born. I believe that proves that your client is an adulterer."

I ducked my head to hide my smile. This was better than reality television!

The judge interrupted the arguing attorneys. "Regardless of who has fathered this child, this couple will agree to a parental agreement for the unborn child. The agreement shall be null and void, *should* the paternity test show negative for the plaintiff. I would suggest that you discuss with your clients in further detail on how to equally divide their assets. We will continue this at a later date." The judge dismissed the couple and called for the next case.

A tall woman with a pile of messy, yellow hair tugged nervously at her red sweater and entered through the small gate.

"You're here for a divorce on the grounds of irreconcilable differences," stated the judge.

"Yes, sir," she responded.

The judge's eyebrows shot up as he scanned her documents. "You've been separated for eleven years?"

"We have been, yes."

The judge chuckled. "What's the rush for a divorce then?" he asked, still laughing.

The woman relaxed and laughed as well. "I just felt like it was time to stop putting off the inevitable."

"Sure, no sense in waiting a long time to get this sort of thing done. I hereby grant you divorced. Please go to the clerk's office for your official decree."

The woman said her thanks and left hurriedly.

I was still smiling when my husband walked through the heavy, wooden doors and into the courtroom. My smile immediately turned to a scowl. Had I known he didn't have to be here for this process, I would have insisted I come alone.

Matthew's face broke out into a wide grin when he saw me. He swooped his dark hair out of his eyes—he looked ridiculous with his emo haircut—and headed in my direction. He was wearing all black and it didn't escape my attention that he was wearing clothes that I had purchased for him. "Do you mind if I sit here?" he asked carefully.

I wanted to tell him to get the hell away from me. Instead, I was polite and merely nodded.

He plopped down in the chair and it squeaked. "It's a lot warmer over here, isn't it?" he asked. "You must've done something about that."

I ignored his comment. I'd take care of his memory later.

"So, how long have you been here?" he asked.

"I actually got here on time."

"Of course you did. Five minutes early is on time for you. I always did admire that about you, Carmen."

"Punctuality? That's something you admired?" I snapped. I stopped myself. I wasn't going to get into an argument with this idiotic man. "That's enough from you until the judge calls us," I said and his lips sealed shut.

We sat in silence as more couples were declared divorced. Finally, the judge called for us. "Matthew and Carmen Ferrara."

Matthew's mouth unsealed and he held the gate open for me as we passed through it and faced the judge. I turned and beckoned for the warm air to follow me and it sidled next to me, my own personal furnace in the drafty room. The movement was so subtle that no one noticed, except for my husband.

There was a rustling of papers as the judge fumbled through our paperwork. We had opted to not use lawyers because he couldn't afford one and I wasn't offering to pay for it. That was something Matthew was learning the hard way: life without a bank roll wasn't as easy as he had thought it would be.

"I see you, too, are suffering from irreconcilable differences," the judge said, looking at us over his reading glasses.

A husband running around with several other women is more like it, but that wasn't an option on the questionnaire when I had originally filled out the paperwork.

"Yes," Matthew and I said in unison.

The judge waved his hands around, feeling helpless. "Is everything in these documents true? You have nothing to add?"

"That's correct," I answered.

"I see that you wish to take back your maiden name of Devereaux."

"I do," I said.

Matthew's mouth dropped open in shock and I bit the inside of my cheek to keep myself from grinning at his reaction.

The judge sighed heavily. "I hereby declare you two divorced. You may go down to the clerk's office to pick up your divorce decree."

And just like that, I was a free woman.

Matthew followed me to the clerk's office, chatting idly about his day and his family as if nothing had just happened.

There were several clerks milling around the dingy beige-and-tan office, busily handing out paperwork. One stopped, took our names, and darted off to retrieve our documents. She disappeared behind a row of gray filing cabinets, but the sound of her shoes tapping against the concrete floor could still be heard.

"My brother's thinking about going back to school," Matthew was saying.

I was tapping a short pink fingernail against the desk, my patience having run dry. "Will you shut up? What do you think just happened here?" I asked.

Matthew stopped, his expression wounded. "I was just trying to make conversation."

"You're my ex-husband and I have no ties to you anymore. I don't care about you or your life."

He gulped. "I thought we'd still be friends, you know?"

I laughed coldly.

"Why can't we be?"

I snapped my fingers and everyone in the room froze except for the two of us. "You cheated on me several times. I worked my ass off while you tried to write a book and what did you do while I was gone all day? You screwed other women. I paid for everything and let me tell you something, you selfish prick. That new lady of yours that you didn't think I knew about, how do you think she's going to take it when she realizes that you're nothing but a broke piece of shit with no ambition and drive? You're lucky I didn't give you a permanently flaccid dick!" I paused, mulling over the idea. I dismissed it immediately. The Council didn't really appreciate it when we interfered like that with a mortal. I wouldn't get in trouble save for a mere slap on the wrist, but it wasn't worth having the point added to my record. I already had one over the hippopotamus incident. You hang a cheating husband over a river filled with hippos and suddenly you're "endangering" someone.

Matthew was looking down at his black shoes, his cheeks flaming. "I was hoping we could be friends because we've known each other for so long that it'd be weird not having you in my life."

"When we part ways today, you will never see or hear from me again," I promised. "You just want to ask for money anyway, don't you?"

Matthew was silent.

"Of course you did." I snapped my fingers and everyone went back into motion as if nothing had happened. I shook my head. "I don't even know why I fell in love with you in the first place."

A red plume of smoke appeared suddenly and a skinny woman wearing a red leotard covered with hearts stood next to us, her smile too white and eager. "Need a reminder why you're in love, you say?" she asked.

I looked up toward the ceiling. "You thought a Cupid would be a good idea now?" The Cupid held up her harp. "Don't you fucking dare start playing that thing," I warned. "We're already divorced."

"Really?" The cupid frowned and pulled a scroll out of her harpsichord. "I see." She shook her fist toward the ceiling. "We've got a communication problem back at headquarters." She shrugged. "Whatever. Well, good luck!" She vanished, this time without the theatrical smoke.

The clerk finally returned and handed us each an envelope. She patted my hand tenderly. "You take that with you, honey, when you go to change your name." She shot Matthew a frown. "Shouldn't take too long."

I nodded and thanked her. I left the clerk's office, Matthew almost on my heels. He shoved his hands into his pockets for warmth as we went outside into the frigid air. "If you ever need help or just anything, please call me. I mean it."

I paused and looked into his brown eyes. They were sad and I knew he was close to crying. I had been that upset, but that was seven months ago when we first separated after my discovery of his infidelity. Less than a month after our separation, I presented to him the divorce papers and made him go through the photos to choose which ones he wanted. I kept a few photos for myself, though I was just biding my time until I could get a proper bonfire going and burn them all. I couldn't erase the memory, but I could erase some of the evidence of our marriage.

"Speaking of erasing," I murmured. Matthew took a step back and I grabbed his wrist.

"Please don't. I don't want to forget."

"If I don't do it, they will and you don't want the Erasers doing it. They're a nasty bunch." The Erasers were actually a group of very nice men and women who quickly and quietly Erased magic from the memories of mortals, but I didn't want them to clean up my mess. That would be unnerving. Matthew hung his head again and his wrist went limp. I pushed back his sleeve and rubbed my fingers against his skin. Most mortals couldn't recognize magic when they saw it, but witches and wizards could create an invisible tattoo to counter this. It was a pain in the butt to get the permit for one, but you just had to write a quick letter to the Council requesting permission for a removal. They generally responded with an approval signature in less than a minute.

Matthew's skin turned red as I rubbed it and he flinched. It did burn slightly, but I was removing a tattoo, not taking him for a walk in the park. Satisfied that it was gone, I released his wrist. His eyes had glazed over and he blinked several times to clear his vision. "Is magic real?" I asked tentatively.

"What?" he asked, confused. "You've got the wildest imagination." He smiled and shook his head.

He followed me to my Volvo and watched me toss my belongings into my passenger seat. He held out his arms expectedly.

"What in the hell are you doing?" I asked.

"I thought it would be nice to hug one last time before you disappear from my life for forever," he answered simply.

I snickered. He was an ass who had brought this upon himself. I ignored his outstretched arms. "Goodbye, Matthew," I said.

His arms dropped pitifully to his sides. "Goodbye," he said softly.

I pulled the door shut to my sedan and started the engine. I watched my ex-husband walk away and I began to giggle uncontrollably.

"Everything go all right?" asked a voice that surrounded me.

"Sure, it was fine as far as getting divorced goes," I answered. I turned up the radio so that I could hear the voice that belonged to my boss, Simon Walters, more easily.

"That's great. Listen, you take all of the time you need."

"I'll be back on Monday."

"Monday?" Simon was sitting in my back seat. He was a short, stocky man who closely resembled a bull frog. He pushed his glasses up on his nose. "That's awfully soon. It's only Friday."

I turned around in my seat to face him. "I know that. I'm going to change my name today."

"Why don't you just use magic for that?"

"It's the red tape. Easier to just do it the mortal way."

Simon nodded and ran his hand over his short, spikey hair that he thought would hide his onset of hair loss. "I get it. You're not going to be alone tonight, are you? You could come over and have dinner. Cindy makes a mean chicken casserole."

I debated. My boss's wife was an amazing cook, even without magic. "No," I finally said. "I'm going to go out and drink away my wiles."

"You're leaving this boat of a car behind, right? Don't know why you bother driving around most of the time."

"Hey, now!" I protested. I put my hands on either side of my steering wheel as if the car had ears and could hear us. "I like my Volvo. Some of us still like to drive around to blend in a little more easily. Some mortals can recognize magic, you know."

"Keeps the Erasers in a job," Simon argued.

"And you're just helping out the economy, right?" I laughed.

He grinned and pointed to himself. "That's me! Listen, Cindy and I figured you'd do something stupid, so here's a cake." He touched the seat next to him and a cake appeared, hovering as if in a bubble. "You start a marriage with a cake. Might as well end it with one, too."

Neon lights began to flash above it. "HAPPY DIVORCE, CARMEN!" it read.

"Thanks," I said. "That looks delicious!"

"Be careful. Teleport if you can't drive!" In an instant, Simon was gone.

I checked to make sure the cake was still in its bubble and pulled out onto the road, heading toward the social security office.

Chapter Two

Hours later, I was standing in the doorway of my townhouse. I hung up my keys on the hook by the door and frowned when I saw the second hook. I waved my hand over it and it was gone, as if it had never been there.

Exhausted, I fell onto my navy blue couch and sighed. It had been a long day, but I was officially Carmen Devereaux again. The thought made me grin and I sat up, beckoning my mirror to me. It hopped off the wall and floated over to me and I stared at my reflection: long pale blonde hair, pale blue eyes, and pale skin. I had tried to alter my appearance when I was a teenager so I wouldn't look so odd, but my mother showed me what women pay in a salon for my hair color and I decided maybe how I looked wasn't so bad after all.

Seeing my long hair, I raised my hands upward and gently touched the top of my shoulders. The length shortened to what I had once heard someone call a lob and I nodded, happy with the new hairstyle. "Thank you, very much," I said and the mirror returned to its space on the wall by the front door.

I was pouring myself a glass of wine when my doorbell rang. "Surprise!"

I smiled. Three women stood on my front porch and ushered past me after I opened the door.

"Just in time! She's already drinking alone!" Tess Lyon said. She put her hand on her forehead dramatically.

"Yes, thank goodness we caught her in time," Siobhan Waters said, her tone dripping with sarcasm. "It's like none of us have ever done that, even without having a good reason." She winked at me.

Enid Wilson was quiet, observing the rest of us. She poured a glass of wine for herself and the others before speaking. "How about a toast?" We raised our glasses. "To Carmen not having the balls to shrivel his dick, which means she didn't get in trouble with the Council and can hang out with her friends tonight!"

"To not shriveling his dick!" the rest of us cheered and clinked our glasses.

"I thought about making it always flaccid," I admitted.

"The Council would have put you on probation," Tess said, flinging her red hair over her shoulder.

"It would have been worth it, wouldn't it, hun?" Siobhan said mischievously.

I laughed. "Maybe."

"What is this? A divorce cake?" Enid was already back in my kitchen for more wine. The neon lights were still flashing obnoxiously. "How clever," she surmised and she began to cut into it with a knife that appeared out of nowhere.

"I have real knives," I said.

"I like mine from home better." She finished slicing the cake into not so equal parts and served them.

"Did Cindy make this?" Tess asked between mouthfuls of chocolate. "Of course she did. I wish the wife of my boss baked like this for me." She frowned.

"That's what happens when you take a mortal job working as a buyer for a department store," Siobhan said. She was scraping the icing off the top of her slice. Enid leaned over and scooped it up with her fork. "I was saving that for last!" she protested.

"You snooze, you lose. Icing's the best part," Enid replied. Her tongue had turned blue from the frosting.

Tess scowled. "Mortals are good bakers. Krispy Kreme is delicious!"

"If you think every single tasty batch they serve doesn't have some sort of sorcery behind it, you're a nut," Enid said. "Their doughnuts are too good to not have a wizard or witch in the kitchen." She ate another bite of cake. "We should get doughnuts later, by the way."

"Is she serious?" Tess asked, looking at me.

"I have no idea," I answered truthfully.

"I'm afraid she's right," Siobhan said. "I dated a health inspector once who checked out one of their kitchens and let me tag along."

"My point is that it doesn't matter if you have a mortal job or not, people are people and they can be good bosses or they can be jerks like mine. It's a universal thing, not mortals versus the magical community," Tess said, annoyed.

"I told you that you can come work with me," Siobhan said.

I started coughing as the wine caught in my throat. "You're a Muse. You're born a Muse, not made into one. How in the hell could Tess work with you?"

"She could be my assistant," Siobhan replied.

"What kind of Muse needs an assistant?" I asked, incredulous.

"Sometimes I might not be able to leave a client for lunch and I need someone to get it for me."

Enid rolled her eyes. "You're a witch, woman! Magic is your assistant." She took a long swig from her glass. "Needs someone to get her lunch. The nerve," she muttered.

"You could always work with Enid," I suggested.

"Enid's job is so boring!" Tess said. "You have to learn history and stuff."

"Better to have knowledge in that brain of yours instead of air," Enid said, laughing.

"Is that a redhead joke?" Tess asked.

"It might be," Enid answered. She collected the empty dessert plates and put them in the sink. I heard the water turn on as she began washing dishes. Enid liked to do things herself most of the time.

"Enid's job is pretty interesting," I said thoughtfully. She worked as a tour guide for a historical company called *The Past is Us*. It took guests through historical events where they could see important moments in history happen live, all from the safety of their invisible train cars. They used to let guests mill around and interact with the people, but their Record Keeper discovered too many events were being altered and had to be repaired, so the invisible train idea was created and utilized instead.

"But you have to know history," Tess insisted. "I like fashion. Besides, I can get away with little things against my boss. I cursed his coffee mug so that its contents turn cold after the first sip." She smiled, satisfied with herself.

"Why even bother with the first sip?" I asked.

Tess waved her hand dismissively. "I did that once, but he yelled at the receptionist and called her incompetent. This way, it drives him crazy every day and no one else gets into trouble. You'd think the guy would learn to use another coffee cup."

We laughed and Enid, having returned from the kitchen, pointed out that there was no more wine left. "We should go out," she suggested.

I shook my head. "Oh, no. I'm done for the day."

Siobhan stood and put her hands on her hips. Her honey-colored hair swirled around her shoulders as she pointed at me and spoke sternly. "Listen here, Carmen. You're a free woman finally and there are endless possibilities for you."

"She means men. Lots and lots of men," Enid interrupted.

Siobhan shushed her. "I'm doing a motivational speech here, Enid." She looked at me again. "We need to celebrate!"

"There's a nice bar downtown," I said.

"Downtown? I think we can do better than that!" Siobhan waved her hands and we were all sitting in a private room that barely muted the loud music outside its walls.

Enid looked down at her clothes she was still wearing from work that day and frowned. "How nice of you to take us to Paris and not bother to change our clothes for us," she said. She smoothed her hand over her yellow polo and it became a tiny, silver halter top. When she looked up from her creation, she saw us gaping at her and shrugged. "Siobhan can't always be the loose one in the group."

I laughed so hard that tears sprang from my eyes. We spent the evening dancing and drinking in Paris, and now we were walking down an alley to a bar somewhere in Ireland that Tess insisted had the best stuffed potatoes she'd ever eaten.

The bar was small, but warm and still filled with locals. They were wearing what I could only imagine as being the itchiest wool sweaters, which made me laugh even harder that they were fulfilling the stereotype. They stared at us when we walked through the door, but Enid's return gaze was harsh enough that they turned away almost immediately.

"Look, a karaoke machine!" Tess said excitedly.

Siobhan flipped through the book of music. "These are mostly nineties songs," she murmured. "Fantastic! I've got Gem!"

"Gem? Get serious. This is a party! No sappy songs. Where's Alana Freebird? Now *she's* got some stuff we can sing!" Enid scribbled her request on a napkin and shoved it into the DJ's pocket.

As Enid belted out old relationship ballads, the rest of us cheered her on from a table we had commandeered near the small karaoke stage. Soon, Siobhan joined her and they sang a duet, swaying back and forth to the music.

The bartender yelled for last call and Tess booed in protest. She chugged her rum and Coke and requested another.

"That's enough for everyone, I think," I said and teleported all of us back to my townhouse. I turned the spare bed into three mattresses to accommodate my friends and left them to sleep off their alcohol. Siobhan was still complaining that we had left too early as I closed the door to their room.

The next morning, I woke up to my head feeling like it was stuffed with cotton. I snapped my fingers and I could immediately smell bacon sizzling from my kitchen. Reluctantly, I wandered out of bed and down the stairs where the bacon was laying itself on a paper towel and the eggs were scrambling themselves.

Tess cheerfully bounded into the room. "Good morning to you!" she said happily, helping herself to orange juice.

"Oh, make her shut up." Enid groaned. She had plopped down on the couch, Siobhan next to her.

"She took some No Hangover before we started drinking," Siobhan said. "Thanks for sharing, by the way."

"I thought you all had already had some," Tess said innocently. She served herself eggs and bacon. "This looks wonderful!"

"If you don't turn down the cheer, I'm going to do it for you," Enid warned. Her hair fell in tangles around her face and her makeup had smeared so much that she looked like she was ready to host a children's party as a clown. She leaned her head against the back of the couch and immediately closed her eyes. "Why is the sunlight so bright?" she muttered.

"Eat and you'll feel better." Tess set the table and motioned for the others to join her.

I held my head in my hands. "Thanks," I mumbled.

"You're welcome!" Tess replied.

As the dishes cleaned themselves, we gathered in my living room. "What are your plans now?" Siobhan asked.

I sighed. I had moved to South Bend, Indiana to go to school and wound up staying after I had met Matthew. I had always wanted to move somewhere else, but didn't because Matthew was close to his family and he didn't want to leave them. They didn't know I was a witch, so it would have been suspicious if we had visited too often. I stayed for him, for his love for his family. "I don't know," I finally said. "I just know I don't want to stay here."

Tess leaned forward and patted my knee. "Why don't you move to Paris? We could be neighbors!" she said excitedly.

"I don't speak the language."

"Speak the language? Don't be ridiculous. Everyone speaks English and you could get a Translator to teach you."

"A Translator would take forever. They get paid by the hour," Siobhan said. "Move to Nashville where I am. It's got everything you could possibly want and you could still drive that Volvo of yours around so you can feel like you fit in with the mortals."

"Am I going to need to defend my sedan two days in a row? I *like* my Volvo."

"I'd say move to Sheridan, but I kind of like having Wyoming to myself."

"No one has a state to themselves," Tess said.

"Oh, I'm sorry. I meant having a place where none of you live so I can get some privacy and peace," Enid corrected herself.

"Does it really matter where you live? You can teleport anywhere. You could live in a cottage in the woods where you don't have a neighbor for miles and miles," Siobhan said.

"No…" my voice trailed off. I was quiet for a moment while my friends watched me. "I think I'll move back home."

"Move back home? What are you, twelve?" Enid asked, incredulous.

"No, not back in with my family. Move back to my hometown. Be close to family, to friends. My stepfamily doesn't know that Mom and I are witches. It'd be nice to see my stepbrothers and their children more often."

"That's what the holidays are for, hun," Siobhan said.

"I think that's a great idea,"Tess said. "I think we all need to go, leave Carmen alone so that she can have some time to herself." She stood up and waited for the others to join her.

Enid motioned for her purse and it slid over to her. She put on her sunglasses tiredly.

"What's with the sunglasses? It's raining outside and you'll be home in a second anyway,"Tess asked.

Enid groaned. "My eyes hurt."

With a soft pop, my friends were gone and I was alone with my thoughts again.

Monday morning arrived too quickly and I found myself back at work, surrounded by the pale yellow walls of my office, going through a stack of permit requests. To my annoyance, they had been dumped in the middle of my desk and on my chair instead of in the box clearly labeled "INBOX." I suppose my coworkers thought it was more of a suggestion than a direction and I waved my hand so the requests landed neatly in a pile where they belonged.

I was looking through one particular request where a woman wanted to enchant her son's tree house to look like it wasn't there so that she wouldn't be in violation of her homeowner's association rules. I shook my head. Mortals and their homeowner's associations were such a pain in the butt. I scribbled my signature of approval on the bottom of the form and folded it. The paper zoomed away toward the green mailbox down the hallway. The woman would have her response within a few minutes and I hoped her son enjoyed his tree house.

Simon knocked on my door and, without waiting for a response, strolled into my office and sat down in an orange guest chair across from me. He placed his stubby hands over each armrest and was smiling oddly at me, his eyes glinting. "I hear you want to move back home."

"How did you know?"

"I have my ways," he said mysteriously.

"The hell you do."

"Okay, you caught me." He spread his hands out, palms facing upward. "Cindy said that, when she got divorced, that was her first move. She wanted to be close to family. Of course, then she met *this* handsome man who convinced her to stay in town."

"Are you telling me you're Cindy's third marriage?" I said, a brow raised.

"What?" Simon's jaw was moving as he figured out my jab. "You're really funny," he said drily.

Chuckling, I reached for another request to review. "Did you want something or did you come in here to try and fool me into thinking you were a mind reader?"

"Actually, I did come in here for a good reason," Simon replied, his tone more serious. "Are you really planning on moving back to North Carolina?"

"Are you going to make fun of my sedan and New Bern now? I know it's a small town, and I won't stay there for forever, but I'd like a change of pace." I leaned back in my chair. "Are you worried there won't be a car to tease me about because I'll just teleport directly to the office? Am I taking away the fun you have during the day?"

"Fate says that your job has to change if you move back home," Simon said bluntly.

"What the fuck?" I blurted. I blushed, not having meant to curse. The news was completely unexpected. "I mean, why would Fate want to change my job? They just assign the Muses each day. I'm not a Muse."

"No, but you're going to be an Influencer."

I shook my head. "I don't know what that is. Is that a new thing?"

Simon blinked at the door and it closed. The room instantly felt isolated. He had blocked it from eavesdroppers. "Influencers are people who coax people into the direction they need to take in order to achieve something great in their lives."

"That's what a Muse does."

Simon shook his head. "You're not listening. Muses inspire. It was a Muse that inspired Adolph Hitler to paint what he did."

"But no one liked his paintings," I pointed out.

"Exactly! And look at what happened: he started another World War. Had an Influencer been around to steer him in another direction, he could have opened up a world-famous truffle shop instead and had several baking cookbooks."

"That's outrageous," I said flatly.

"It's not," my boss insisted. "Fate saw that he could have had a different path if he had someone there to gently steer him in another direction."

"Why call it Fate if there are other options?"

Simon waved his hand dismissively. "I don't know. 'Optional Paths' wasn't as cool of a name for that department? It doesn't matter. They recently created the position of Influencers, though it's a secret."

"Why make it a secret?" I asked tentatively.

Simon was silent.

"It's a secret because they are used on witches and wizards," I said slowly.

Simon nodded. "Bingo."

"I chose to move to New Bern and Fate decided my job had to change?"

"I don't make the rules. You made a choice and this is what happens with that choice."

I frowned. "I'll report to Fate, then?"

Simon laughed and stomped his feet gleefully on the carpet. "Do you report to Fate? Oh, that's a good one!"

"Simon," I said, my voice low.

Wiping tears from his eyes, he stopped and cleared his throat. "We all report to them. Not with paperwork, but they're like Elf on the Shelf. They're always watching."

"You mean Santa Claus," I corrected.

"No, I mean Elf on the Shelf. Santa can't watch everyone by himself. The elves are there to keep a closer eye on things. Quit looking at me like that. Fate doesn't have elves working for them. They're union and Fate doesn't like working with union workers, but that's also a secret."

"Naturally," I said lightly.

"You'll still report to me. We can't have people knowing what your real job is, so we're going to have an android do your job while you Influence."

My jaw dropped. "You're replacing me with a robot?"

"No, no, no. Not a *robot*." Simon almost spat the word. "An *android*. Much fancier. Newer technology. It will look just like you. No one will notice, I promise."

"You're telling me Nolan, who has worked next to me for the last ten years, won't notice a robot has taken my place?"

"If someone really needs to talk to you, you'll pop back here. You'll get a signal and poof, there you are, ready to chat." Simon was teetering back and forth in his chair. "I'm so excited for you! This is a great opportunity!"

"This doesn't make sense. If I'm out Influencing, how are people not going to put two and two together that I'm both here, in this office, and also out there, steering people onto a different path?"

Simon looked down at his brown leather shoes. "Uh, that's complicated, but mostly Fate figures that if you're in North Carolina, no one will realize that it's not really you here, in Indiana."

"How convenient."

His eyes brightened. "Isn't it? Anyway, when are you planning to move?"

"I guess next week," I muttered.

Simon clapped his hands. "This is wonderful! An Influencer in my own presence!" He stood up to leave.

"Simon, how do I know who to Influence?"

My boss stopped in the middle of my doorway. "I think Fate gives you something."

"Like a hit list?" I said sarcastically.

Simon turned to me and grinned. "Well, yeah."

Chapter Three

"Hi, Mom!" I exclaimed.

"Jesus, Mary, and Joseph, you scared the hell out of me!" Evelyn Cleary, my mother, leaned down to pick up the tongs she had dropped. She swirled her hand over them and they were clean again. She was still holding them as she hugged me. "I'm so sorry I wasn't there on the day you got divorced, sweetie, but I got the impression you'd want to be alone."

"It's all right, Mom." I quickly recounted what happened, including my new position with Fate. I knew I was breaking a rule by telling her, but my mother was an excellent secret-keeper. She had been a spy before I was born, but that was the extent of my knowledge on that because, as she had said, it had been top secret work. There was a piece of the Berlin Wall in a shadow box on display inside her home, though she never admitted that was what the object really was. I had stumbled upon its true origins when I was a teenager at a museum and realized one of the blocks of broken wall on display had a piece where my mother's keepsake would have fit perfectly. I never asked her about it, though. She wouldn't have told me anyway.

Using her pinky, Mom pushed her light brown hair away from her face, her red mouth a thin line. "That's quite the promotion. I met one once…" her voice trailed off, a twinkle in her eye.

"Who was he?"

Mom's lips pursed. "I can't tell you."

"It was Dad, wasn't it? That's why you know he was one and that's why you got divorced."

She patted my cheek lovingly. "That's right, dear." She turned her attention to the large grill in front of her, using the tongs to flip the steaks. "Your father is a great man, but the job came first for him."

I looked around at the large backyard where we were standing. The pool was bright blue and inviting, even in December. Mom and Lewis, my stepfather, had made it heated and used it often. They loved to swim when it was cold outside, especially when it snowed. It seldom snowed in New Bern, but they took advantage of it when they could.

"How do you plan to explain to Lewis why you're moving here?" my mother asked. She had put the steaks on a plate to rest and was running a scrub brush over the grill to clean it.

"It would be easier if you just told him what we are."

Mom shook her head vigorously. "Oh, no. I told my second husband and went through hell with him. He took advantage of me. That's why we were only married for a few months."

"Lewis isn't a jackass, though. He's a good guy. Stop being like a 1960s sitcom and do it already. You've been married for twenty years. He loves you for who you are."

My mother was biting her bottom lip, thinking. She shook her head again. "No. I'm not ready. It hasn't hurt him not knowing. I just have to be careful about when I use magic."

"You use magic all of the time," I pointed out.

"Do you think he really notices that the coupons aren't from the newspaper? He thinks I scour the magazines and Internet for those." She smiled mischievously. "He called me a 'wiz with money.'"

"A *wiz*? You have to be a man to be good with finances?" I asked.

"Carmen, stop." My mother laughed. "He doesn't know the difference in terms for us, that one is for female and one is for male."

"He would if you told him," I pushed.

Mom held the tongs and was pointing at me with them. "I. Am. Not. Saying. A. Word."

I held up my hands defensively. "It's your decision. I'm just trying to make your life a little easier. I didn't hit thirty-two just by being pretty."

The loud rumbling of a truck could be heard in the distance. "Lewis is almost home. You better get out of here. Come back this weekend and we'll look at places for you to buy. Tell him you were offered the chance to work from home and you chose to move down here. Off you go, now." She leaned up on her toes to kiss my cheek. "Love you, dear!"

As Lewis's truck pulled into the driveway, I snapped my fingers and disappeared.

The weekend arrived quickly and I found myself sitting in my car, a map spread out in front of me. I was only in my driveway, but I didn't want to travel for fourteen hours just to have my car for Lewis's benefit. I needed a place where I could teleport without being seen. I picked out a spot and closed my eyes, concentrating hard.

The Volvo lurched forward and my eyes flew open, seeing nothing. I was in a garage, which meant I had really overshot myself. I raised my hand and the garage door opened without a sound. There was a golf course in front of me and I could tell by the houses lining the road that I had wound up in my mother's neighbor's garage. Carefully, I pulled out the sedan and steered left onto the road. Within a minute, I was back in another driveway, this one belonging to my mother.

I honked the horn and Mom rushed out of the house as if she hadn't just seen me a few days prior. "I'm so happy you're here, sweetie!" she said, throwing her arms around my neck. "Come in, come in. I've got dinner ready. I made your favorite!" She turned around, her favorite navy blue apron with the White House crest on it blowing in the wind.

I followed her up the stairs to the front porch where Lewis was waiting. "Hi, Lewis," I said, hugging him. I had always thought Lewis to be a great man and was happy that he had married my mother. "I see Mom's been keeping you busy." I motioned toward the front yard adorned with reindeer, an inflatable Santa Clause in a helicopter, and several other decorations that would put a department store's display to shame.

Lewis inhaled deeply and ran his hand through his short, white hair. "She keeps me occupied all right. I hardly ever get a day off."

"I don't think you could handle just watching the television all day."

His ice-blue eyes looked longingly toward the sunset. "A man can dream."

Sharing a laugh, we went inside where Mom was waiting for us. She had already set the table, even going so far as to use her "fancy plates" for the occasion.

"You didn't have to go to such trouble, Mom," I said.

Mom waved her hands dismissively. "It was no trouble at all. I wanted you to feel welcome." She handed me a plate and ushered me off to the kitchen where she had food set up in stations for us to take. I gave myself a generous helping of her roast and potatoes before sitting down in the dining room. She sat across from me and looked at me expectedly.

"Your Christmas decorations are beautiful, Mom," I said before taking a bite of the roast.

"Thank you, sweetie. Lewis and I spent a lot of time trying to get these up." She looked at her tree. In the glow from the lights, she looked positively radiant. "I just love going down memory lane when we take out the ornaments."

"Yes, and the stories I get to hear year after year never get old," Lewis said. He caught Mom's eye and smiled. I knew that he loved hearing her stories. He cleared his throat and added, "How was your drive? Must have left really early this morning. Did you take a vacation day or did you call in sick?"

"I took a vacation day," I answered, hating having to lie to my stepdad.

"Was traffic bad when you hit Raleigh? You had to have hit rush hour."

I looked down at my plate. "It wasn't as bad as I thought it would be."

"At least you left early enough to miss morning rush hour in Indianapolis," Lewis said, piercing a piece of potato.

"Carmen won't have to worry about making that drive anymore. Isn't that right, dear?" Mom looked at me pointedly.

I cleared my throat. "That's right."

Mom put her hand over her husband's. "Carmen is transferring here!" she said excitedly.

"Great. More kids back at home."

Mom slapped his arm playfully. "Hush. You know you like having the kids around."

"Wait, who else is here besides Finn?" I asked. Lewis had two children from his first marriage, one of whom had never left town. The other, Randy, had moved to Atlanta where he was a safety manager with a wife, a child, and another on the way. We hardly ever spoke because he was too focused on his burgeoning family.

"Cecily wanted to be closer to home, somewhere where she felt like she had more support for her and the children," Lewis answered.

"You mean she wanted free babysitters and she can get them here where both sets of grandparents live," I clarified.

"That's an excellent translation," Lewis said, laughing. He shrugged. "The more, the merrier I suppose."

Mom nodded. "It'll be nice having babies around the house. I can bring down your old toys."

I groaned. "Mom, no one wants to play with old Barbie dolls and Cabbage Patch kids. They all want something tech these days."

Mom shook her head in disagreement. "That's only because they have been conditioned to think that technology is more fun than the toys that make you use your imagination. They'll have fun with them," she said confidently.

"As long as you call them 'vintage,' Cecily won't mind. Otherwise she'll think they're just old toys you've kept in hopes that it'd be my own kids playing with them."

"It's all about how you put the spin on things. I'm surprised you never went into marketing." Lewis took a long drink from his Diet Coke before he set it down on the table. "Where will your new office be?"

I swallowed my roast, mulling over my answer before replying. "They're going to let me work from home, actually. All of the permit requests are uploaded and I hardly ever have to speak with people, which works out very well." It was true that it had been rare that I had spoken with someone regarding a request, but I always set up a meeting and just popped in a predetermined meeting place should one be required.

"I hope you'll be able to actually work from home. You get a lot of people who need a change of scenery or just can't manage to get anything done because they can't separate their home from their work life," my mother chided. I looked at her, my eyebrows raised. Was she really fussing at me for a job I wasn't even going to be doing anymore? Noticing my expression, she set down her fork. "Is anyone ready for dessert?"

As Mom gathered the plates, Lewis put his elbows on the table and leaned forward. "I think you're very lucky and I'm happy for you. Most work from home jobs are scams where companies just want you to sell crap no one needs." He nodded. "I'm proud of you and I'm excited you're going to be living here near us. Your mother misses you."

Another puzzled glance at my mother and she ducked her head downward as she set the dirty dishes into the sink. She was really good at acting like a parent whose child lived a few states away whom she hardly got to visit. She'd hate it if I told her it was being deceptive instead of keeping a secret.

"How long is your company going to give you to find a new place?" Lewis asked.

I stood up to help Mom with the dessert. I reached over her and pulled down three small plates which she promptly filled with her famous apple pie. "About a week," I said, really unsure of Fate's time table for me.

"A week?" Lewis' s eyebrows were raised in surprise. "That doesn't seem like a long time. If you're going to buy a house, escrow itself is usually about thirty days. Renting won't take as long, but they still do those background checks and make sure you can afford your rent."

Mom sat down and I served everyone dessert. Mom's pie-filled fork hovered in the air as she suggested slowly, "Carmen could stay with us for a little bit."

I almost choked on baked apples. I hadn't lived at home in fourteen years. I had moved out a couple of months after high school graduation and into the dorms at Notre Dame. After graduating from there, I started working in the permit office and purchased a townhouse where I had been living for the last ten years. "That's awfully nice of you, Mom," I began.

"Don't argue with me." She sat up straighter in her chair, pleased with herself. "I love having company!"

"I'm your daughter. I'm not *company*," I corrected.

"That's too bad that you want to put a label on it because company doesn't have to help with chores." She flashed a smile before eating another piece of pie.

I sighed. Lewis looked at me, his expression sympathetic. "Welcome back home," he said.

"We look for houses starting tomorrow," I declared.

A few days later, I watched myself fold my hands together and smile pleasantly. "How may I help you?" I asked sweetly.

I groaned. "This is the android that's supposed to fool people into thinking it's really me?"

Samuel Francisco—his parents had an interesting sense of humor—rushed to the android's side. "What? No? She's great!" the technician said defensively. "I spent all weekend tweaking her to act just like you."

"Tweaking?" I asked.

"We keep basic models in the warehouse," he explained. "We adjust them to look like exact replicas of the people they replace. The personalities require a little bit more of a hands-on approach." He began to absently stroke the android's hair.

"Stop that," I ordered.

"I'm just fixing it," he replied, smoothing the white-blonde hair into place.

"I know, but it's weird. Listen, she's too chipper. I'm never that way."

Samuel shook his head. "Yes, you are. When customers visit, you are very pleasant."

"Really?" I asked hopefully. "You think so?"

"No," he admitted, running his hand through his shock of bright red hair. "Call it a personality upgrade, but management will like it and so will the customers."

"Oh," I said, deflated. "I don't think she'll fool Nolan," I said, speaking of my coworker.

"Nolan won't notice, trust me." Samuel was now adjusting the vertebrae in the back of the android's neck. The android remained perfectly still, her eyes looking forward at nothing. "You tilt your head a little when you're skeptical. Now she will, too." He smiled, satisfied with his work.

"Nolan is my work buddy. He'll know."

Samuel straightened. "I'm good at my job. Awesome, in fact. No one will be able to tell, I promise. That's why they have me. It's a seamless, smooth transition." He looked at the android and blinked rapidly.

The android relaxed and stood up. She walked around to the front of the desk and gave me a hug. Her embrace was warm and it was surreal being hugged by myself. "We'll take care of you, Carmen," she said assuredly. "I'll call you if I need you, but trust in Samuel's work. He's the best."

"You're programmed to say that," I pointed out.

The android tilted her head to the side and I snorted. The technician had been spot on with his observation. "No, I don't think so," she finally said.

Defeated, I grabbed my purse and looked at my office once more. I'd miss it, but I was looking forward to my new career direction. "See you around, Samuel, Carmen," I said.

They waved at me in unison.

My townhouse was still a mess from Friday night's festivities before my friends and I had gone bar-hopping. I waved my hands and everything returned to its place. I hung up my purse and paced as I waited for the realtor to arrive. I needed to get my townhouse on the market and, as I waited, I realized that potential buyers might not appreciate the colors I had chosen to paint the walls. I roamed from room to room, snapping my fingers and adjusting the paint from bright, vibrant colors that flowed beautifully to varying shades of beige and white. I ran my hand along the floor and the Spanish tile I had previously chosen so carefully rippled and turned into dark brown hardwood.

The kitchen didn't match the new décor and I looked over my cabinets and countertops, my hands on my hips. I enjoy a good home improvement as much as anyone, though I thought the new styles were very boring. Regardless, they sold homes and I clapped my hands together twice. The cabinets turned inside out, showing off their new Shaker style. White subway tile raised from the surface and the countertops dipped inward, then back out as they became a sparkling white quartz. I wasn't a fan of how bland everything was, but I hoped the neutrality would help it sell faster.

With the countertops newly shining, the doorbell rang loudly and I answered it. Patty Ricardo, my realtor, stood on the front porch. Her black suit and coat were coated in snowflakes and she brushed them off quickly before stepping into my home. Her brown eyes were bright and appreciative as she entered. "This is perfect!" she said excitedly. She hung up her coat and walked into the living room. "Look at this floor, how gorgeous!" She reached down with a red-manicured hand and ran her fingers along the wood. "It looks so new! You've been here for ten years, you said?"

"That's right," I answered.

"This will be great if people have kids. This floor seems indestructible."

"I've recently done some remodeling," I admitted.

"Ah," Patty said knowingly. She looked at the furniture, which had not been changed. "I suspected as much. The styles don't match, but that's ok because you'll have your belongings out before we show it, correct?"

"Yes."

"Mmhmm," she murmured, doubtful. "Will you have help packing everything?"

"I will," I answered, starting to get annoyed with her. Magic was always a great help.

"Excellent," she said, walking into the kitchen. "This is right on trend." She ran her hands over the countertops. "A risky choice with the sparkling countertops, but it comes together beautifully."

"Thank you," I said. She didn't need to know that I had gotten my ideas from the Home and Garden channel.

After looking through the rest of the townhouse on her own, she rejoined me downstairs. I waited for her to speak while she perused her notes. "I think this won't take any time at all to sell, even though you're putting it up around the holidays."

"The holidays?" I asked, puzzled.

Her red lips parted, surprised. She caught herself quickly and said, "Sure, the holidays. People decorate for Christmas, they want to spend time together with their families. They don't want to worry about moving this time of year."

I looked out the window, hiding my frown. I hadn't thought about that.

"Don't worry, Ms. Devereaux. This townhouse is in a great location, it's been remodeled with new everything, and turnkey is what people want. You'll sell it for twice as much as you paid for it."

"Twice as much would be wonderful," I said absently. The snow was really beginning to churn outside.

"It'll go on the market first thing tomorrow morning," Patty promised. "We'll have a contract in no time!" She reached forward and I shook her hand. Her handshake was delicate.

Sliding into her coat, she said, "We'll talk soon!"

I watched her walk to her car. She was practically beaming as she slid into her heated leather seats. As she backed away, I noticed it wasn't snowing anymore and closed the door. Turning back toward my living room, I stopped in my tracks. There was snow churning even faster on the other side of the window and I went out onto my small back patio. There was a privacy fence around the space, but I looked around to make sure I was alone. "Hello," I whispered.

The snow stopped, falling to the ground at once. It formed into a tiny snowman, though it had no eyes, nose, or mouth. It moaned as if trying to speak through closed lips. I held out my hand and buttons appeared, which I carefully arranged to create a face.

"You couldn't spring for a hat, could you?" asked the snowman. "It is cold outside."

A beanie floated down and rested on top of his head.

"A beanie? What am I, some hipster teenager?"

"It's a toboggan."

"That's a sled."

"You can use the same word for more than one thing."

"Yeah, and that's why I called it a beanie. To avoid the confusion." The snowman looked upward at his hat. "I guess this will do," he grumbled.

"Is there something you wanted?" I asked, starting to grow impatient.

"I'm Lenny the Snowman."

I chuckled and Lenny cut me off. "I don't make fun of your name, so don't go making fun of mine." He teetered a little as he huffed. "I'm almost eighty years old, so treat me with some respect."

"I'm sorry," I said, a hint of laughter still in my voice. "What can I do for you, Lenny?"

"I'm going to be your liaison to Fate."

"I thought I answered to Simon."

Lenny huffed again. "I'm your direct link. Think of me as a compass to help you when you need it."

"I haven't even started to Influence yet," I said. The sun had fallen behind the horizon and the temperature was dropping quickly. I rubbed my arms.

"Genius, aren't you?" Lenny's button eyes were narrowed. "I'm here to tell you who to help."

"Ah," I said simply, not wanting to further aggravate the snowman.

"Abby Windsor." A photo fell next to Lenny and I picked it up. She was my age with chestnut hair styled into a pixie cut and warm brown eyes. She was a little heavier, but her smile was happy and she looked friendly. "She's a teacher for middle school children," Lenny was explaining.

"How am I supposed to meet her?" I asked.

Lenny scowled. "I don't know. You figure it out."

"You're really helpful."

"I don't need your lip. It's been a long day. Do you think you're the only link I have?"

"Sorry," I apologized once more.

"Here's the other one. A male."

I paused, stunned. A picture appeared of a male in his mid-thirties with a neatly trimmed beard, dark brown eyes, and was wearing a camouflage baseball hat. The hair underneath was also dark brown but it was thinning, which is why he wore the hat. "Finn. You chose my stepbrother?" I asked, incredulous.

Lenny leaned closer to the photograph. "That really your kin?" he asked.

"Yes."

He laughed so hard he started to cough, little flecks of snow puffing out into the air. "I guess Fate decided you're the best one for the job."

"What's wrong with Finn? He's a construction worker who duck hunts on the weekend when it's in season. He's happy."

"He's got a bigger role to play. You're going to help him find it."

"What is it? What about Abby? What are they supposed to do?" I prodded.

"I don't even know that."

"Then how am I supposed to Influence them down their better paths?"

"You'll know. That's why you were chosen for the job. Listen, it's late and I've got another person to get to. He lives in Florida, which is going to be hell for keeping this body together. You don't mind if I keep the buttons, do you?" Lenny was already fading.

"Thanks for the help," I said.

"Yup." Lenny's voice was all that was left and then, like the sun, he was gone.

Percy Pattinson was a tall, very attractive man. He also was well-aware of this and he walked smugly through the large house, arms spread wide as he explained the details of what the seller had done. "They've installed this crown molding, which is just something you don't see often these day. It really polishes the room, don't you think?" He flashed a smile, his teeth bright white and perfectly straight. His hazel eyes twinkled.

"It does," I answered politely. "This house is much bigger than I had expected."

"I assumed it would be for you and your boyfriend."

"No. It's just me."

Percy feigned surprise. "Aren't you just a strong, independent woman," he said.

"Oh, yes, I have a job that pays me well and I take care of myself. It's a really different way of doing things this day and age," I said, not holding back my sarcasm. I smiled sweetly.

His eyes widened. "I didn't mean anything by that," he said, trying to backpedal. "I just meant that it's nice seeing someone who can take care of herself without any help."

"Yes, that makes it sound better," I said, walking away toward the front door. "Show me something else, Percy."

"Of course." Percy locked the house while I waited. He rushed down the front steps and opened the door to his overly priced BMW, a fake smile spread across his tan features.

I slid into my seat and stared out the window as Percy took us to the next house. Elm Street was lined with trees, all bare this time of year. The house sat away from the curb, a beautiful lawn in front of it. It was an older home and reminded me of England. The roof was made of rust-red slates and the siding was a textured beige. There was a large deck off the side of the house and I thought that tall hedges would offer more privacy.

"This house was built in 1936," Percy explained. "If you like this, wait until you see the inside."

The front door was heavy and had beautiful carvings etched in it. It opened into a large living room filled with light, and there was a fireplace that was crackling warmly. A curved archway divided the living room and the dining room, which boasted an antique chandelier.

"The light fixture will stay," Percy said, as if reading my mind. "The owner thinks it's too perfect for the space to take it away."

"How thoughtful of them," I said, walking into the kitchen through the swinging door.

"You can remove this door so it's open to the kitchen," Percy suggested.

"What? Then what will hide the mess in the kitchen that I've made when I have guests?"

Percy swallowed. I turned away and smiled. I needed to lighten up on him a little, though I did want to see the rest of the house alone. I pointed to a chair and Percy sat down, claiming he needed to rest and he'd meet me back in the kitchen. I left him to his thoughts and explored the rest of the home, loving that it had a library. Downstairs I found a full bar and family room with the floor tiled to resemble a shuffleboard. This home was perfect.

"Percy?" I said, entering the kitchen. "I'm finished."

He stood, the light reflecting off his expensive Italian leather shoes. "I have a few more houses for you to see."

"No, I'd like to make an offer on this one."

"Before your townhouse in South Bend sells?"

I could feel my eyes narrowing. "Are you going to continue being a sexist pig or are you going to be my realtor and put in the damn offer?" I snapped. Between him and Patty, my patience had run thin with real estate agents.

Percy cleared his throat and flashed another one of his award-winning smiles. "My apologies. I'll get that offer put in and get back to you. Meanwhile, I'll take you back to your mother's."

He was thankfully silent on the way back to my mother's neighborhood. It was only the middle of the week, but I felt like I had made plenty of progress. Pulling into the driveway, Percy mumbled something.

"I'm sorry, but I couldn't hear you."

"I wanted to apologize if I offended you. I just don't see a lot of single women around here with their act together, you know?" Percy said. He had dropped his smug act.

"Oh," I replied, feeling awkward. "No worries."

"I hope you get the house," he said before leaving.

Mom was waiting anxiously in the living room. She was wringing her hands as I walked through the door. "What did you think? Did you find anything that you liked? I can't believe you didn't want me to come along!"

"I did find a house and I put in an offer." I sat down in one of her antique, mauve chairs. She had to have enchanted it because it was far more comfortable than it looked.

"That's wonderful, sweetie! Listen, you have a message from a Patty Ricardo. She said she couldn't reach you on your cell and called here."

"How did she even get this number?"

"I might have added it to your card when you weren't looking. You know you can't trust those cellular phones and I don't know why you won't enchant yours."

"Sometimes I'm not upset if I'm out of range," I murmured, looking over the message my mother had taken. "Give me a second, Mom." I got up and went upstairs to call my other realtor.

"I have great news for you! There were a few couples that went through your townhouse and they've put in offers today. I haven't gotten back to their agents yet because I couldn't reach you."

Trying to hide my excitement, I instructed, "Take the highest offer and let's get it closed."

"That's the great news! You've got a couple who can offer all cash and close in a couple of days."

"What? Is it a flipper?"

"No, it's not a flipper. Some couple who just received money from a deceased grandparent. They don't want a mortgage payment, so they're going in with all cash."

"Let's do it, then."

"I'll let them know! Are you going to be back to sign the paperwork or do I need to DocuSign it to you?" Patty asked. I knew she was already spending her commission in her mind.

"I'll be back tomorrow."

"Just so you know, this rarely happens this fast. It's like you were meant to leave as quickly as possible."

"I bet," I replied, hanging up the phone.

"Everything is just falling into place!" Mom rounded the corner and into the bedroom I had claimed as my own temporarily.

"Mom, you can't listen to my phone conversations."

"I'm your mother. You know I can be nosy. But you love me anyway."

I did.

A week later I found myself frantically waving my arms to rearrange my furniture in my new home. I knew Fate had stepped in and had someone speed up the closing process for the older home Percy had shown me. I wish I knew who that person was so that I could thank him or her.

Lewis had insisted we gather everyone together to move my belongings inside after the movers arrived with the moving truck. My mother had politely turned him down, explaining I wanted to take care of everything on my own. "We're family. We help each other," he had insisted.

"Really, Lewis, I'll be fine. I'm paying the movers to do it all," I had lied. I wanted to tell him the truth, that there were no movers at all because I could just transfer my belongings in an instant.

Now I was frowning at the layout I had chosen. It didn't flow very well.

"I think your problem is that you've made the fireplace the center of the room instead of the television," Siobhan said, suddenly popping in next to me. She looked around critically.

"There's a whole room downstairs for entertaining," I replied, unsurprised at her intrusion. Siobhan had never needed an invitation to visit, something that she decided herself after college. "That's where the big TV will go."

"You want me to worry about drunkenly crashing into your nice Samsung during your house warming party?" Her candy-cane colored nails blurred in front of her as she waved her hands and the couch slid over another two feet. "That's much better."

"I wasn't aware I was going to have a party. You'll have to let me know when you're inviting people to my house. Also, I don't like that there. I want a conversational spot that's cozy." I beckoned and the couch moved back to its original spot.

Siobhan grimaced. "All right, that's good, but you need more seating if you're going to be just sitting in here and talking." Her bright green heels clicked against the blonde wood floors as she walked to the seating area. She chose a spot between the couch and loveseat and bent down, placing her hand on the floor. As she raised her hand up, an overstuffed chair appeared and stopped growing when her hand reached her waist. She snapped her hands and it became the same blue as my other furniture. "It needs a little something extra," she said to herself. She placed her hands on top of the new chair and French text flowed out from underneath until it covered the entire piece. She snapped her fingers and matching blue, text-covered pillows appeared on the couch and loveseat. "How's that?" she asked brightly.

"I can't read French," I said, circling her creation. I sat down in it. It was extremely comfortable.

"Tess can teach you." Siobhan giggled. "She'll love what it says."

"Maybe I don't want to know."

"Maybe you don't." Siobhan chuckled again. "Your party is going to be next Friday, by the way. I'll take care of everything since I'm basically throwing a party in your home. Is there anything that you need? This is a great time to ask for gifts."

I stared at her. "This is why we made fun of you for suggesting that Tess could have been your assistant."

Siobhan jutted her chin defiantly. "You could use taste other than your own."

"What's wrong with my taste?"

She jumped off the side of the chair and spread her arms. "It's a little old-fashioned."

"The house was built in 1936," I argued. "It has a laundry shoot."

"But *you* weren't built in that year," she said. If she knew only that, technically, I was just built recently. My android was fitting in nicely and doing my old job very well.

"Not everyone likes the flashy stuff that you do. Your home looks like the Tate Modern."

Siobhan smiled proudly. "Thank you, Carmen. That's the nicest thing you've said to me in a while."

"No offense, but I'd rather Tess help me with decorating. She's more open to classic design."

"You mean old."

"Classic," I corrected. I conjured a small, marble table with two matching chairs and slid them against a wall away from the seating area.

"What's that for?" Siobhan asked curiously.

"I'll let you make me a chess set if you stop bitching about my design choices."

She wiggled her fingers and geometric figures began to take shape, starting as small puddles and then rising upward. They steamed as they cooled and she flashed a grin. "How's that?"

I groaned. She had created simple rectangles for the king and queen, squares for the pawns, and I wasn't quite certain which shape she had chosen for the rest of the pieces. I hadn't done very well in geometry class. Who uses rhomboids anyway? "Sure," I mustered.

The doorbell rang and, glad for the interruption, I answered it.

"Hello, Carmen!" Percy Pattinson said. He was wearing another award-winning smile and a dark green sweater that emphasized his eyes. He was also carrying a bottle of wine.

"Hi, Percy," I greeted, stepping aside so that he could enter.

Siobhan marched forward, her hand held out to shake his. "Hello!" she said.

"Percy Pattinson, this is Siobhan Waters, my good friend. Siobhan, Percy is my realtor."

I watched my friend playfully smack Percy's arm. "You brought a gift? How sweet of you!" she said, flirting. She took the wine from his arms. "Carmen, why don't you show me where this goes in the kitchen? Don't you move, Percy. We'll be right back."

Inside the kitchen, I added the bottle to the wine rack. Before she could even ask, I answered her, "Yes, you can sleep with him."

"I never said anything about sleeping with him. We're just going on a date."

I stared at her.

"I will *probably* sleep with him, yes, but we're going on a date first," she corrected. "You really don't mind?"

"Not at all," I assured her.

"Any tips for him?"

"Be the damsel in distress. He hasn't quite caught up to a woman's ability to take care of herself."

"Oh, really? I can do that."

I followed her back to the living room. "Percy, would you like to join us for a little while?" she asked. Siobhan already had her hand over his arm and was steering him toward the sofa.

"For a little while," he said.

"Isn't it a little chilly in here?" she asked. "I'll start a fire."

"Have you had a chance to make sure the chimney is cleared out?" he asked timidly.

I sat in my new chair. "I'm sure it's fine," I answered. I really didn't know nor had I thought about it before now, but I thoughtfully bit my lip and the fireplace was safe to use.

"I'm just having the hardest time getting this match to light," Siobhan said, feigning frustration. She held it out for Percy. "Would you mind?"

Percy joined her by the fireplace and struck the match easily. Siobhan looked at him like he was her hero and I stifled my snicker. She was really something else when she was on the hunt.

He threw the match over the logs and I saw Siobhan's nose wiggle as the flames immediately roared to life. "Wow, that's quite a talent you have!"

Percy's cheeks reddened. "I didn't do much."

"Sure you did," Siobhan insisted, looking deeply into his eyes. "You made me warm." She smiled.

I wanted to puke. With his back to me, I motioned at Siobhan to wrap up her charade. She nodded.

"I'd love to buy you dinner as a thank you," she offered sweetly.

Percy cleared his throat. "That's not necessary, but I'll be happy to take you to dinner."

Siobhan pretended to think, nervously running her hands over her silky hair. "All right. Carmen, would you like to join us?"

I almost said yes just to screw with her. Instead, I said, "No, I have too much work to do here. You two go and have fun."

Percy held out his arm like a gentleman. "Shall we?"

Siobhan looped her arm over his. "We shall."

I watched them leave, Percy closing the door behind them with a small wave to me. Siobhan needed to hang around more playwrights instead of artists to give them inspiration. She was a star performer.

Chapter Four

With my home completed and the party just a couple of days away, I decided it was time to get to work. I knew I needed to speak with Finn, but I also needed to find Abby Windsor. Lenny had told me she was a teacher, so I spread out a map in front of me, marking all of the middle schools in town.

After looking up the phone numbers for each school, I scribbled the number next to their location on my map. Taking a deep breath, I punched in the numbers and a high, tight voice answered.

"Grover."

"Hi, yes, I'm calling to ask about the next parent-teacher night. Will Ms. Windsor be there?"

"Who?" came the shrill reply.

"Ms. Windsor."

"We don't have one of those at this school," the voice snapped before hanging up on me.

"No wonder the kids love going to school these days," I muttered to myself. I marked out Grover Fields on my map and reluctantly dialed the next number on my list.

Several frustrating minutes later, I was staring at my last two options. I chose West Craven Middle School and was relieved when the receptionist kindly assured me that yes, Ms. Windsor would be at the conference. I thanked her and hung up, circling the school on the map and, taking the photo of Abby, I placed it beside the circle. I checked the clock. School would release soon and there was no time like the present to get started.

I drove to West Craven and parked across the street. The bell rang and students began to pour out of the brick Y-shaped building, Abby leading them in the front. The picture Lenny had given me had been recent; she matched it perfectly. She stood by the buses and I watched her guide kids to the correct bus, help a child who dropped his backpack, and switch her weight back and forth from each foot as she waited for the last bus to leave. When the last one took the final busload of children, she walked back into the building.

Feeling stupid, I realized the teacher's parking lot was in the back of the building. I held out my hand and a small, discreet tracker in the shape of a fly appeared. It buzzed, ready for action, in my palm. "Follow her, okay?"

The tracker fly buzzed in response and flew across the street. It landed on the top of her brown hair, which she swatted immediately. I cringed, expecting her to have squashed it. The fly buzzed, offended, and landed on her shoulder instead. She couldn't feel it through the thick cotton of her plum-colored sweater.

I unfolded my map and spread it out once more, this time across my passenger seat. I was pleased to see that my tracker was still with her. It was showing me that she was in the parking lot. I waited a beat longer and saw her exit on the map, then looked up and saw her turn right out of the lot. I followed her slowly, hoping she wouldn't notice. Though, didn't only spies notice people following them? Abby was no spy.

Abby turned into a small shopping center and parked her Ford Focus. I chose a spot nearby and watched as she twisted to reach into the back seat and retrieved a bag and bright purple yoga mat. She slid a headband over her short hair and walked inside a studio that offered hot yoga classes.

I swore under my breath. Tess had once dragged Enid and me to a hot yoga class after she insisted we enjoy a Mexican restaurant that had just opened. Enid had to put a silencer charm on her own butt because she couldn't stop farting. I began to laugh at the memory. Poor Enid.

Snapping my fingers, a similar gym bag popped up on my lap. "Ahem," I said and a yellow yoga mat slid out from underneath my seat. "Thank you." The yoga mat wiggled. I grabbed the bag and mat and followed Abby into the studio.

An incredibly thin woman greeted me. "Welcome to Hot Yoga for You! You're new. I never forget a face."

"I am," I said. "I'd like to try out a class today."

"Good for you! Classes are twenty-five dollars each, but we offer a punch card for one hundred dollars that allows you to come to five classes! That's like one whole free class!" She ran her fingers over the keyboard and asked for my name.

"I thought introductory classes were free," I said.

A dark look crossed her face, but she quickly shook her head and smiled even wider. "We're so confident that you'll love us, we know you'll want to sign up today!"

"Uh-huh," I said doubtfully. Even with Enid's amusing gassy derriere, I hadn't particularly enjoyed the yoga itself. At that moment, Abby exited the bathroom and I rummaged through my bag, fished out my wallet, and handed the lady my credit card. I could always erase my information later if needed.

The lady returned my credit card and asked me to sign my receipt. She reached underneath her desk, found a membership card, and punched a hole in it. "Enjoy!" she said cheerfully. Then she turned away, waiting for the next sucker to come through the door.

I changed quickly and found a spot next to Abby in the back of the studio. We both stretched, me mirroring her movements but never looking her in the eye or speaking to her.

The yogi entered the studio, walking lightly on his feet. He was tall with a dark beard that was fashionably unkempt, his long hair pulled back into a bun. He wore loose, striped linen pants and a matching top. I thought it looked like a set of pajamas I owned as a child. "Hello, my beauties," he said, his voice low and husky.

I discreetly rolled my eyes. This man was the epitome of a yogi stereotype.

His eyes were roving over the students and landed on me. "I see we have a new student," he said. "What is your name?"

"Carmen," I answered.

"Everyone, turn to Carmen and welcome her into our fold."

Suddenly, everyone was looking at me and, in unison, said, "Welcome, Carmen!"

"Thanks. Good to be here," I said awkwardly. These people reminded me of *Children of the Corn*.

"Let's get started on this beautiful day," the yogi began. "Let's all be a tree."

I looked at the others for guidance and placed my left foot onto my right inner thigh. This was actually easier than I thought.

Abby grunted next to me as she struggled to find her balance. Her foot dropped back onto her mat. "Crap," she whispered.

"This pose makes me want to make like a tree and leave," I whispered.

She looked at me and laughed under her breath. She regained her position, adjusted the headband that held back her short hair, and we went through the next hour sweating and trying to hold poses that were almost impossible. Or maybe I was just terrible; I hadn't decided how much I wanted to wound my own ego yet.

"Lie back into corpse pose and breathe in, then out," the yogi said soothingly.

I was flat on my back, my eyes closed. "Now this is more my speed," I whispered.

"Mine, too," Abby whispered back.

"Do I hear talking?" asked the yogi. "This is a time for peace and inner understanding. Breathe in, now out."

"Yes, thank you for pointing out how I need to breathe," I said softly.

Abby giggled.

The yogi ignored us, but another woman shot us a nasty glance.

When the class was finally over, I rolled up my mat and put it in between the handles of my gym bag. "Sorry if I got you into trouble," I apologized.

Abby looked around the room and back at me. She smiled as she removed her sweat-soaked headband and stuffed it into her bag. "This is meant for rejuvenation, but these people take it a little bit too seriously."

"I noticed. Laughter is good for the soul, too. Do you think they know that?"

Abby laughed. "I doubt it."

I held out my hand and she shook it. "I'm Carmen. Carmen Devereaux."

"Abby Windsor. It's nice to meet you."

"You, too. Hey, I know we're a hot mess, but do you want to get some coffee?"

Abby's face brightened. "That'd be great! I know just the place."

I followed her to a small coffee shop nearby aptly named *The Coffee Company*. It was nestled between an antique store and custom frame shop. Inside were several square tables with comfortable chairs and a beautifully carved coffee bar where orders were taken. The aroma was a mixture of vanilla and various coffee beans. Light jazz played in the background.

"This is my favorite place to get coffee," Abby said. "I can't stand that other chain. They have no individuality. Who has a siren for a logo? You're supposed to stay away from those." She shook her head and stepped up to the counter to give her order, a peppermint mocha. "'Tis the season!" she said, raising her cup.

I ordered a simple vanilla latte and we sat at one of the tables. "I don't remember this place being here when I was growing up," I said, looking around the room.

"You're from here?" she asked. She took a sip of her mocha and winced at its heat. She set it gingerly back down on the table and pushed it away from her so it was out of the way while it cooled.

"I am," I admitted. "I've been gone for about fourteen years now. I just moved back."

"How old are you, if you don't mind me asking?"

"I'm thirty-two," I answered.

"Me, too!" she said excitedly. "Wasn't it a little harder to turn thirty-two than it was to become dirty thirty?"

I laughed. "It was! There are no more milestones to hit until fifty."

"What brought you back here?" she asked.

"You know, the typical story. I went to Notre Dame for school and met a boy. I married him, he cheated, I divorced him, and I moved back home."

"Oh," Abby said quietly. "I'm really sorry to hear that. That couldn't have been easy for you." She checked her mocha again and, finding it to be the right temperature, took a drink.

"It's all right. His cheating made it easier to get over him. Now I have family that seems to be coming out of the woodwork telling me that I never should have married him."

Abby laughed. "Isn't that how it goes, though? I dated a man for four years and I was head over heels for him. My parents and friends told me over and over again that he was no good for me."

"Why did you break up?" I asked. I could smell her peppermint mocha and was regretting my plain vanilla latte.

She blushed and looked sheepishly down at the table, not meeting my eyes as she spoke. "He had just gotten out of the military when I met him and was living back home with his parents. He was looking for another job. The man is a really great chef, actually. When he cooked for me, I thought he would be great at a restaurant." Her voice grew softer as she became more embarrassed. "He never did get a job. He continued living at home and mooching off his mom and dad. When we went out, I paid. One day we were at the movies and trying to decide between two new releases. He insisted we see both and was kind of being a jerk about it. You know how much movie tickets are these days. I didn't want to pay that much for four tickets and he wasn't offering to foot any of the bill. It was then that I realized he was a loser who had no ambition and would be content for the rest of his life letting others take care of him. I already take care of children all day. I didn't want to take care of another one."

"You work with kids?" I asked, feigning ignorance.

Abby looked up, proud. "I do. I work at a middle school with special needs children."

I raised my brows, surprised. Lenny hadn't told me that. "You must have the patience of a saint."

She shook her head. "Some days are more difficult than others, but they're so rewarding. These kids get looked over so often by so many people who either don't want to or don't know how to deal with their differences. I want them to learn and to feel normal when they're in my classroom." She took another drink of her mocha, draining it. "I'll get off my soapbox now," she said, putting her cup on the table.

"It's not a soapbox. It's not like you're preaching to me how I should become a vegan now that I've taken a hot yoga class."

Abby's face broke out into a smile. "They're so serious there, but it's the only hot yoga studio in town." She poked at her stomach. "I've been hoping the heat would help reduce this. I also take a cardio kickboxing class. Those people are intense, but in a more fun way."

Why hadn't she gone to the other class today? I would've enjoyed that way more and not been out one hundred bucks. "There's a difference in what healthy looks like on people. That receptionist? She's painfully skinny. I wanted to ask her if she wanted a cheeseburger. I may be body shaming here, but when I can see your collarbone and hip bones sharply jutting out, maybe it's time to eat solid food and ease off the liquid diet."

"She's probably a size zero," Abby interjected bitterly, unconsciously glancing down at herself.

"Can she run for a mile or more and not get winded? Can she stand there and hit mitts and make her training partner have to step back because she was throwing a little too hard? Can she do a push up or pull up? Can she lift more than ten pounds?" I asked.

Abby thought for a moment. "Probably not," she finally said.

"I bet that you can," I pointed out.

She sat up a little straighter in her chair. "I can do all of those things."

"That's right. So which is healthier? A size zero that can do some yoga poses in the heat or a size fourteen that can do all of those things and only gets better each day?"

"Are you some kind of inspirational speaker?" she asked curiously.

I chuckled. "No, I am definitely not," I said. "I work at a permit office," I added. I assured myself that, technically, it wasn't a lie considering there was an android in my image and personality doing my old job.

"Like building permits?" she clarified.

"Sure," I said.

"That sounds like a really exciting job you have there," she said, laughing. "How did you get involved in that?"

"I got a degree in architecture. I didn't want to actually be an architect because people in those firms seem a bit stuffy, so I went with permits where I could review the plans. It's not a bad living. When I leave the office, the job can't follow me home." Sometimes the job *had* followed me home. Requests would get confused or pushy and pop up randomly inside my refrigerator and I'd have to tell them the right address before they'd leave and show up on my desk at work.

"Did you get another job like that or are you looking for something else?"

"It's all mostly online now, so I can work from home."

"That's nice. Some days I wish I could stay at home, but then fall break or Christmas break or a snow day shows up and I get time to myself. It's not from the kids. It's from the other teachers. They can have cliques just as bad as the students," Abby said darkly.

I watched her carefully for a moment. "Do the other teachers leave you out of things?" I asked cautiously.

Abby bit her lip. "They do," she admitted. "I've always been kind of an outcast myself. I don't look like you, so I never really fit in with the popular crowd. I know that I'm a little overweight. That's always been a struggle for me. I'm not good with men. Sometimes, when I go to school, it feels like I'm in high school all over again."

I swallowed, unsure of what to say next. "Looking like me won't get you in the popular crowd," I began. "Being tall with such pale skin, hair, and eyes opens up for a lot of teasing about being a vampire. I was awkwardly thin until I started playing volleyball and my muscles finally figured out what tone was. Suddenly my height was an advantage and, with my teammates, we did really well in matches. I gained more confidence and people saw that and quit teasing me. It seemed like it wasn't going to be worth it for them to tease me when I would just brush it off easily. You just need to remember that you're an adult, you're a great teacher, and you take care of yourself. Be confident in yourself because you're the one who made yourself successful. Those other teachers will open up to you, I bet, if they saw that in you. Show them the real you, the one you are showing me."

"You sure you're not some kind of motivational speaker?" Abby asked jokingly.

"Why? Would you pay me a lot of money to hear me speak?"

She laughed, her eyes crinkling. "Those speakers do seem to make a lot of money, don't they? We paid an anti-drug and alcohol speaker to come to the school and he charged us six thousand dollars."

"What? I would have done it for five hundred less."

"See? Wrong line of work."

I shook my head. "No way. I'd make a horrible speaker. I'd want to talk about real issues."

Abby frowned, her brows narrowing. "What's more real than talking about not doing drugs or drinking?"

"I'd separate the boys from the girls. I'd tell the girls to not be skanks and I'd teach the boys to be able to tell the difference between who you take home to mom and who you don't, and those are the girls you don't even want to date."

A huge guffaw escaped Abby and she quickly clasped her hand over her mouth. "That's the funniest thing I've heard all week! That would be more practical, but I don't think the principal would go for it. You'd be better off scattering pamphlets on the ground and hope the kids picked them up."

"I guess my career in that field ended before it even began." I leaned back in my chair and crossed my arms. "How disappointing," I said sarcastically.

"How long do you think you're going to stay in town?" Abby asked, serious.

"I just bought a house over on Elm Street."

"Haven't had any nightmares yet, have you?"

I laughed. "That's *punny* of you." I uncrossed my arms. "No, it seems to be working out so far. I haven't met my neighbors, but I'm sure I'll get around to it soon enough. My mother is just upset that I didn't buy a house next door to her."

Abby groaned. "I live in an apartment a few streets over from where my parents live. Now *that* can be a real nightmare." She made her voice shrill. "'Abby, why don't you come over and help me with the yard? Why don't you come over and paint that wall for me? Abby, you don't have a social life, so spend all of your time doing projects for me.'"

"Your mom sounds like a special kind of lady."

She shook her head. "I love her, but she drives me crazy sometimes. I need to buy a house on the other side of town and maybe she won't bother me so much. I think she drives by my complex to see if my car is there and that's how she ropes me in. She sees that I'm home and am not doing anything better."

"Why don't you buy a house, then?" I asked.

The corners of Abby's mouth lifted a little. "I'd like to, but I don't think I can afford it."

"Why don't you find out? Think about how much money you spend on rent each month. Surely that money could be put to better use going toward a mortgage payment, something you can own yourself." I had finished my latte finally and gently tapped the table. The cup refilled with peppermint mocha. I tasted it and frowned. It didn't even come close to what the barista had created for Abby. I tapped the table again and the cup emptied.

Abby hesitated, unsure.

"I could help you," I offered. "I bought my townhouse in South Bend and then this house here. If you decide to move out of your apartment, that is."

"Maybe," Abby said, her voice trailing off.

I looked out the window and noticed it was dark outside. It rarely snowed in North Carolina, but it did get cold and I shuddered. "I guess it's time to go and face the outdoors."

She nodded. "This was fun. We should do this again. You could come with me to try out the cardio kickboxing class. We could go next week."

"That sounds great," I said, scribbling my number on a napkin for her. "Just give me a call."

Abby stuffed the napkin into her bag and we left, parting ways in the parking lot.

"Lenny!" I shouted. I was standing outside in my new backyard.

The snowman appeared, his body not as dense this time when he had to create his own snow. "What? I was at home watching my stories," he complained.

"Lenny, what in the hell am I doing? Abby's a nice woman and I can see us being good friends, but how does that Influence? I can't be friends with every person I'm meant to change."

Lenny's button mouth became a straight line as he fought off a snide remark. "You won't be friends with all of them. This one, though, you *need* to be her friend."

"She does seem to need someone."

"You'll help her. You're doing great. Just keep doing what you're doing," Lenny said reassuringly.

"Are you just saying that because you mean it or are you saying that because you want to go home and watch *Real Housewives?*"

The snowman waved his stick arms up and down. "I like those shows! I got a thing for the guy that hosts the reunions. He's got great hair," he said defensively.

"I think he's taken, Lenny," I said.

He bobbed up and down. "A snowman can dream! Do I show up and poke holes into your fantasies? No, I don't." He tried to cross his arms, but the sticks wouldn't bend.

"Sorry," I apologized.

"It's not sincere, but I'll take it. Is that all you wanted? Look, if you're going to doubt yourself every step of the way, then just start sending emails. I'm not interesting in hearing you whine."

"I wasn't whining," I protested.

"Lenny, I'm new to the job and unsure of myself. Fate wouldn't have any clue what they were doing choosing me to Influence, so I'm going to question what's happening," he said, pitching his voice high, trying to mimic me.

"You know they're canceling the Atlanta edition of *Housewives*, right?"

The snowman's button eyes grew bigger. "They are not!" He looked frantically toward the ground, his stick arms quivering. "I need to get home and check! Remember, email if you're just going to whine!" With a poof, he was gone.

Feeling a little better, I went inside to my kitchen. There was a fire crackling in the living room and my house felt warm and inviting. I turned on the stereo and Christmas music began to softly play. I hadn't put up a tree yet, which was a tradition I preferred to do by hand rather than by magic. This was my first home that I purchased by myself in years and it felt great wandering from room to room, knowing I was by myself and my options were endless. I wasn't ready to date again, but it was nice living for just myself and not having to worry about taking care of anyone else.

I whipped up tortellini with Alfredo sauce, ate happily and, too lazy to do the dishes myself, snapped my fingers and they began to clean themselves. "You can go back into the cabinet when you're dry," I told them.

I showered and crawled into bed. The heavy comforter was soft and I motioned for more pillows to pile up behind my back so that I could sit up without slouching. I pulled a notebook out of my nightstand and began to write down the possibilities for Abby's future. She was a teacher who wanted to fit in yet also wanted her own identity. What was she destined to do with her life? I sighed with frustration and turned the page.

I wrote Finn's name at the top. I loved my stepbrother and we got along well, but we had never been close. He worked for a small, local contractor doing honey-do work around town and duck hunted when it was in season. I usually bought him something hunting related during this time of year and he always loved it. The more duck calls, the better. When he couldn't hunt, he liked going to bars with his friends and drinking beer. I frowned. He did that a lot, actually. He used to waste entire paychecks at the bar until Lewis and my mother stopped loaning him money. He had a roommate at a place where rent was really cheap and I always thought he could do more with his life if he had a better role model.

My head shot up and I stared at the wall. Me. I was going to be that role model. But how could I make him want to change his direction and go on the path he was meant to take? How would I even know which path he or Abby should take? I sighed again and slouched down against my pillows. I'd figure it out. I had to.

Twinkling white lights floated in the air, their reflections gleaming and shining brightly off the fake snow Tess had created in my backyard. She wanted to add the lights to the inside of the home, but I had told her it would be a bit too much. "Lights are romantic. I'm trying to set a mood," she said.

"It's a housewarming party around Christmastime. It would be inappropriate to be romantic."

"Give the woman a break. She lives in Paris. The City of Love," Enid chimed in.

"Thank you," Tess said gratefully.

"You're welcome. We all know a shriveled up snail would turn you on at this point, you frog transplant." Enid playfully stuck out her tongue at Tess.

Tess's mouth opened into an O shape. Her jaw tensed and relaxed for a minute while she tried to retort with something clever. She wound up shaking her head and walking into the kitchen to help Siobhan with the food and drinks.

"She used to be better than that," Enid said, dejected. "It takes all of the fun out of teasing her if she won't fire back."

"I think she gets a little sensitive when you talk about her home like that. She really likes it over there."

"She doesn't like her job," Enid said.

I shrugged. "That's her own fault. It's a fashion capital. It's not like she can't move on to another store or work for a designer directly." I lowered my voice. "It's not like she couldn't give herself a magical edge."

Enid pretended to be shocked. "Are you saying she should break the rules?"

"I'm saying she could make it so that her resume continues to creep to the top of application piles and stay there so that the hiring manager keeps seeing it. That's not breaking any rule." As a witch or wizard, we weren't supposed to interfere with the natural order of things like applying for a job. It wouldn't be fair to the mortals if we always gave ourselves first dibs. The Council had made it clear we were to remain honest. Sometimes honesty sucked.

"I do like how you decorated for the holiday," Enid said, admiring the tree and other decorations. "It's very…" her voice trailed off.

"It looks like a department store threw up in my house," I finished for her.

"I wasn't going to say that. I was trying to be nice."

Siobhan and Tess joined us in the living room. "Tess, I think it looks beautiful. We should all be so lucky to have your taste," Siobhan said admirably.

"Suck up," Enid and I said in unison.

Tess blushed. "Thank you." She glanced around the room. "I might have gone a little bit overboard, but this is Carmen's new house for her new life and I wanted this celebration to be special."

"Speaking of which, we got some help to serve the hors d'oeuvres and drinks tonight," Enid said. She whistled and in marched several gnomes, their eyes gleaming with excitement.

Enid bent down so that she was on their level. To the gnomes in the green pointy hats, she said, "I've got several trays in the kitchen. Just pick them up and ask the guests if they'd like anything from the tray. When the tray is empty, just take it back to the kitchen and put it on top of the stove. They'll refill themselves." She turned to the gnomes in red hats. "You'll do the same, but just put the tray next to the fridge and they'll refill with drinks. Everyone got that? Come get me if you need anything and you're welcome to anything you want."

The gnomes rocked excitedly back and forth in their black boots and nodded. "Yes!" they yelled in unison. The tallest gnome at two and half feet motioned toward the kitchen. "Let's get to work!" We watched them march single file into the kitchen.

"Are those my neighbor's garden gnomes?" I asked, suddenly realizing why they looked familiar.

"What? Of course not. I brought my own," Enid said indignantly.

I was quiet.

"Yes, yes those would be your neighbor's garden gnomes," Siobhan admitted. I looked at her and Enid, my brows knitted. "She'll never suspect that they're gone."

"You even changed their outfits," I accused.

Siobhan put her hands on her hips. "They looked ridiculous in those outfits she had them wearing. Besides, they needed uniforms for the party. I'll change them back before the morning."

"Don't worry about it. We didn't even take all of them from her yard. She won't notice anything missing," Enid said, trying to reassure me.

"You have *ten* gnomes in my house."

Enid's eyes widened. "Is that how many there are? I never bothered to count." She looked at Siobhan. "We just took ten gnomes and Carmen's neighbor still has several more. I think our friend moved next to a nut."

"She's not a nut. She's eccentric," I said, defending Mrs. Crouch.

"Is she rich?" Enid asked.

"I don't know. I guess," I answered. "She had a lot of clocks on her wall when she invited me over for tea and cookies. She said that she liked to watch time move from every angle."

"You're right. She's eccentric," Enid said.

"She's right. If she wasn't rich, then she'd be a nut." Siobhan shrugged. "That's how the world works when it comes to its crazy people."

"You know my family is coming to this party and they're going to ask about the gnomes," I pointed out.

"No, they won't. They're just going to see little people as our caterers," Siobhan said smoothly. "Unless they can recognize magic. Your family can't, can they?" She was starting to get worried.

I thought of all of the things my mother had done without Lewis noticing. "We'll be fine."

"I heard you went on a date with Carmen's realtor," Enid said slyly to Siobhan. "How did that go?"

Siobhan grinned mischievously. "We had a nice time," she answered simply. She lowered herself onto my loveseat and crossed her legs.

Tess paused from fluffing one of the pillows on the couch and studied Siobhan. "You like the guy," she blurted. "You genuinely like him."

"How can you like a guy with a name like Percy?" Enid asked. She looked at me. "Didn't you say he's a bit sexist?"

"He's not sexist," Siobhan interjected. "He's old-fashioned. He opened doors for me, he didn't try to split the bill, and he didn't expect anything from me when he brought me back here."

"I can't believe you didn't go ahead and put out. That's your status quo," Enid said.

I shot her a nasty glance. She was going a little too far.

"Knock it off, Enid," Tess warned.

"We all know that Siobhan is the slutty one of the group," Enid said, her voice rising.

Siobhan cleared her throat. "Ahem," she said. "Every group has that one slutty friend and, Enid, I suppose you're right that it is me."

Enid nodded in agreement.

"But that's only because I've got you beat by one," Siobhan added.

Tess and I exchanged glances, remaining silent.

Enid glared at Siobhan before she burst into laughter. "You're right. It is just by one."

I let out a breath of air that I didn't realize I had been holding. Siobhan and Enid were dear friends, but sometimes Enid was known to cross the line.

"Are you going to see him again?" Enid asked, her tone lighter.

"I might. He knows that I live in Nashville and wouldn't be able to visit him often." She nodded in my direction. "But who knows?

I might find myself moving here to be closer to my friend. Maybe I could be the neighbor on the *other* side and have garden gnomes of my own. What do you think, Carmen?"

I shook my head. "You shouldn't have to ask. I wouldn't change my life for a man unless I was absolutely sure it was going somewhere. Even then I'd be hesitant."

"Oh, you're just sour grapes after your divorce. Why am I asking you anyway?" Siobhan said bitterly. She pouted.

"Because you love me and you value my opinion," I answered sweetly.

"Narcissist," she retorted, tossing a pillow across the room at me.

"Hey! I just arranged those," Tess said, snatching the pillow and putting it back into its place. "Go get changed," she ordered. "We have a party to throw." She looked pointedly at Siobhan. "And change the text on that chair. 'Hail to the V' is not appropriate for guests."

Siobhan smiled wickedly and the text glittered before being replaced.

Tess frowned. "You can't put curse words on Carmen's furniture."

The text glittered again, this time reading, "Tess is the best."

"That'll do," Tess said, smiling.

Within an hour, my new home was bustling with people. Siobhan had borrowed another gnome from my neighbor and made him the bartender for the bar downstairs. She sheepishly apologized, promising she wouldn't take anymore from Mrs. Crouch's yard.

I wandered through the crowd, happily chatting with old friends that I hadn't seen in a while and catching up. One had a cat on a leash, claiming it was his emotional support animal.

"You needed an emotional support animal?" I asked, doubtful.

My friend looked around and whispered, "No, but Mr. Pickles is a real ice breaker with the ladies."

"Good for you," I said before excusing myself. The doorbell was ringing and I answered it, finding my mother and stepfamily. "Welcome to the party!" I greeted warmly.

Mom stepped inside first, Lewis following closely behind her. "This is some turnout you have!" she said. "It's almost as big as the party you had in high school."

"You knew about that?"

She raised a brow.

"Of course you knew about it."

"Not much gets past her," Lewis said proudly. He leaned in and lowered his voice so that only I could hear him. "Except for how much I really spent on my new sports car."

I laughed, watching my mother shaking her head behind him. She mouthed the words, "I *do* know."

Cecily Cleary shoved a stroller through the door. "You could have made this baby accessible," she snapped. "It's hard enough getting around while being pregnant."

My stepbrother, Randy, gently patted her arm. "Honey, you're only three months along. It's not that bad, yet." He looked at me apologetically. "I'm sure Carmen didn't expect us to bring Apple. Otherwise, she would have gotten a ramp."

Cecily sniffed and flipped back her long, dark hair. "Can you do something about this music? It's too loud. And the lights outside, I get what you're going for, but they're too bright. I need to put Apple down for bed soon." She pushed the stroller past us and into the kitchen.

I looked at Randy. "I'm *so* glad you brought your wife."

"I told her it wasn't your typical housewarming party, but she said if she couldn't come, then I couldn't come and I wanted to support you," Randy said, his voice small.

I hugged my stepbrother. "I'm glad you're here," I said. I wanted to add that I wished he'd let his balls drop and stop letting Cecily be such a jerk.

"You think that's bad, try riding in the car with them on the way over here," a voice said behind me.

I turned around to see my other stepbrother, Finn, standing in front of the door. He was tall, lanky, and was wearing his usual baseball cap. He was sensitive about his thinning hair, though it didn't stop Randy from teasing his little brother about it occasionally. I hugged him, too, and tugged him further inside so that I could close the door. "Finn!" I said excitedly. "How have you been?"

"Not bad. Working. Drinking. Same shit," he answered simply.

"Are you still working for the same company?"

"Yeah."

"What about your roommate? Are you still living at the same place?" I prodded.

"Yeah, it's all the same. No changes since the last time you were home. You, though. Look at you. Finally got rid of that asshole." He shoved his hands into his pockets and looked down. "Sorry," he said softly.

I waved my hand. "Oh, no. It's okay. Really. You were the only one who protested us getting married. I should have listened to you."

"I'm not always dumb."

"You're *never* dumb," I argued. Changing the focus, I asked, "What about you? Are you seeing anyone?"

"Cecily offered to set me up with one of her friends."

Rigid, I stared at my stepbrother.

He laughed. "I told her no, thanks. I'd find a lady on my own."

I relaxed. "We don't need two of them in the family."

"Hell no," Finn agreed. "To tell you the truth, I'm not looking right now. I found that the best relationships happen when you stop searching."

"I was unaware you've had a great relationship," I said carefully. Finn had dated women on and off for years, though he had never been with one for more than a few months. He was like Siobhan in that matter.

"That's why I've stopped looking. A woman will come to me. Eventually."

"That's right," I said. "Have you been doing anything else outside of work other than going to the bar?"

Finn's brown eyes flashed for a moment. "I did start to take some guitar lessons, but I stopped."

I tilted my head, thinking. "Why did you stop?"

"I just didn't have time for it."

"You really didn't have time or you didn't make time?" I asked.

He laughed. "You caught me. I didn't make the time."

"You should make the time. Get you out of the *Midnight Cowboy* a little more often," I suggested, referring to a local bar.

Finn nodded and thoughtfully stroked the stubble on his chin. "I guess I could. I enjoyed it when I did it. I did spend all of that time learning to read music. I'd hate for it to go to waste."

"Then go for it. We can have a jam session."

"What do you play?" he asked. "I didn't know you played anything."

"I can hit the buttons with pre-recorded songs on the keyboard."

Finn laughed again. "Fair enough." He looked around the living room. "Hey, are those gnomes serving drinks?"

My eyes widened. "No, they're not," I stammered.

He squinted. "Sure looks like it to me, but I guess they prefer to be called little people."

The doorbell rang again and I answered, not sure who else it could possibly be.

"Hi, I'm an Eraser," said a large man dressed as Santa Claus.

"I don't think we need one," I said, frowning.

The Eraser looked past me, at my stepbrother. "I think you do."

I sighed. "Fine." I stepped aside so that he could enter. "Could you at least wait until the party is over? There might be more he'll notice," I asked.

The Eraser smiled. "Sure," he said easily. "You don't have any of those spinach pinwheels, do you? Those are my favorite."

Two hours later, I thanked everyone for coming to my housewarming party. When they didn't take the hint that it was time to leave, I began to hustle people out of my home. My family had already left except for Finn, who had asked if I could give him a ride home. Cecily was complaining about having parties in the evening instead of during the day when children could enjoy them more as she dragged Randy and Apple to the car.

Finn was currently deep in conversation with Enid. She was explaining her job to him, though she made it sound like she worked at a museum instead of a company that literally transported its guests back in time. It was too bad outsiders weren't allowed to know about witchcraft. It had taken decades to get the Council to change its mind about being able to tell spouses. I didn't know if they'd ever budge on their decision to let extended family in on the secret. I paused and shuddered. Cecily would be even more of a pain in the ass if she knew that witchcraft was real. It was easy to picture her demanding I provide everything her family needed so that she could keep Randy underneath her watchful eye twenty-four hours a day.

The crowd thinning, I noticed the Eraser. He took another pinwheel, this one made from cinnamon and marshmallow cream, and thanked the gnome who had given it to him. "That's a great choice, sir!" the gnome said.

"You've got good taste," the Eraser replied with equal enthusiasm.

The gnome squealed with delight and scurried off to the kitch-
en. Siobhan and Tess followed him, hopefully to gather all of the
gnomes and return them to Mrs. Crouch's yard.

When he was finished eating his treat, the Eraser walked over
to Finn and held out his hand to shake it. "I don't think we've met
yet," he said.

Finn's eyes glazed over as the Eraser's magic rippled through
him.

"Kind of funny how Carmen got elves to serve at her party,
isn't it?"

Finn's head tilted and his eyebrows knitted in concentration.
"No," he said, almost dreamily. "They're gnomes."

The Eraser shook his hand harder. Finn looked like he was vi-
brating and I shot a warning glare at the Eraser. "What did you say
the caterers were?" he prodded.

"She got little people to dress up as elves. Good theme for the
holidays, but it feels kind of wrong in a way. Politically, I mean," Finn
muttered.

The Eraser released Finn's hand. "Pleasure to meet you, Finn!"
he said cheerily. He inclined his head slightly toward my stepbrother and headed in my direction. "What I do doesn't hurt them at all.
It just looks like it does. I promised that I would never hurt a mortal. It's easier for the ones that don't recognize magic at all. I suppose
people like Finn keep people like me in business." He flashed a grin.
"See you around, Carmen!" In an instant, he was gone.

There was a loud crash and Enid and I excused ourselves to join
Siobhan and Tess in the kitchen. A gnome was sulking on my bar
stool, his arms crossed. "I don't want to go back to the yard! I want
to stay here!" he cried.

"That's where you belong," Tess said soothingly. "You have someone over there that loves you dearly."

The little gnome sniffed. "She dresses me in funny clothes."

"Don't you like them?" Siobhan asked tentatively.

The gnome took off his green hat and rubbed his hand over his bald head. "I don't mind them."

"Then what's wrong?" she asked.

"I don't like being near the tree by the sidewalk. I get peed on by dogs." The gnome replaced his hat and fresh tears sprang out of his eyes.

"We'll move you," Tess promised.

He cried even harder. "But then one of my brothers will get peed on!" He shook his head sadly. "I couldn't wish that on them."

"Oh." Tess looked at the rest of us, unsure of what to do.

"I'll help you out with them," Siobhan said, stepping forward. She touched the tip of his hat and he began to glow a bright, neon green. As the glow faded, she said, "Now you're waterproof." To prove it, she filled a glass with water and poured it over the gnome's head. It cascaded off around him, never touching him.

The gnome's eyes widened and he hopped off the bar stool. He hugged Siobhan's shins, thanking her repeatedly until she gently pried him off her. "I'm ready to go back now," he said.

"All right." Siobhan and Tess clapped their hands in unison and the gnomes went back to their normal state. Another clap and they returned to their former positions at my neighbor's home.

"Is everything okay?" Finn asked, popping his head in through the swinging door. "Is there a problem with the caterers?"

"Oh, no. No problem at all. They just left," Enid answered easily.

"That was fast. Must be a great company," Finn murmured.

"Are you ready to go home?" I asked.

"Yeah." Finn looked at my friends, his eyes glazing over once more. "It's been weird, ladies." He waved and returned to the living room to wait for me.

I frowned. "Does the Eraser's magic have aftereffects?"

"It shouldn't," Tess said. "I've never heard of anything like that."

"Maybe he's just stoned," Siobhan offered. "He could have shared."

Enid snickered. "Maybe he was around a Muse for too long. That can make you feel a little buzzed."

"That's not true," Siobhan said defensively. "You know that's just a myth."

"Guys, thank you for this wonderful party," I said before Enid could retort.

"We're glad you enjoyed it," Siobhan said warmly. "I won't even complain anymore that you let Tess finish helping you decorate."

"How nice of you," Tess said drily. She held out her arms. "Group hug!"

We closed in around Tess, Enid grumbling that adults shouldn't still be doing group hugs. Tess shushed her immediately. When we parted, they disappeared without a sound.

I met Finn in the living room and grabbed my keys from the hook by the door. "Where are your friends?" he asked.

"They're cleaning up the kitchen for me," I lied. I hated that it was getting easier to be untruthful to my family.

"That's nice of them," he said, shrugging into his coat.

"It is," I agreed. I motioned for him to exit and I followed, locking the door behind me.

My stepbrother was quiet on the way back to his apartment, deep in thought.

"Did you have a good time?" I asked.

"What?" he asked, glancing at me. "I did. You have a lot of friends. They seem like good people."

"They are," I said. "I've known most of them for a long time now it seems."

"What about childhood friends?" he asked.

"I lost touch with them over the years," I answered, lying again. The truth was that no one else had been magical when I was growing up and Mom had restricted my playtime with other children until I was old enough to understand not to use magic in front of mortals.

"That's kind of sad, don't you think? You move back home and the only people you know in town are your family. You don't have anyone to go to complain about how crazy we can be," he said, a smile in his voice.

"I'll make friends."

"How? You work from home. You won't even get to get out and meet people," Finn argued.

"I went to a yoga studio and made a friend just this very week," I said indignantly.

Finn snorted. "You want to be friends with a hippie?"

"She's not a hippie. It just helps her relax," I said, defending Abby. "She's a nice person. She's a middle school special needs teacher."

"Hmm," Finn said thoughtfully. "No, she's a hippie."

I reached over and pulled off his hat. "You take that back!"

"Hippie! Carmen's hanging out with dirty hippies!" he said, laughing.

I rolled down the window and held his hat outside like it was my hostage. "You take it back!"

"No, not my hat! Not one of my dozens of hats!" he cried.

Laughing, I gave him back his hat and rolled up the window. He hastily put it over his thinning hair. "Fine, she's not a hippie. I'm sure she's one of the normal people who do yoga, but I swear, if I come around you and you've stopped taking showers and start asking me to hug a tree, I'm going to drag your ass to hippie rehab."

"They don't have a hippie rehab," I pointed out.

"Sure they do. It's in a basement where I tie you to a chair and make you watch the news, commercials featuring meatball subs, and you listen to Metallica. I'll only need twenty-four hours to convert you back to normal."

"I can see how that would convert a person," I said.

"Damn right. This is my turn, by the way."

Turning left, I noticed the street lights had faded and it was practically pitch black. When we approached Finn's apartment building, I had to wiggle my nose to get a few porchlights to turn on just so that I could see the building numbers.

"This is a pretty private area," Finn mumbled.

"Must be," I agreed.

"This is me," he said. He hopped out of my sedan and stood next to the door for a moment before ducking his head back inside. "It's good to have you back," he said softly before closing the door.

I watched my stepbrother walk to his apartment, making sure his way was well-lit.

Chapter Five

"Jab, cross, burpee!"

"Why don't you jab, cross, and burpee?" I muttered, dropping to the ground to do a push up. I jumped my feet toward my hands before leaping upward, my hands outstretched in the air.

Abby panted in response as she drove her jab into the heavy bag in front of her.

She had texted me the day before and invited me to her cardio kickboxing class. We dove right into instruction and I had to admit that it was love at first sight for me. The red-and-gray gym was large, bright, and clean with several rows of different types of punching bags hanging from a well-constructed metal rack. The instructor had proudly told me before class started that he had welded it together himself before sliding the waiver of liability across his desk for me to sign.

Class was almost over and we were doing a burnout session. My arms felt like lead hanging by my side and my hair was so drenched with sweat that it looked like I had just gotten out of the shower. I certainly didn't smell that way.

The timer buzzed loudly and all movement halted immediately. I was breathing heavily, but I felt wonderful. I followed Abby to the bleachers where we had set our belongings. Parents were beginning to fill them up as they filed in to watch their offspring train for the children's class that would start in ten minutes. "Excuse me," I said to a parent, motioning for him to move his feet. He lifted them slightly and I grabbed my gym bag.

"Good class?" he asked.

"Yes," I answered, fishing out a towel and wiping sweat from my forehead.

"I'm just here to watch my son, Alfred. His mother is out with her boyfriend now."

"That's so nice that you let your wife have a side piece," I said, smiling brightly.

Abby's face reddened and she briskly walked away. She was already in the locker room by the time I caught up to her, bent over with laughter. "I cannot believe you said that to that man!" She gasped.

"Who hits on someone at the gym?" I asked.

"You're sweaty. You look like crap. You definitely don't have a nice scent on you. I'd say you're at your worst. If he hits on you at your worst, then I say go for it because he'll think you're a goddess with dry hair and fresh deodorant."

"Who are you calling stinky?" I asked, feigning anger. "I think I smell like a daisy."

"Yeah, one that's still a seed buried under layers and layers of earth and some of those layers are poop," she replied. She dug out her toiletries and went into one of the shower stalls. She closed the curtain and the water came on, quickly followed by a squeal. "Takes a little while for this warm up!" she shouted.

While waiting for the water to get warm in the next stall over, I retrieved my own toiletry bag. I stuck a toe inside the curtain and, finding it to be suitable, began to shower.

"Did you sign a contract?" she asked.

The lather from my shampoo dripped down and I wiped it off my cheek. "Not yet."

"I like how it's a flat fee for the entire month instead of the punch card that the yoga studio uses."

"That is appealing to me," I admitted.

"I think I'm going to drop yoga once my card is full. You're the first decent person I've met and I've been going there for months." There was a faint squeak as she shut off her water. "I know why I started going there. Why did you? That doesn't seem like your kind of place. I don't mean any offense because I don't know you that well, but I'm just curious."

I finished my shower and reached for my towel. It wasn't on the hook by the stall. Instead, it was lazily draped over my bag and I beckoned for it. "Get over here," I whispered furiously. It dropped off my bag and hovered over the floor for a moment before floating over to my outstretched hand. Drying myself off, I answered, "I just moved back into town. It was a new place. I thought I'd try it out." I thought about what Finn had told me. "I work from home, so the opportunity to meet people is slim. I guess most yoga people aren't my kind of people either."

Dressed, I pulled back the curtain and found Abby squeezing excess water out of her short hair. She slathered some curl cream into her palm and rubbed her hands together to spread it before slicking her hands back through her hair. "I was going for the increased flexibility. I think I wind up more irritated by the time I leave," she said. She stuffed the rest of her belongings into her bag and I followed suit. I hurriedly French braided my own shoulder-length hair and regretted not drying it as soon as we faced the harsh wind outside.

"Let me drop this off in my car," she said. I watched her carefully and ran my hand over my head, drying my hair quickly. I pointed at her, making her hair dry as well. I hoped she wouldn't notice the sudden change.

I was already waiting in my Volvo and had hurried along the heater. New Bern wasn't nearly as cold as South Bend, but thirty-two degrees is freezing no matter where a person is located. "Is *Smithfield's* still open?" I asked. My mouth watered just thinking about their grilled chicken. That was a lie. I was thinking about their fried chicken, but I felt guilty for wanting fried food so soon after a workout.

"That place will never go away and thank goodness for it!" Abby answered.

We pulled into the parking lot and stood in line to order. I told Abby I would take care of the bill as a Christmas treat and she chose a table next to a window. We waited quietly until our number was called and we carried our trays to the table. The silence wasn't uncomfortable as we sank our teeth into the delicious chicken that a certain colonel couldn't top on his best day.

"How's your house coming along?" she asked, scooping up coleslaw with her fork.

"It's fine. I'm finished now."

"Already?" she asked, a perfectly arched eyebrow raised.

"I had some help," I admitted. "My good friends came down to visit over the weekend and one of them did most of it. She works as a buyer for a department store in Paris."

"Paris?" Abby's eyes lit up. "I would *love* to go to Paris! I hear it's so romantic."

"I don't know about romantic, but it's a nice city to visit. They have good Italian food."

"Italian food? You went to France and all you can say is their *Italian* food was good?"

"Imagine you're fifteen years old and you don't speak a word of French. It's your first visit and you're with your dad who takes you into a nice restaurant. The only word you can sort of translate is 'shrimp' and you order it, expecting a delicious French concoction. Instead, you receive several poor shrimp, with their heads still on, their little eyes blackened and tentacles still sticking out of their heads. That wouldn't leave a good taste in your mouth either."

Abby held her fork in her hand and was pointing at me with it. "You know shrimp don't have tentacles, right?"

"Whatever, you know what I mean," I said, laughing. "My point is, when you see several full, dead shrimp surrounding a peeled potato, then you'd love the Italian food more."

"Wait, did you say the potato was *peeled*?" Abby put the back of her hand to her forehead. "My goodness!" she said, thickening her Southern accent. "Shrimp and a peeled potato! Whatever shall I do?" She waved her hand frantically in front her chest. "It's just too dreadful! The vapors! I have got the vapors!"

I laughed so loudly that other patrons turned to stare at me. What in the hell was I supposed to do to Influence this woman? She seemed like she was on the right path. She had a great career and she could take care of herself. What did Fate have in store for her other than what she was doing? Working with special needs children made her a saint already in my book.

"I do have a question, though," she said, her accent back to normal. "Did your friend come in all the way from Paris just to help you decorate?"

I wanted to tell Abby that yes, Tess had done exactly that. Instead, I told her, "Oh, no. She just came here first before heading up North. I think she really wanted to see how I was doing after my divorce." That last part wasn't entirely untrue.

"I couldn't imagine going through something like that," Abby said, shaking her head.

"Hopefully you won't have to. It could have been a lot worse than what it was."

"Does he try to contact you?" she asked timidly.

"No," I said flatly. It didn't take magic to block phone numbers these days.

"I'm happy you have your new home and can start over. I was actually wanting to ask you about that." Abby's voice lowered and she suddenly had something in her throat that she struggled to clear.

I pushed our empty plates out of the way. "Sure, ask away."

"My rent is due at the first of January and I was thinking about the difference between a mortgage and a rental payment." She paused, tried to find her words. "I've been living at my apartment since I got out of grad school, so that's been eight years now. That's almost seventy thousand dollars in rent."

She went quiet again and I waited for her to continue.

Finally, she spoke again. "That's a lot of money down the drain on a place that isn't my own. Renting has its advantages like I didn't have to replace the fridge when it went out, but you're right, I would rather have my money going to something that I can *own*. I paid off my car this year and it felt so great that I bought myself a bottle of merlot and went crazy with it. By crazy, I mean I drank it and watched bad reality TV that no one wants to admit they watch."

I chuckled. "Sounds like my kind of night!"

"It was fun," she admitted, smiling at the memory. "I wanted to ask you, since you mentioned it last time, if you were serious about helping me work out buying a house."

"Absolutely. Whatever you need, here I am," I promised.

She relaxed, obviously relieved. "I was worried about asking because we just met last week, but I felt like we've been friends for years." She stopped herself, embarrassed.

I nodded encouragingly. "No, I understand what you mean and I feel the same way. It's too bad we didn't go to school together because I'd have all sorts of blackmail stories on you."

"No. I was kind of boring as a child and as a teenager. I went to school like I was supposed to and never skipped classes. I made good grades and never really got into trouble," Abby said quietly.

"Oh." I shifted in my chair. "I cannot say the same."

Her brown eyes shined. "What did you do?" she whispered, leaning over the table.

"I got busted for skipping classes," I answered.

"That's it?" She was disappointed.

"Okay, I'll tell you the worst thing. I set the auditorium on fire."

"You're joking!"

I was nodding my head. "I'm dead serious. There was a group of us working late after school on the prom committee. There was a stage in our auditorium and it had these thick, red velvet curtains that hung down. Someone had brought in sparklers and I was playing with them. I guess I got bored over what the theme should be and, without realizing it, got too close to the curtains. Velvet burns really fast, but I put it out quickly."

"You must have gotten grounded for weeks and suspended."

"I didn't get suspended. I had a good *talking to*."

"You got lucky! You can't bring that kind of thing to school anymore." She grinned. "I'm fairly certain you couldn't have brought them in then, either. But that's a great story!" She laughed.

I felt guilty for not being able to tell her the entire truth. I had shot off fireworks from my fingers so that I could show the other members of the committee—witches like me—that we could pull it off without mortals realizing it wasn't magic. Unfortunately, a firework had hit the curtains and they went ablaze quickly. It was hot, smoky, and dark. One of the members created a light that shined powerfully out of her palms while the rest of us dipped our hands into the air, grasped water, and threw it onto the flames. With the fire out, I waved my hands and the curtains were back to normal and nothing was damaged. The Council did find out because the girl who shined the light had ratted me out to her mother who was on the board. Her mother did talk to me, though it was more to explain that I could have just stopped the flames without "all of the theatrics."

"If you don't mind," Abby said, interrupting my thoughts, "would you go look at houses with me? I don't know much about inspections and I was hoping you could guide me."

"Sure. I already know a good realtor. He's kind of a pig, but he grows on you."

"I hope you're going to actually buy your gifts," Mom chided me. She grabbed my elbow and guided me into a large department store where we were immediately assaulted by perfume.

"If you like Poison, try Arsenic!" a saleswoman said, spritzing the air. "It's the latest creation from Moo!"

"Is the slogan, 'Be that toxic person in someone's life?'" I asked drily. Mom tightened her grip and pulled me away from the now very-confused looking saleswoman.

"You could be a little nicer," my mother snapped. "It's Christmas."

"I can't have fun around Christmas?"

"Sometimes you think your jokes are funny when they're not."

I shrugged. "As long as I think I'm funny, my self-esteem will be upheld."

Mom's lips formed a thin, straight line.

"Care to try some lipstick, ma'am? I can show you some tricks to make that pout look fuller!" said a young male. He held a tube of lipstick in his hand like it was a wand.

"No, thank you," Mom said tersely. She let go of my elbow and walked away hastily toward the purses.

"He was just trying to help."

Holding a bright yellow tote bag, she glanced at me out of the side of her eye. "What do you think about this for Cecily?" she asked, brushing off our slight disagreement. She always did that when she found a subject distasteful and wanted to move past it. My mother was an expert at gracefully changing an unpleasant subject.

"I think she'd have a fit about the color." I began to whine, "Why, oh why is this yellow? For God's sake, woman, don't you know the kids? The kids! Yellow will show stains! And this doesn't have a long strap to go across my chest? Do you think I'm an octopus with enough arms for the kids' things *and* a tote? Well, let me tell you that I am no octopus. Just a mere, annoying, pregnant mortal!" I paused for a moment. In my natural voice, I added, "She might not call herself annoying, but the rest I feel is accurate."

Despite her best effort, Mom laughed heartily. "If Randy loves her, then we should love her. She is a part of this family," she finally said once her laughter died down.

"You don't have to try and sell her to me," I said. I cleared my throat. "I promise I'll behave."

"And?" Mom prompted, an eyebrow raised.

"And I will try to like Cecily more. She's easier to handle in small doses."

Mom nodded in agreement. "That's true." She found a designer diaper bag in black with a long, thick strap. She ran her fingers over the buttery soft leather. "This is nice. Surely she'd like this." She checked the price tag. "I don't think I like Cecily enough to spend that much."

"You could just create one yourself."

"I have a Christmas budget. Don't you think Lewis would notice if the money wasn't missing? He would question where all of the gifts came from when the money for them is still in the account."

"You could tell him the truth. I hear that's always something that a husband and wife should do."

"I might one day," Mom said casually. She sauntered near a beautiful periwinkle purse and began checking the pockets and zippers.

I knew she was only saying that to placate me, but I decided to drop the subject anyway. "Is that for you or Cecily?"

"Are you kidding? This is for me. You're right. I'll just create that diaper bag for Cecily and spend the money on this beautiful purse for me." She checked the price and smiled. "I like me enough to spend this."

"What about Lewis? Won't he notice you have a new purse?"

"Carmen, this is a spring bag. I'll store it for now and, when spring comes around, I'll use it then. Lewis probably won't even notice. Men don't notice that stuff." She looked across the racks of purses to the salesman who offered her a lipstick tutorial. "Except for that man. He'd notice, but then he does apply makeup better than I do. I might come back and let him give me a makeover."

"I'm sure he'd be happy to do it," I said quickly. "Are you almost done with this store?" I asked.

"Why, am I keeping you from an important appointment?" Mom asked sarcastically.

"No, but I'd like to finish my list today and we can't do that when you're shopping for yourself."

"What did you get for me?" my mother asked, taking the periwinkle purse to the checkout counter.

"That's a secret."

She swiped her debit card and punched in her PIN. "I haven't even told you what I want yet," she murmured, signing her name. She tucked the card back into her wallet and looked at me. "I want a pretty necklace."

"Great. I'll get you one for your birthday or Mother's Day," I replied. I took the plastic bag containing her new purse and we left the department store, entering the wide hall of the mall. Its carpeting was thick along the sides, but worn thin in the middle where it had seen years of traffic. The rest of the mall hadn't seen an update since I was a teenager, but it was one of the few places to go in New Bern and was just as busy as ever.

Mom pulled a piece of paper out of her pocket and tried to read it. She rifled through her purse until she found her reading glasses and, after donning them, began to read again. "That's better," she said, more to herself than to me. "Just you and Finn and I cannot buy something for you with you here. What about you? Who is left on your list?"

I pulled out my own piece of paper and scanned it. "Finn."

"Do you have any idea on what to get for him?"

I smiled. "I do."

The guitar was blonde wood with a shiny, protective coating. The Les Paul was from 1959 and absolutely beautiful. "This is a good idea for Finn."

"That's a nice gift, but it costs five thousand dollars," Mom pointed out.

I waved my hand dismissively. "I'll create one," I said simply. I took out my phone and began to photograph it sans flash in the climate-controlled room.

"You can't get him a guitar. Finn doesn't have much money and he'll feel badly that he can't buy you something as nice," Mom argued.

"I'll tell him it's a knockoff," I said, gingerly removing the guitar from its rack to photograph the back.

Mom shifted her weight from foot to foot, thinking. "Lewis and I will buy him six months of guitar lessons, then," she said. "He was taking them, you know, then he stopped."

I replaced the guitar and turned to look at my mother. "I do. He said he didn't make the time for it."

She smiled sadly. "He couldn't really afford it, but he was getting pretty good for the short amount of time he spent practicing."

"Why doesn't he try to change his job if he isn't doing that well?" I asked carefully.

Mom sighed deeply. "He's afraid of change," she admitted. "He's a great kid. I say kid and he's barely two years older than you are." She laughed softly. "He was offered a job in South Carolina, but he chose not to take it. He's got his dad here and his mom is an hour away. His friends are here."

"His friends aren't the best influences," I pointed out.

"I know that. They're fine mooching off their parents when they spend money on beer and cigarettes instead of paying their bills," Mom said, bitter. "Finn knows better than to expect us to do that for him," she added quickly.

The door to the climate-controlled room opened silently and a music store employee entered. "May I help you ladies today?" he asked, his smile a little too wide and eager.

"No, thank you," I answered.

"I see you're eyeballing that Les Paul. That'd make an excellent Christmas gift!" he said encouragingly.

"I think I'm going to go a different route for my stepbrother," I said.

"Oh." The employee's shoulders drooped.

"I could use the name of a great guitar teacher," Mom said.

The employee straightened and smiled, if possible, even wider. "I know a great person to teach guitar!" he gushed.

Then he handed my mother his card.

Chapter Six

Back home, I scrutinized every photo I had taken of the guitar. I let go of my cell phone and it hovered in the air while I placed my hands over the top of my dining table. Concentrating hard, I moved my hands as if actually feeling the instrument beneath my skin, starting with the headstock. I twisted my fingers to form the tuning keys and tuning pegs, then the nut and the rest of the neck. The fret board came next, followed by the body. The electronics came last and, finally, the small details that made the decorative yet functional pieces of the guitar.

I could physically feel my forehead relax when I opened my eyes and peered down at the new instrument I had created. I compared it against the pictures and mentally gave myself a pat on the back.

I delicately picked it up and strummed the strings, satisfied with the sound. I couldn't wait to see Finn's face when he opened this gift. I waved my hands and wrapping paper snaked its way around the curves of the guitar. A bright red ribbon tied itself into a perfect bow around the instrument's body.

I motioned for the guitar to go away and it rose from the table. "Go on," I said.

It fell back to the table, stubborn. My eyes widened. "I forgot the amp. I suppose Finn will need that to play you, won't he?" I snapped my fingers and an amp appeared. Only really intricate pieces needed the amount of concentration I had used for the guitar and I was relieved that amplifiers weren't on that list. It wrapped itself, though it completed itself with a green bow. Satisfied, the guitar rose again from the table and zipped back toward the hall closet, the amp following closely behind it.

Phone still floating in the air, I motioned for it to follow me as I went into the kitchen. It was getting later and I looked through my pantry and fridge, not quite finding what I wanted. "Ask Siobhan if she's busy," I instructed my phone.

"Not at all," came Siobhan's quick reply.

I closed my eyes and thought of Siobhan's colonial-style home. When I opened my eyes, I was standing by her back door, hand poised to knock.

She answered the door while my hand was still in the air. "Fancy seeing you here on a work night," she said.

"I had a hankering for the *Blue Bird Café*."

"You know, they're having one of my favorite comedians at *Zanies* if you want to join me this weekend," she suggested, leading me to her garage.

"We're driving? There's no parking over there," I protested, ignoring her question.

"You know there's no place to pop in undetected over there."

"What about the bathroom? And I can't make it this weekend."

Siobhan opened the door to her Audi. "Look, I just traded up and I like this car. I get it now with your Volvo. We're driving."

I slid into the passenger side and she started the engine, the garage door still down. "I'm not suicidal yet."

"Drama queen," Siobhan teased, raising the garage door. She eased the green sedan out into her driveway, then looked both ways before pulling onto the street. "What are you really doing here? Is this something about your new job as an Influencer?"

I said nothing.

"I'm a Muse. I can sense those things. Don't worry, your secret is safe with me."

"I didn't know you could do that."

"That's why I'm good at secrets. There's a lot of things I can do that you don't know about because Fate wants it that way."

"I need a favor," I admitted.

Siobhan cursed at the traffic. "I shouldn't have taken sixty-five," she muttered.

"Nashville doesn't really stop having a rush hour when it comes to this highway."

"It's not that bad," Siobhan said defensively. "The trade-off is that there is so much more here than in your little town."

"I like my little town. It has character."

"Nashville has plenty of character, too. Just take a stroll down Broadway." Impatient, she began to swerve in and out of lanes.

"Tourists frequent that street, not so much the locals."

"You do if you want to go to *Puckett's.*" She sneered when another driver flipped her off.

My mouth watered at the name of the restaurant. Nashville *did* have a lot of amazing places to eat.

Siobhan pulled off onto the exit and into a residential area. We passed the café and parked a few blocks away. She lovingly ran her hand over the hood of the Audi, placing an anti-theft charm on it. "That's how you stop a thief in a questionable neighborhood," she said, grinning.

We began walking toward to the café, silent at first. Finally, I prodded, "What about my favor?"

"What about the comedy club?" she retorted.

"You know that falls on Christmas Eve, right?"

"Really?" Siobhan stopped and looked at me. She tucked her honey-colored hair behind her ear and pouted. "Where has the year gone?" Worried, she asked, "Should I get something for Percy?"

"You haven't been together for that long, so make it something small."

We started walking again, Siobhan wringing her hands in thought. "I can see the show and my family in the same night," she grumbled, more to herself than to me.

We approached the *Blue Bird Café*, seeing the throng of customers that already waited outside. The café was a small restaurant with seating so crowded that you wound up eating with strangers. They could have had more tables if it were not for the makeshift stage for live music, but this was Nashville and live music is basically everywhere. Cozy was the best word to describe the café, but the food was incredible. The breakfast was especially wonderful and we were lucky enough that they served it all day.

Siobhan gave our names to the hostess and swirled her finger when the hostess wasn't looking so that our names climbed higher on the list.

"That's cheating," I murmured.

"It's not. It's prioritizing," she quipped.

I hugged my arms around my body and shivered. "You'll probably get another ice storm," I noted casually.

Siobhan snorted. "When don't we get an ice storm here? I miss regular snow. I can drive on that."

A waiting customer laughed. "I hear that!"

Siobhan nodded in his direction, then shifted her focus back to me. "I'll do it."

"I haven't asked what I wanted yet."

"You wouldn't ask if you didn't really need it."

"Finn just needs a push. Between Mom and me, we're getting him a guitar and the lessons. I was hoping that, if you were there for the first lesson, it would inspire him to stick with it. I have a feeling that this will take him somewhere important."

Siobhan pursed her lips. "Playing the guitar will change his path?" She was doubtful.

"I think so."

She cupped her hands around her mouth and breathed warm air into them. "All right, then," she said, her voice muffled.

"Waters, Devereaux!" called the hostess.

Those still waiting for a table groaned in protest. Siobhan lowered her hands and smiled brightly. "That's us!" I watched her practically bound toward the entrance and into the heated interior. She turned and beckoned for me.

Feeling guilty that I didn't feel guilty about magically cutting the line, I followed.

My heater was on full blast with a little magical boost as I waited in the parking lot for Abby. The temperature had dropped significantly in North Carolina and I was actually looking forward to hot yoga. We both had punch cards to finish out and we agreed that I'd pick her up after school.

I watched Abby emerge from the school building, a relieved look on her face. It was the day before Christmas Eve and only a half day for the teachers and students. Abby had admitted that she enjoyed the breaks as much as the children did, and I knew she was looking forward to a week of peace.

A short, slender woman with long, silky black hair and eyes a startling pale brown followed closely behind Abby, almost marching. She reached out and grabbed Abby's arm so fiercely that the motion spun Abby around to face her. Abby dropped her turquoise tote and the woman cruelly looked down upon her as she bent down to pick it up.

Abby's face darkened as the woman spoke harshly to her. Abby kept her head down shyly as she mumbled a reply and walked away, her eyes on the ground.

I got out of the Volvo. "Abby!" I called cheerfully, waving my arms wildly. The black-haired woman shot me a nasty glance, her eyes filled with hate. I squinted and a gust of wind hit her so hard in the stomach that she doubled over, falling to her knees. "You okay, ma'am?" I shouted sweetly.

The woman hastily stood up and brushed away the dirt that had collected on her knees. She cursed under her breath when she realized she had grass stains. Another squint and another gust of wind knocked her back onto her butt. She sprang up as quickly as she had gone down and almost ran back inside of the school. I smiled to myself and felt something in my pocket. It was a note that read: *That wasn't nice, but I like your style. −Simon.* I chuckled. I hadn't realized he had been watching and hoped it wouldn't count against me later.

Abby excitedly grabbed my wrists after strolling across the parking lot. "Did you see that?" she asked. She was talking quickly, something I noticed she did when she was happy. "I don't know how that happened, but that was wonderful! Miss Priss needed to be knocked off her high horse!"

"Who is she?"

"She's an English teacher named Lauren Lennox. She's awful." Abby scowled as she spoke of her.

We got into the car, Abby putting her hands up by the vents to warm them. It reminded me that I needed to buy my friends gloves for Christmas. I absently ran one thumb over the other and the present I had bought for Abby changed to a pair of deep purple cashmere gloves with a matching toboggan. An almost matching set appeared in my hall closet, though it was bright green to match Siobhan's eyes.

"What did she say to you?"

Abby placed her hands into her lap and stared at them. "She said it must have been nice to have special needs kids so that I can play all day while the normal students and teachers have to do real work," she answered softly.

I felt my jaw tighten in anger.

"I told her she knows it's not that easy and she just laughed at me."

"Why don't you tell her to blow it out her ass and not take that kind of crap from her?"

Abby shook her head vigorously. "I could never do that. Lauren is the kind of person that was the most popular girl in high school and she's like that here."

"You teach middle school."

"It doesn't matter. The teachers act like they're still in high school. They have cliques and everything." She sniffed. "It's really frustrating. They're not exactly welcoming to me and I have been nothing but nice to them. They think I spend my days watching movies and playing games, but that couldn't be further from the truth. The kids I teach…" her voice trailed off.

I pulled into the yoga studio's parking lot, but said nothing, waiting for her to finish.

"They have real problems. They barely know the alphabet or how to count. We're working on basic math skills and the games I create or the ones I use that someone else made are designed *specifically* for children whose minds haven't progressed the way a normal student's has. They might be games, but they serve a purpose. My students may not be rocket scientists, but I hope I am preparing them to live in a world where they can be semi-independent because that is the best-case scenario for them. Most of them will always need someone to help them and that breaks my heart." Her eyes had welled up with tears and I handed her a tissue she didn't see me create. "I'm sorry. I just love those kids, you know? I wish I could do more."

"What do you think you could do?"

She sat quietly, thinking. "I saw something once, but I couldn't get that off the ground. Not by myself, anyway."

"What's that?" I prompted.

"Just a special kind of place for kids outside of school." She flashed a nervous smile, dabbed at her eyes. "Let's go inside and be trees," she said, changing the subject.

I nodded and got out of the sedan, popping open the trunk for our gym bags. Noticing the wrapped presents, she pointed. "Those are wrapped beautifully."

I reached in and grabbed two of the packages. "I was going to wait, but these are for you."

Her eyes widened. "Hold that thought." She hurried to the passenger side, opened the door, and grabbed something out of her tote. She returned holding two mason jars with neat little red and white bows tied around them. "I hope you like hot chocolate and brownie mix!" she said.

We switched packages and I opened the jar of hot chocolate. "You even added the mini-marshmallows! I love those!"

"Cashmere gloves and a hat? These are so nice! You didn't have to go to the trouble."

"You're my friend. It was no trouble, I promise." I smiled at her. "Thank you! I can't wait to bake those brownies."

"It's my grandma's recipe. I don't just give those out to anyone."

I lowered my voice. "I won't tell a soul."

Abby laughed. She tucked her gifts back into her tote and placed the mason jars inside the cup holders. "I needed that. Thank you, Carmen."

I gave her a hug. "Anytime, Abby."

We entered the yoga studio, the stick-thin receptionist nowhere to be seen. "Maybe she fell between the floor boards," Abby joked.

Laughing, we pushed open the glass door to the main studio. Candles were lit everywhere and incense was strongly burning. Women and men were already lying on their mats, quietly waiting for the yogi to arrive.

Abby and I copied them, though whispered amongst ourselves from the back of the room. "This reminds me of the sorority I almost joined," she said quietly.

"You? A sorority?"

"I know, I know," Abby whispered hastily. "I wanted to find a group where I'd fit in and I was hoping a sorority was the answer."

"You know women who join those are usually called 'frat mattresses', right?"

"What?" Abby asked, confused. Her eyes grew rounder as she understood the phrase. "That's just wrong."

"Wrong are the women who fit the stereotype. Not that you do," I added quickly. "Why didn't you join?"

"It was the money. I didn't realize they charge a fee each semester. I didn't want to pay for my friends. I could do just as much work as they did with other volunteer groups on campus."

"I didn't know they did charity work."

Abby snickered. "They say that they do, but I rarely saw them when I was at various school functions." She inhaled deeply. "They mostly threw parties and complained that they couldn't share an actual home like the fraternities because then they'd be considered a brothel." She giggled. "I suppose some of them did behave as if they lived in one."

"Ouch," I said.

"If the shoe fits," she replied.

The yogi finally arrived, the receptionist not far behind him. They both appeared disheveled.

"Looks like she's a yogi mattress," I said softly.

Abby's laughter filled the room. The yogi glanced at her harshly and she shrugged. "If the shoe fits," she repeated quietly as the session began.

"I don't know why we had to come all the way over here. Don't they know how difficult it is to get Apple in and out of her car seat?"

"Honey, it's because Dad and Evelyn have the biggest house to accommodate all of us," Randy said, trying to soothe his wife.

Cecily crossed her arms over her burgeoning belly. "It will be different when this baby comes. Then they'll *have* to come to us. It will be just impossible to get Apple *and* an infant into their car seats."

Finn caught my eye and shook his head. There was a lot of tongue-biting when it came to Cecily.

"Would you mind helping me with something in the kitchen?" I asked Finn.

He eagerly rose to his feet, happy for an excuse to leave his brother and sister-in-law.

"What could he possibly help you with in the kitchen?" Cecily asked incredulously.

I smiled, leaned over, and patted Cecily's knee. "You just sit your pretty little pregnant butt on that couch and let us take care of all the work. After all, you did just make that long, exhausting trip of three miles to Mom and Lewis's house."

I could feel her jaw working angrily as I walked away from her. Finn stifled a laugh until we reached the kitchen. "You know you can't talk to her that way. It will upset Randy," he chided.

I bit my lip. "I know, but sometimes I just can't help myself. She is insufferable!"

"Not to our brother. Maybe she'll grow on us," he said hopefully. "Maybe the rush of hormones from the new baby will mellow her out."

"Aren't you the optimist?" I said, opening the refrigerator. I pulled out the deviled eggs and took off the lid. I offered one to Finn and he grabbed two. I took two as well and replaced the Tupperware.

"Are you eating the deviled eggs already?"

Finn and I whirled around guiltily, our mouths full. Mom was glaring at us from the other entrance, her hands on her hips. "No," I said, my voice muffled from the deviled egg.

Finn ducked his head and shoved the entire second egg into his mouth. He gulped. "She offered it to me. I thought it was okay," Finn said quickly.

I finished my own egg. "Bus driver," I replied.

Finn held up his hands like he was driving a steering wheel and pretended the other hand was on the gear shift. "Driving forward," he said, leaning forward. He moved his hand backward and took off his hat, using it to wave at me. "And then driving back to make sure I got you."

Mom's face cracked into a smile. "It's okay. There are more in the fridge out in the garage. I just knew you two would steal a bite before dinner."

"We already ate those," Finn said, his face serious.

Mom's eyes became steely, her mouth a thin line.

He held up his hands in front of his chest, palms outward. "I'm just kidding!"

My mother laughed and Finn relaxed. She shooed us out of the kitchen so that she could check on her prime rib.

"Your mother is a real character," Finn said.

"Don't I know it!" I opened the patio door and we went outside into the cool night air. Finn turned on the patio heater and joined me, sitting in the chair next to mine.

"I wanted to thank you again for your gift. That is an amazing guitar." He shook his head. "I cannot believe that it's a knockoff of the '59 Les Paul. Whoever you got to make that could make a fortune."

"It's just an old friend who likes to do that in her spare time as a hobby," I lied.

"I love it. I wish I could've played around with it more this afternoon. Damn that Cecily," he grumbled. He had excitedly hooked up the guitar to the amp after he unwrapped his gifts and strummed a few chords before Cecily complained that it would wake up Apple from her nap.

"The world revolves around her and the offspring."

"Doesn't leave much for Randy, does it?" He sighed. "If he's happy, though…" Finn stopped, lost in thought.

"I hope you'll take advantage of those lessons and make the time for them. I know you have so much potential. I'd hate to see you waste it," I said carefully.

My stepbrother looked at me thoughtfully for a moment. "You're not just talking about playing the guitar, are you?"

I blushed, caught. "I just think you don't give yourself enough credit. You could do better if you wanted to, you know."

"I like my job," Finn said simply.

"Don't you want to be able to live in a nicer apartment without a roommate? To be able to pay all of your bills and still have some extra to put into a savings account? To not have to ask your dad for help?"

Finn's eyes flashed and I knew I had gone too far. "I don't have to ask for help."

I took a deep breath and pushed onward. "I know you're going hungry when you can't afford to eat. You might not ask for help anymore, but you're still going without."

Finn jumped up from his chair so quickly it almost fell over. "I don't have a fancy job like you that allows me to have a fancy house. I didn't go to school."

"Whose fault is that?"

He turned away from me and I saw his shoulders slump. "It's mine."

I was quiet for a few moments, thinking. Finally, I said, "Finn, what if you moved into my house? There's a room downstairs with a full bath. It would be your own space and you could stay until you've saved up enough money to really get you going and you can do something better."

"Would I even get the wet bar in the family room?" he asked, his voice small.

"What? No way, we have to share that. That's a family room. You can't just take over the bar." I was grinning.

Finn tapped his chin thoughtfully. "I suppose I will think about it."

"You do that." I gestured toward the door. "We better get back inside. We can't let everyone else suffer in Cecily's presence. It's Christmas, you know. She's like the gift no one wanted."

Chapter Seven

"You've lost your damn mind!" Simon's voice was so high, he was practically squeaking. He paced the length of his office, taking brief moments to glance at his collection of antique fishing hooks hanging from the wall. He finally stopped and sat down heavily in his high-back pleather office chair.

I stared at him, surprised. He had called earlier that day and demanded I get to the office immediately. I remained silent in my chair.

Simon sighed and steepled his hands on top of his large desk. His voice lower, he said, "I just cannot have you risking Finn living with you."

"He's my brother. He needs my help," I replied simply.

Simon vigorously shook his head, his jowls swiveling with the movement. "No, he's your *step*brother and he does *not* need to live with you. You *know* he can see magic and you know mortal family members outside of spouses are not allowed to know about us."

"If we can tattoo mortals to see magic more clearly, is there not one they can get so that they won't?" I asked timidly. Simon was usually a happy man, but he was absolutely furious with me at the moment.

"No, there isn't a tattoo! That's why there are Erasers! Which you might as well invite them to live with you as well because you're going to need one on a daily basis!" He flattened his palms against his walnut desk. "You will rescind your offer." He spread his palms over the desk, then back together. "You will apologize and tell him that you're just not ready to live with someone again after your divorce." He repeated his hand movement. "That's final."

I sat rigid in my seat, my own anger beginning to churn hotly. "It's my gut feeling that he needs to get out of the environment he's currently in. I'm an Influencer for a reason and this is what I think needs to be done. He needs someone to support him, to be there for him. That someone is me. You've got to trust me on this," I said, trying to keep my anger from boiling over.

Simon caught my gaze and watched me, unblinking, for several moments. He relaxed and sighed, this time in defeat. "You're stubborn."

"It is *my* house," I pointed out.

"That Eraser did like your cooking. I suppose you could get the same one to return who won't cause such a fuss if you need him to." Simon tilted his head thoughtfully. "No magic in the house."

"No magic when he's around," I argued.

My boss nodded. "This isn't a long-term situation, is it?"

I drummed my fingers impatiently on the armrest. "I don't know what his alternate path is, so I don't know. What will happen to him if he continues down his current path?" I asked curiously.

"Nothing," Simon answered simply.

"What do you mean *nothing*?"

"I mean nothing. He'll get up, go to work, and repeat the process."

"That's not bad. A lot of people follow that pattern."

Simon narrowed his eyes. "He'll work at his job where he will never advance and he'll never feel good enough to try. He'll date women from time to time, but they'll be nobodies, just people to warm his bed. The worst one will appeal to his softer side and be a worthless piece of crap who refuses to work but says she needs the money to stay at home with her kids while her estranged husband works. That's right, she'll still be married but will claim she's getting a divorce." Simon shook his head. "She's not getting a divorce. She'll just continue to accept Finn's help because he has a good heart and he genuinely believes he's doing the right thing. She'll break his heart and he'll become bitter, never have a meaningful relationship, and die an unhappy man."

"Oh," was all that I could muster.

"You're going to ask me about Abby, but I can't tell you that."

"Is it worse than Finn?"

"No."

"Then why won't you tell me?"

"Because I don't know," Simon replied sheepishly.

There was a hard, fast knock on the door and Simon called for the visitor to enter. My android joined us by taking a seat in the chair next to mine. "Sir?" she said and I shuddered internally. It was eerie watching and hearing myself.

"What do you need, Carmen?" Simon asked, tired.

"I seem to be malfunctioning."

Simon jumped to his feet and rushed over to the android. "What's the problem? I'll call Samuel right away."

Android Carmen shook her head sadly, the ends of her pale blonde hair brushing against her collarbone with the motion. "I was asked a question today and I didn't understand it."

I chuckled. "That's not a malfunction."

"It is when you're a perfect android," Android Carmen snapped.

"What were you asked?" Simon asked.

"I was asked, 'Why did the chicken cross the road?' I don't understand this. Why *would* a chicken cross the road? What business does the fowl have in doing this? Surely there's chicken wire to keep it enclosed in its pen?"

Simon and I exchanged glances and I rose to my feet. I patted him on the shoulder. "You have fun with this," I said, trying to contain my giggle.

"You're not going to help with this?"

"I would, but it's funnier for me if I leave you to it." I smiled brightly and slowly faded away as Simon stood in front of me, his mouth open in frustration.

Abby ran her hands over the carvings on the bar as she looked in awe at the room around her. "I cannot believe you have a real bar in here!" she exclaimed. "I want one of these!"

I had invited Abby to my home to hang out for a little while before Percy picked us up in an hour to look at houses for her. "I didn't want this. It was just a bonus, really."

"What a nice bonus to have! I love this house. It's very charming."

"Thank you," I said warmly.

She paused outside of Finn's room. He hadn't moved in yet, but we had plans to do that over the weekend. "Kind of bare in here, isn't it?"

"It is," I agreed.

"Everything else is classic but it looks like you forgot your guest room. Or were you going to use this for storage because you have another guest room upstairs?"

I shook my head. "I did have it decorated, but my stepbrother is moving in with me. I want him to make it his own."

Abby's face darkened. "You're letting your stepbrother move in? Why? I thought you liked living alone."

I frowned, not understanding why Abby was upset. "I think he's not in the best place right now and I offered him my place until he found something better down the road." I was talking about his place in life, but Abby misinterpreted my words.

"Ah," she said and ascended the stairs that led to my kitchen. She ignored my bar stools and leaned over the counter, shuffling her paperwork. She had made an Excel form with her salary, current expenses, and how much she had leftover each month. "There's no way I could afford a house like this on my teacher's salary," she said, bitter.

"Wait a minute," I said. "What's with the attitude?"

She rubbed her temples. "I'm sorry," she muttered, looking at the countertop.

I softened my tone. "Seriously? What's wrong with you?"

"I'm just in a mood. I don't need a house this size. I just need something small and that I can call my own so I'm not wasting money on rent anymore." She still wouldn't look at me.

"Who put you in a mood?" I asked, knowing the answer as I spoke.

"It's Lauren Lennox." She spat the name. "She heard I was house-hunting and told me I might as well live in a studio apartment because I was going to remain alone."

"Don't let that bitch get you down," I said sternly. "People like that are just miserable and they make fun of others so they can feel better about themselves."

"Classic bully tactics, I know. I hear about this at the assembly we have once a year."

"You could always tell her to fuck off," I offered.

Abby inhaled sharply. "I could never do that. I don't have that in me."

"Sure you do. You just need to be more confident. We've talked about this. Confidence isn't just sexy. It's a necessity for getting what you want out of life, or at least trying."

"I'll work on it," she said. She scanned her finger down her list of expenses. "I wish I could get rid of this one. It costs me over a hundred dollars a month just to color my hair."

"Stop coloring your hair." I flashed a smile. "See? One problem solved already."

Abby's lips pursed briefly as she tried to hide her grin. "I wish I could. I want it back to my natural hair color, but I don't know if the stylist can't figure out how to do that or if she doesn't want to because I'm income to her." She eyed my pale blonde hair. "Do you color yours?"

"No, I never have. Any other color would just seem odd with my skin tone."

"You are basically translucent. If I hadn't seen you out in the sun, I would have thought you were a vampire."

"How original," I said drily.

"I know, sorry." She laughed. "I remember you telling me about the kids picking on you."

"I'm pretty good with hair color. I could dye it for you if you'd like."

"You'd do that for me?"

I nodded. "Of course. Listen, I dyed a friend's hair recently and I still have a bunch of different brown shades. I'm sure I could mix them to match to your roots." As I spoke, I wiggled my fingers so that an assortment of hair coloring mixture appeared underneath my bathroom sink.

"Do we have time?" Abby asked, looking at the clock.

"We have almost an hour. I'm really good at this." A pang of guilt hit me. I hated how easy it was becoming to lie and any woman could tell you it takes more than an hour to change the color of your hair.

Abby took a seat on my vanity chair and I draped a towel around her shoulders. "All over color, please," she said. "My eyebrows might help if the roots aren't long enough."

"Sure," I murmured. I grabbed two random bottles and told her I would mix it in a bowl from the kitchen. I pulled a plastic bowl from a cabinet and held my hand over it. I gripped the air as if one of the bottles was being held and tilted my hand. A perfect mixture flowed from the empty space in my grip and into the bowl. I snapped my fingers and a brush materialized.

"Have you ever noticed how the solution looks like it is purple?" Abby asked when I had returned. She peered into the bowl. "Except for yours."

"I think it's a difference in brands," I said hastily. I put rubber gloves over my hands and proceeded to paint her hair in sections.

"What about a dryer?"

"Have you ever been to an Aveda salon?" I asked.

"No."

"You should. They're the best! They offer a neck and shoulder massage while your hair is in a masque. That's all complementary. Anyway, they use natural products and they don't need a dryer to let the product set."

"I don't think we have one of those here," Abby said gloomily.

"No, but maybe one day," I said hopefully.

I finished covering Abby's hair in color and waved my hands over it, trying to be as casual as possible. I wanted to ensure it wouldn't fade over time and she'd never have roots again until she chose to visit another salon and color it a different shade.

"That was fast," Abby said forty-five minutes later. "We're kind of cutting it close, aren't we?"

"Percy can wait a minute if we need him to," I shouted over the sound of the hairdryer. Once completed, I put a dab of Moroccan oil into my hands to smooth her hair.

I finished styling her hair and handed her a mirror so that she could see the back. "I cannot believe how good this looks! It looks like I've never colored my hair in my life."

"I'm glad you like it," I said, throwing the towel I had used into my hamper.

The doorbell rang. "Right on cue," Abby murmured, still looking at herself.

I opened the front door, Abby padding down the hallway behind me.

"Hello, ladies," Percy said. He straightened his dove gray suit jacket. "Are you ready to find your new home?"

A month later I found myself grilling chicken in the frigid cold that threatened snow. Say what you want about a famous former boxer's indoor grill, but few things beat the taste that charcoal creates.

Finn had moved in and I was surprised at how well we got along as roommates. Admittedly it was a harder transition than I had expected to not use magic as often at home and Tess had pouted that she couldn't just pop in anymore, but things were working out smoothly. He was taking weekly guitar lessons and, thanks to Siobhan, was picking it up quickly and his interest wasn't waning. His instructor had said that he absorbed in a month what it had taken other students six months to grasp.

I had learned quickly that he seemed to spend the majority of his paycheck at local bars and I had to have a serious conversation with him. I had explained that I had offered my home to him so that he could save money and, hopefully, find something more fruitful to sustain him. I didn't mean for him to move in and decide that he'd only have enough money to pay the rent we had agreed upon. He had balked initially, claiming that he was a "grown-ass man" and could spend his money as he pleased. I told him that, at his rate, he'd wind up in a broken-down, rusty single-wide trailer, with an equally crappy car that wouldn't start most days to take him to his lousy job. I knew I was being extremely harsh, but he needed to hear it. He had been so angry with me that he had stormed out of the house.

When he returned, he apologized and said that no one had ever been so blunt with him. "I guess I needed a figurative foot up my ass," he said quietly.

Abby had since found a home and it was going to close soon. Her landlord was giving her a little trouble over having to find someone to move in during the middle of winter and she had almost agreed to stay longer. I told her that the occupancy of the apartment wasn't her problem and she didn't need to feel guilty for wanting to do something great for herself. The house was roughly one hundred years old and needed some work, which I had promptly promised to help her with.

I flipped the chicken and closed the hood of the grill. I paced and stamped my feet to keep warm and noticed the churning of snow nearby. Worried, I glanced toward the back door leading to the kitchen.

"Don't worry, he can't see me," Lenny said dismissively.

"He can see snowmen," I argued.

Lenny rolled his button eyes. "I know that. I meant he can't see me from this angle."

"Uh-huh."

"Really!" Lenny had upgraded his arms and these were able to bend. They were currently placed on his hips.

"Is there something you wanted to tell me or did you just show up because you forgot to record the latest reality show?"

"Don't be ridiculous, Carmen. I don't watch all of them. I do have standards, you know. Watching bachelors and their damn roses got old."

"Sorry if I offended you," I said insincerely.

Lenny sniffed, not noticing my tone. "It's okay."

I lifted the lid and checked on my chicken. It was close to being finished.

"That smells wonderful," Lenny said, leaning forward. The wave of heat hit him as I closed the lid and he shuddered. "Watch it!" he snapped. "I'm stuck to ice cream, milkshakes, shaved ice, and smoothies. Anything cold or frozen."

"I can't imagine why."

Lenny's eyes narrowed. "Is that a snowman joke?"

"Of course not," I said quickly.

"Listen, the reason I'm here is to let you know that you're on the right track."

"Really? I feel like Finn is doing better, but what about Abby? Nothing has changed except for the house she bought."

"The house is what sparks the real change," Lenny said mysteriously.

"She's going to become a house flipper?"

Lenny snickered. "No."

I was growing impatient. "Listen, I'm getting really tired of this cryptic crap. You have to give me something else here." An idea popped into my head. "Is this about Lauren Lennox? She's a bully that's on Abby's case a lot. Abby's been doing better about sticking up for herself, though it's a slow process and only when I'm near."

He threw his stick arms in the air. "She's meant to buy something else. Before you go running that mouth, I can't tell you what. I'm sorry, but that is the best that I can do for you right now."

I smiled. "Thank you, Lenny." I meant it. I lifted the lid again and began piling chicken onto a plate I had conjured. I touched one, made it cold, and handed it to Lenny.

His button mouth widened into a smile. "Thanks!" he said, shoving the whole piece of chicken into his mouth. His button lips smacked together. "Delicious! See you later!" he yelled, his form bursting apart into little snowflakes.

A chicken bone lay where he had been and I frowned. Lenny had left me the equivalent of his poop.

"What's that stuff?" Abby greeted me at her front door. She had on old clothes with various holes, and her short hair was pulled off her forehead with a purple paisley bandana.

"It's spackle," I answered.

"I don't think I need any."

"Did you pull out any nails?"

Abby nodded.

"Then you need spackle."

"Oh." Abby moved to the side to allow me to enter. Her front door connected to an enclosed front porch, which was perfect for spring and fall months. In February, it was freezing and we hurried back into the main part of the house. Pale gray light poured through the windows. It barely highlighted one of the best features of the house: an intricate, colorful stained-glass window in the living room that Abby had fallen in love with as soon as Percy had led us through the door.

"Do you know if there is hardwood floor underneath this carpet?" I asked. The carpet downstairs was a luxuriously soft chocolate brown that added warmth to the old home. Upstairs, however, was another story. Abby had asked Percy if the owners had run out of money with the carpet downstairs because the bedrooms and hallway on the second floor were covered in a cheap, threadbare vomit-green carpet. The real estate agent hadn't been sure and promised to check, though Abby and I knew he'd never ask such a rude question to the owners themselves.

"It's beautiful!" Abby said excitedly. "Daddy ripped up all of it. That saves me a ton of money not having to replace it. I was sure I would have to spend a small fortune trying to match what's on the first floor."

I inhaled sharply. "Your dad ripped up the carpet even though he knew we were going to paint?"

"Yeah! Wasn't that nice of him? My daddy is such a sweet man."

"I'm sure he is," I murmured.

"What's wrong?"

I hesitated. I had grown up in a home where my mother was close to expert level with power tools and, even though she was magical, she knew how to do all sorts of repairs and building projects. Each of my bookshelves and quilt rack had been built by her. She'd taught me the fundamentals and I had to remind myself that not everyone was as lucky as I was to have someone teach me the basics.

"We're going to paint and you were going to replace the flooring anyway. It's counterproductive to rip up that dingy carpet and expose the hardwood before we finish our project. Do you have a drop cloth?"

Abby shook her head. "No. Daddy said we would just have to be extra neat. He and Mom did buy some painter's tape for me." She had led me into her kitchen where the counters were stacked with paint brushes, trays, and tape.

"This is good," I said. "Look, I brought a drop cloth with me because I didn't know if we'd need an extra. Let me run out and grab it." I rushed to my Volvo and reached into the backseat, a drop cloth materializing in my hands. When I returned, Abby was already upstairs, a large, five-gallon bucket of paint sitting in the middle of her bedroom. She grunted as she lifted it and I spread out the drop cloth. I handed her a spackling knife and she held it limply in her hand.

"Won't the paint just cover the holes?"

I laughed. "No." I held my own tool and dipped it into the spackle. I slid a small glob over a hole and smoothed it over the wall. "That's how you patch a hole properly. When the spackle dries, we'll run sandpaper over it to really smooth it."

Abby looked hopelessly around her room. "They must have had at least fifty pictures hanging up in here."

"Do it right the first time and you won't have to do it again later." I groaned. I sounded like my mother.

"I've been talking to a man," Abby said casually as she smeared spackle over a hole.

"Oh? How did you meet?" I asked curiously.

Abby ducked her head, sheepish. "At school. He's the school security guard."

"I don't remember having a security guard growing up."

"With all of the things going on nowadays, most schools have one or more. It just depends on the size." She moved onto the next hole. "His name is Eric Short. We've been talking for a little while now."

I raised a brow. "How long is a 'little while?'"

"Three weeks."

"Three weeks! You didn't tell me."

Abby reddened. "I didn't want to say anything if I didn't think it wasn't going anywhere."

"Has he asked you out yet?"

She shook her head. "No. We flirt a lot. It seems like he makes excuses to stop by my room more often. He's talked about going out, but hasn't asked."

"Have you asked him?"

"I did, but he said maybe."

It was my turn to shake my head. "Good luck with that," I said and continued my work.

Abby paused, spackle tool held in the air. "What? What's wrong?"

"He's just a work flirt."

"A work flirt?"

"You know, someone you flirt with at work but nothing ever comes of it."

Abby beamed. "No, he just said he's been busy. He's coming by later with a ladder for me to borrow."

"That's nice of him," I said, trying to sound neutral.

"Just wait until you meet him. He's a good guy," she reassured me.

As if on cue, the doorbell rang. "Do I look all right?" Abby asked. She looked down. "I should change!"

"You're working. He knows that. He won't care what you're wearing."

She rushed down the stairs and I looked at the rest of the holes left to be repaired. I quickly checked out the other two bedrooms to see how much damage they had. They were worse than the master bedroom and I brought my hands together in a silent clap, the holes closing immediately. Hearing Abby and Eric coming up the stairs, I rushed back and continued spackling as if I had never left.

"Hello," I said warmly, holding out my hand.

Eric Short glanced down, noticing the extra spackle that had dried on my skin. "Hi," he said tersely, his eyes roaming around the room. He was barely taller than Abby and wore a hooded sweatshirt over cargo shorts. He shoved his hands into his kangaroo pocket and walked around inspecting our work. Abby dragged in the ladder behind her, Eric never offering to help.

I put my hand back at my side. "Sorry, I didn't realize my hand was dirty."

"No problem. If you were as good as I am, you wouldn't spill a drop." He nodded toward the paint. "Nice color you chose, Abby," he said.

"Thank you," Abby said, almost shyly. She pointed to the ladder. "And thank you for the ladder. Carmen and I are going to need this soon."

"No problem," Eric repeated.

"You're a security guard at the school?" I said. "I bet the kids look up to you."

"I'm a police officer," Eric corrected snidely. "We all take turns each year patrolling the school. This year just happens to be my turn."

"That's good. Keeps things fresh," I replied. Inwardly I cringed. This guy was a jerk.

"You have no idea." He turned toward Abby. "I'm really sorry, but I need to go. I just don't feel well."

"What's your malfunction?" I asked wryly.

Eric's head swiveled in my direction, his eyes flashing. "I had a rough week."

I laughed. "You work as a security guard at a middle school. What could possibly have made your week so rough?"

Abby shot me a warning glare.

Ignoring me, Eric said, "I'll see you later, Abby."

"Let me walk you down."

"No, I got it. You ladies have fun up here." Eric tipped a hat that wasn't on his head and exited.

I waited for the front door to close before speaking. "Abby."

"What?"

"Abby, you're a smart woman. You're dumb when it comes to that guy. He's a jerk. He's just a work flirt."

She firmly shook her head. "No, he's a nice guy. If he was just a work flirt, he wouldn't have let me borrow his ladder."

"If he was really interested, he would have tried to score brownie points by offering to help. Abby, he didn't even carry the ladder upstairs for you."

"But he brought it all the way over here," she said, her voice faltering.

I said nothingand concentrated on filling in the leftover holes.

Abby lowered herself onto the floor, her legs crossed. She put her head in her hands. "Damnit," she said. "He's not actually interested in me, is he?"

"Work flirt," I repeated.

"He loaned me his ladder," she said in protest. She was grasping at straws.

"Booty call for the ladder."

Abby was quiet for so long that the spackle was nearly dry.

Finally, she spoke.

"Damn boys."

A few hours and one coat of primer later, Abby and I were seated around her kitchen peninsula—she had grumbled that she would have preferred a real island—and enjoying takeout. She expertly grabbed bits of rice with her chopsticks. Frustrated, I reached into the bag and took the wrapped plastic spork.

"Some of us know how to fix holes in the wall and paint." She picked up a single grain of rice. "Some of us have skills using eating utensils."

"Chopsticks are not a normal eating utensil," I protested.

"Over a billion people use them and that's before you count people in other countries."

"Don't judge me," I said, laughing as I tried to pierce my shrimp with the spork.

"Oh, I'm judging you. I'm judging the shit out of you." She snapped her chopsticks together, mocking me.

"I'm never eating Chinese around you again," I grumbled, a smile on my face.

"Yes, you will because you love *Tsunami* as much as I do."

I finished my meal and reached for the fortune cookies. I held out my hand for her to choose one and she eagerly opened it, her face falling as she broke it open and read the tiny scrap of paper.

"You will avoid a disaster," she said glumly. "I should have eaten takeout weeks ago."

"At least you got a fortune. Mine just told me the Chinese word of the day."

Abby grinned. "Maybe the lottery numbers will work."

I handed her the fortune. "Have at it."

She took it and put it into a kitchen drawer. "For down the road, maybe."

Chapter Eight

M usic wandered softly through the house, slow and melodic. It was comforting to hear as I unloaded groceries onto the counter. I looked outside at my car and, making sure that no one would be coming upstairs anytime soon, whistled. The last of the groceries lifted out of the Volvo's trunk and floated toward the open back door. They settled on the counter and the trunk slammed shut.

The music became harder, more rock and roll, and I found myself dancing to the beat while I put various food and beverages into their correct place within the cabinets and refrigerator.

"You're why we can't go out in public together," Finn said.

I paused, my face holding a deer in headlights expression. I hadn't realized the music had stopped. Blushing, I laughed. "You could learn some moves from me."

Finn shook his head vigorously. "Hell, no!"

I pointed at him. "I know. This is a sexy dance that will attract others. It doesn't matter if they're male or female." I began to pat my head while rubbing my other hand in a circle on my stomach as I swayed my hips awkwardly back and forth. "Coordination. That's what's hot."

Finn groaned. "Stop it."

I kept up the motions and sauntered next to him. "Come on, Finn. This is awesome. This is what all of the kids are doing."

"Are they having a seizure?"

I burst into laughter and stopped. I walked back to the counter and leaned against it. "You love me. I'm your favorite stepsister."

"You've got a funny way of keeping up your self-esteem," Finn replied wryly.

"Someone's got to do it. Are you done with your lesson?"

"Until next time." Finn and I turned toward the top of the stairs where Roach, the guitar instructor, was standing. He held one guitar in a hand and brushed his spikey turquoise hair off his face with the other.

"Thanks, man," Finn said, shaking Roach's hand. "I'll see you next week?"

"Right on." He looked at me. "See you later, Carmen." He opened the back door and exited, his heavy cologne wafting in his wake.

Noticing my scrunched nose, Finn said, "I should have told him at the first lesson that I was allergic to perfume and cologne."

"I wish you had, too," I replied. "It sounds like you're doing really well."

Finn nodded excitedly. "It's coming so naturally to me. Could you tell the difference between when I played and he played?"

"No," I said. I hadn't even realized that both of them had taken turns playing, having assumed it was all Finn.

A grin stretched across his face. "Maybe you should pick an instrument and we can jam together like we talked about."

"You know the ice cream shop down on Main? On Wednesdays after the owner closes, she opens it up to local musicians who just want to play together."

"Loretta does that? Is that why she closes so early?"

"She plays a wicked accordion."

Finn stared at me, waiting for me to laugh. When I didn't, he said, "Oh, you're not kidding." He tilted his head back and forth thoughtfully. "That could work." He looked shyly at his shoes. "Would you go with me?"

"Of course."

"Great," he said quickly. He walked across the kitchen and started opening cabinets.

"Your coffee is in the cabinet over where it always is."

"No, I was looking to see what you bought. Thought I'd make dinner for a change."

I raised an eyebrow. "You never offer to make dinner. Or breakfast. Or anything. You're great at helping with the prep work, though."

He pulled out a box of angel hair pasta with merlot wine sauce and set them next to the stove. "I was thinking that women like men who cook."

"That's a definite plus," I agreed.

"I should learn. I've been watching you. It doesn't look that hard."

"Or maybe I just make it look easy."

Finn guffawed. "Right," he said sarcastically. "I figured I'd give it a try. I'm good at playing the guitar, so why not have another hidden talent that chicks would dig?"

"Women don't like to be called *chicks*. We don't cluck or bob our head up and down."

"Sometimes women do." He grinned wickedly.

"Gross, get your mind out of the gutter." I groaned at him.

"Okay, okay, maybe *women* will appreciate the talent."

I sat down on one of the barstools. "Let me give you a hint, Finn. Women are just happy when a man offers to help. It doesn't necessarily matter what it is, but it is nice when a woman comes home from work and her significant other doesn't even ask; he just starts dinner. There's something to be said about kicking up your feet and all you have to worry about is doing the dishes after you're finished eating. Dinner doesn't even have to be fantastic. This is one where the thought really does count."

"Wouldn't the cook do the dishes?"

"No. It's a trade-off. One cooks and the other cleans."

"Balance is a big deal, then?"

"Balance is a big deal," I echoed. I gestured toward the ingredients lying next to the stove. "Now get to work."

"I think we're finally done!" Abby stepped back from the wall and beamed. She lovingly ran her fingers over her new cabinet pulls and new quartz countertops. "This looks like a whole new home!"

I nodded in agreement. In the last six weeks, Abby and I had worked each weekend painting her home and renovating the bathrooms and kitchen. She had taken my advice and painted the cabinets to save money, but installed new pulls and she used her savings to splurge on gorgeous white quartz tops. She'd made sure the vanity in the bathrooms matched the cabinets and counter in the kitchen to help with the "flow of the home" as she had called it. I was against her buying the sparkling quartz because I was afraid she'd tire of it quickly, but watching her admire her handiwork made me realize that I was wrong. She was in love with her new home and nothing would change that.

"We can finally move in the rest of the furniture."

My eyes darted to the basement entrance. We had stored all non-essential furniture in it so that we would have less to move out of the way while we worked. Her parents had hired movers as their housewarming gift to her, but I dreaded having to relocate some of the heavier pieces. That was definitely a task for which I'd have to mentally prepare.

"Why not go ahead and do it now? We can get that chore out of the way."

So much for time to mentally prepare. I followed Abby down the steep steps and looked warily at a large, heavy wooden dresser.

Noticing my expression, Abby said cheerfully, "I know we can handle that. With all of those kickboxing classes, I feel stronger. Don't you?"

"Sure," I said quietly, contemplating how we were going to move everything. Taking a risk, I put my hands on either side of the dresser and willed it to be lighter. I willed too much and it almost came off the ground. Hastily, I backed off and the dresser grew heavier yet remained maneuverable. "I can't do this alone," I said.

Abby placed her hands underneath it and we lifted at the same time. "This isn't nearly as bad as I thought it would be! Those classes have really paid off!"

I said nothing, deep in concentration.

Reaching the foyer, we set down the antique. "Is this where you want it?"

She nodded. "It's an extra dresser. I've got one for the spare bedroom that isn't as nice, but I want something I don't mind everyone seeing down here. I'll store winter gear in it so I can just grab it on my way out each morning."

"You won't need winter gear for too much longer."

"Thank goodness! I'm so tired of being cold. I'm ready for the summer!" She poked at her stomach. "Maybe this will be ready, too."

"You'll be fine. You look better than you think. Besides, once summer is almost over, you'll be looking forward to fall because you'll be so tired of the heat."

She laughed. "That's why I love four seasons. Just when I'm tired of one, here comes another for me to enjoy."

"We should go stand-up paddleboarding in Beaufort when it's nice," I suggested.

"That would be fun! I haven't done that in a long time. What about paddleboard yoga? That's really taking off now."

"Why would you want to spoil the fun with yoga?"

Abby grinned, a mischievous twinkle in her eyes. "I think it'd be hilarious to watch you keep your balance on one of those boards."

"Thanks, jerk," I said, my tone light.

Her face darkened. "I'd like to see Lauren fall off one."

"When are you going to just tell her to shove off?"

Abby sighed. "I keep hoping that if I'm nice to her, she'll be nice to me."

"She's just a bully."

"I never thought I'd still be bullied as an adult." She sank down onto the floor, her back against a wall and her knees pulled to her chest.

Joining her, I said, "That's why you have a talk with her. If you can't work it out, then go to your principal and tell him that Lauren's created a hostile working environment."

Abby bit her lip. "I'm afraid that will make it worse. It's pretty awful now. I hate going to work because I dread seeing her. I'm fine when I'm with my kids, but she's not even holding back her nasty comments when we're in the hallways now."

"You need to talk to the principal," I urged. "You work in a middle school. You're not actually *in* middle school. It might help if you point out that the students can hear what she says and they would think that it's okay to speak to each other that way."

She laughed softly. "I think she's forgotten that, but so have some of the other teachers. It's a different animal from elementary."

"I didn't know you taught elementary school."

"I did up until a few years ago. I had been working with third grade special needs children."

"Why did you stop?"

Abby looked at me. "I don't have a choice where they put me. I'm special needs, but I'm not specific to a grade or anything. They put me wherever they need me."

"How could they not need you back at the elementary school?"

She motioned her hands outward, as if encompassing the entire town. "This isn't a big town. It's the Good Ol' Boy Network. You know as well as I do that it's not about what you can do, it's about who you know. Especially in a smaller town."

I nodded reluctantly in agreement.

"That was my case," she continued. "Someone who is important has a relative who didn't want to leave the area and they asked where that person wanted to be, and they said the place where I was. That left me displaced from my job and they found me another position at the middle school. There used to only be one special needs teacher. Now there are two of us."

"Is the other teacher good to you?"

"She is for the most part. She's happier for a smaller classroom so that she can have more one-on-one time with the kids. She's also been there longer and she's older, so she's got the attitude of someone who just doesn't put up with people's crap."

"Why can't you get that attitude? I told you it's all about confidence."

Abby shook her head sadly. "It's not that simple. I'm a nice person who doesn't like confrontation. I can only do so much for myself and then I start to feel badly because I don't want a fight. I just want to go to work and be left alone so that I can just focus on the kids. They're what's important."

"There's your solution. Ignore her."

"Like the silent treatment?"

I snickered. "No, not like the silent treatment. Just ignore her. Pretend she doesn't exist."

"That's the silent treatment."

"You say tomato, I say potato."

"I don't think that's how that goes."

"Sure it does. I can't stand tomatoes."

Abby laughed and I was happy to hear it. She rose to her feet. "Why don't we finish this and grab some dinner? Something wildly unhealthy for us because we have to have burned a zillion calories from all of this labor."

"What did you have in mind?"

"The hibachi grill sound good to you?"

My mouth watered at the thought. "Perfection."

After moving the rest of the furniture, we enjoyed the food tricks from the chef at *Imperium*.

I drove back to my house, my belly full of delicious shrimp sauce and steak. I parked and carried in the takeout I had brought with me in case Finn was hungry. He pulled his truck in behind me, his eyes on the ground as he followed me inside.

"Thanks," he mumbled, grabbing the takeout bag away from me. He shoved off his boots and tossed them down the stairs before sitting on a barstool and opening his Styrofoam box. "This is still fresh and hot," he murmured.

"Yeah, I left straight from there," I said.

"It's almost like magic."

I froze.

"There are a lot of peculiar things that happen around here," Finn continued behind mouthfuls.

"Like what?"

"I don't know. I can't put my finger on it."

I looked at him closely. "Finn, are you drunk?"

"No."

"Have you been drinking?"

"No."

"Then what's your problem?"

He put down his fork. "I don't know, Carmen. Things are just funny. They don't always add up."

I remained silent, though internally my thoughts were running a mile a minute. I was so careful to not use magic when Finn was near and I made sure that my friends knocked on the door instead of just popping in like they used to do.

There was a knock on the door and I excused myself. I answered it to find the same Eraser who had been at my housewarming party. "Don't suppose you have any more of those hors d'oeuvres, do you?"

I stepped out onto the front porch, closing the door behind me. "You can't go in there."

"I take that as a no."

I waved my hand and spinach-artichoke pinwheels appeared in a clear container. "Here," I said, placing it into his hands.

"That's not all that I need to do here."

"He doesn't even know what he's talking about."

"That doesn't matter."

"If he doesn't know what he finds peculiar, then how will you know what to Erase?" I argued.

The Eraser looked at me thoughtfully. "You ought to be more careful."

"I am!" I insisted. "I never use magic when he's around. Or at least not in the same room."

"What about your job? You're supposed to be working from home according to your family."

"He's at work all day. He can't possibly know that I'm not here."

"Did it ever occur to you that he comes back here for lunch?"

"How did you know that?"

The Eraser shifted uncomfortably. "I have to check in once in a while," he admitted.

"Do you know the truth about me?"

"I do."

I swore. "What's the point in all of this secrecy about what I'm really up to now?"

He shrugged. "You got me. You know how Fate likes to be Fate. They like their games. It was pretty hilarious watching one of those vendors back in South Bend ask out your android. That Sam Francisco did a pretty good job."

"He goes by Samuel for a reason," I pointed out. "Did someone really ask the Carmen android on a date?"

"Scout's honor," the Eraser said, holding up his hands in a peace sign.

"I don't think that's right."

"Whatever. I had to go up and Erase his memory, but not before I watched the other Carmen blubber her way through an excuse. Simon had to come in and lead her away."

"I bet Simon's having a hell of a time with all of that."

"He is, but you know Simon. He rolls with the punches."

"How do you know Simon?"

"I get around. Not like that, but I wish! Sorry, I'm off topic. I do get around, though. Lately I've been assigned to work with you more often. From a distance, obviously. It'd be weird if I was here all of the time."

"Oh, yes, because you keeping tabs on me from afar isn't creepy at all," I said drily.

"I'm going to have to come in there and take care of Finn for now."

"You come past this door and I'll hang you upside down by your toenails over tapioca pudding." I couldn't allow the Eraser inside and make Finn feel worse than he already did.

The Eraser scowled. "That's just gross."

"And painful."

"I have a job to do. He'll be happier once I do it, I promise."

I shook my head. "I think he's upset about something else."

"I'll pose as a delivery guy and get him to sign something. I can touch him when he reaches for the pen. He'll never even know I was here."

"Tapioca pudding. Don't even try me," I warned. "I'll talk to him. If he's still upset, you can come back tomorrow and take care of him."

"I ought to go to the Council and file a complaint," he grumbled.

"Go ahead." I swallowed, hoping the Eraser wouldn't notice my nervousness.

He sighed. "Fine. I'll come back tomorrow if he's still behaving this way."

"Thank you for being so nice and understanding about this."

"No problem. That and I'm a little scared. I heard what you did to your ex-husband. You probably really wouldn't give a damn if I filed a complaint, would you?" He stared at me for a moment. "No, you wouldn't." He turned to walk down the steps leading to the sidewalk. "See you tomorrow," he yelled.

"Don't count on it."

Finn was finishing his dinner when I returned to the kitchen. "Who was at the door?"

"No one important," I lied.

"See? It's things like that that are weird. People don't just show up at people's houses, but your friends seem to drop by whenever."

"That's not true. They come by once in a while on the weekends. There's nothing wrong with having visitors."

My stepbrother closed the takeout box and took it over to the trash can. He dumped it in and turned back toward me. "It is when they don't even live nearby," he snapped.

"What's your real problem, Finn?" I asked softly.

"It's weird being here."

"I don't think you're telling me the truth."

"I am!" Finn insisted.

I leaned against the counter and caught his gaze. "Liar," I said bluntly. "You can't possibly be this upset that I have friends who drop by once in a while to see me. You're either picking a fight just to pick a fight or something else is bothering you."

Finn sighed, defeated. "I'm sorry," he muttered. "I'm having a tough time at work."

"Why?"

"I realized today that there isn't much room for advancement. I could be a foreman and then that's it for me."

"You could be a project manager," I pointed out.

Finn frowned. "I don't have an education."

"Go back to school."

"At my age?" he asked, incredulous.

"People of all ages are going back to school these days. The days of people in their late teens and early twenties being the only students are far gone."

"The truth is that I don't know if I want to do this anymore. It's not very fulfilling."

"Is there something else you'd rather do?"

Finn shook his head. "I don't know. I'm good at what I'm doing now. I build things. I fix things. People need construction workers like me so that they can live more comfortable lives." He absently removed his baseball cap and ran his hand over his hair. "I don't know what else I could do. What makes me happy doesn't pay my bills."

"What makes you happy?"

"Going to the bar, drinking beer, and talking to women." Finn smiled sheepishly and I laughed.

I leaned across the counter and patted his shoulder. "If that was a profession, there would be a lot more happy people in the world. Maybe you could find something on the side that would help you feel better. What about playing guitar at Loretta's? We haven't done that yet."

A smile tugged at the corners of Finn's mouth. "I suppose we could go do that."

"You can get paid by day for something you're good at, and be ogled by night for something you're also good at doing."

"Who is ogling me?"

"You know they say that guitar players get all of the action. Don't you know your band trivia? Singers, guitar players, and drummers are the most popular. Bass players, not so much."

"Bass players are underappreciated."

"I had a crush on a bass player once," I admitted.

"You had a thing for a musician?" Finn asked.

"I did. I was about nineteen and there was this guy, Warren."

"His name was Warren? Sounds like a winner already," Finn said sarcastically.

"Shut up, Finn. He was hot. He had messy brown hair that, nowadays, I'd say he needed a haircut. I was into it back then."

"I bet he threw one of those wool beanies over it. He probably even wore it during the summer because he thought it looked cool."

"Would you shut up and let me finish my embarrassing story?" I didn't want to give him the satisfaction of knowing he had been absolutely correct in his observation.

"Go on. I love to hear about other people's misfortune."

"Thanks. Maybe." I flashed a grin and continued. "He played for a band that I had heard at one of the bars. I liked their music so much that I would make sure I saw their shows whenever they played. Warren caught my eye one night while he was playing and I just felt this connection."

Finn groaned and rolled his eyes, but said nothing.

"We started talking about their set and we would do that after all of their shows. I kind of became a groupie."

"You were a loser."

"Groupie."

"Loser."

"A huge fan of their music," I compromised. "I overheard one of his bandmates ask him if he liked me and I was so happy when I heard Warren tell him that yes, he did. Warren would never ask me out, though, and I was too shy then to do it myself. Instead we just kept talking after shows. One day I told one of my friends, Avril, that I had a crush on him. She had known him longer than I had and just said that it was nice that I liked him. I told her I didn't know what was wrong because Warren hadn't asked me out yet and she told me she'd find out for me."

"That's kind of childish. Why not just have her give him a note from you that asks, 'Do you like me? Circle yes or no?'"

"Ha ha, Finn," I deadpanned. "I was a teenager." I dramatically tossed my short hair over my shoulder. "I was nowhere near the level of sophistication that I possess today."

My stepbrother snickered.

"We went out that night to watch the band play. After they were finished, Warren sauntered over to our table. His eyes got really big when he saw Avril and I just remember she gave him this extremely sweet smile before asking him, 'Hey, Warren. How's your girlfriend doing?'"

Finn inhaled sharply. "What!" he exclaimed.

"Warren muttered that she was doing just fine and walked away. I don't know why Avril didn't just tell me. She always had a flair for the theatrics, but either way, my crush ended immediately. *That's* why bass players can't be trusted."

"I still say they're underappreciated."

"We can agree to disagree."

"Are you kidding? That guy was so smooth that he had you following along for weeks. That's an underrated skill set right there."

I wanted to tell my stepbrother that an underrated skill set was me ensuring that each of his strings broke in the middle of every set for the next month, but I had to keep that to myself. I had popped into a restroom stall at the various places where they played and walked out long enough to point at the strings on his bass guitar, see his frustration as they sprang apart from the headstock, and return to the stall where I'd disappear. That had been really fun. I smiled at the memory.

"Karma's a bitch. The guitar player went off to medical school and the band broke up, never to play again."

"I don't know if that's karma. That just sounds like life got in the way."

I narrowed my eyes. "Can't you just let me have this?"

It was Finn's turn to pat me on the back before heading toward the stairs that led to his bedroom. He shouted over his shoulder, "Nope. Someone has to be realistic in this house."

Chapter Nine

"Finn's on the right track. He's close to where he needs to be. Abby, on the other hand, is a different animal."

I crossed one leg over the other and clasped my hands together on top of my knee. "I don't know what to do about her. She's a nice woman. I wish she'd stand up for herself more when it comes to Lauren Lennox, but she just won't do it. She claims that she doesn't like confrontation and won't tell anyone else about it. I don't mind being there for her to vent, but I can't help her. Not in the way that she needs. I know she's supposed to do something else, but I need more details so that I can guide her in that direction."

Simon was listening, his eyes focused on his expanding collection of antique fish hooks, but his thoughts were miles away.

I waved one hand in front of him. "Simon?"

"I know what we need to do," he said slowly.

"That's great because I'm fresh out of ideas. I've been encouraging, I've been helpful with her buying and fixing up her house. We exercise together. I've been her friend, Simon. How does being her friend help her reach her path?"

"Because you're a witch."

"She can't know that."

"Which is why we're going to have to be very careful about what we're going to do. When I say 'we,' I mean you." He grinned.

A feeling of dread began to wash over me. "What?"

"A memory trip."

"No fucking way," I blurted. Memory trips were used for people who really needed an attitude adjustment, not just a gentle push to guide them in the right direction. Ebenezer Scrooge is the most famous known person to have taken a memory trip, but that's only because he got greedy and sold his story to a young author.

Simon grabbed a pencil and jotted down a note for himself. "I need to tell Samuel that he needs to add those little bombs you like to use into the android." He read his note and scribbled over it. "Never mind. More trouble than it's worth."

"I'm not doing that. It's too risky. I haven't even done one before."

"It's not that hard. I'll put together the permit and I'm sure it will get approved. I can't imagine Fate saying no to this. Abby needs the nudge."

I unclasped my hands and stood up. "I am not doing this, Simon. It will expose us. You need to let an experienced person do this."

"You want one of the Ghosts?"

"Not Future. He's still sensitive about his adult acne and keeps his face covered. It makes him look creepy."

"Future thinks he looks mysterious."

I rolled my eyes. "Oh, please. We all know what he's hiding under that hood. He needs to just nut up and go to the dermatologist. What about Past or Present? All three of them can go in whichever direction, but they just choose to have a specialty."

"It needs to be you. You're the Influencer."

"I'm not a time traveler, Simon! I wouldn't even begin to know which events to show her that will push her in the right direction." I could feel myself growing frustrated.

Simon's voice lowered. "You're doing this."

I frowned and returned to my chair in front of my boss's desk. I knew that tone well. There would be no more arguing. "Can I at least ask for help from one of them? They can pinpoint the events I need for her to relive more easily."

"That's fine. I'll have Past send you the information."

"What about a pill to give her afterward so she'll think it was all a very vivid dream?"

"A pill? Just take her out for some pie."

"Pie?" I asked skeptically. "How does pie make a person think that a literal trip down memory lane was nothing but a dream?"

Simon shrugged. "I don't know. I don't make the rules. Just make sure that she has some pie when you're done."

"Does it matter which kind of pie?"

"Apple, but that's just me being partial to the stuff. It really doesn't matter which one she chooses. She could choose a fruitcake pie if she wanted, but those aren't too good." He suddenly looked around the room anxiously. "Don't tell Cindy that. She thinks I loved her little creation over Easter dinner." He scrunched his nose. "It didn't even *smell* good." He reached into the mini-fridge he kept next to his desk. "Do you want a slice?"

"Why would I want something that you hated?"

"I'm trying to get rid of it."

"It's been a couple of weeks since Easter. I think you can toss it because it's old."

"No. Cindy always enchants her food so that it lasts at least a month." He looked dreamily out the window. "If only she had made an apple pie."

"Maybe next time," I said hopefully.

"You take this pie off my hands and I'll make sure Past sends you the information by tomorrow evening."

"Deal."

The next night I sat alone in my office, the windows open with a faint breeze rifling through the room. Flowers and trees were blooming as April was turning into May. Spring permeated the air and I loved it. I had already done my winter-summer switch in my closet, the warm clothes safely packed away downstairs until fall approached.

I yawned and stretched, focusing my attention back to my computer screen. I jumped out of my chair, startled to see Past staring at me. She chuckled to herself and floated out of the computer and over to the window. "It's a really beautiful evening, isn't it?" she said.

"Yes," I answered.

She turned back to me, her blue hair swaying around her. "I remember a night similar to this one back in the eighteenth century. Those were simpler times, weren't they?"

"I'm sure that time period has its pros and cons." I had heard that Past was a little odd. Clearly that had been an understatement.

Past looked at me sadly. "You poor thing. You don't know. You have such a short life in comparison to mine."

"Yeah, the thought keeps me up at night." I leaned against the window behind my desk and crossed my arms.

She reached out and touched my face. Her hand was freezing. "You're pretty, at least."

"Thank you," I said, suddenly blushing.

"I suppose you want the information Simon promised you." Past floated over and hovered over my leather guest chair.

"I really appreciate you taking the time to map out the key points I need," I said, my tone now sincere.

She fished into the pockets of her white gown that suspiciously looked like a certain Duchess of Cambridge's wedding dress for the information. Past was known to enjoy trends, though she was usually a little bit behind. "I believe this will help you," she said. The paper turned solid in her hand and she placed it on the edge of my desk.

I looked over it carefully. She had put everything in an outline form, complete with notes on what I needed to say. "You really went into detail here, Past. Thank you."

"I had to. You're an amateur at this."

"That's what I told Simon! I asked why you couldn't do it."

"This is your journey."

"Past," I said bluntly. "We both know that's a line. It's the person of interest's journey. It doesn't really matter who the guide is because it's all a dream to them anyway."

"Okay, it doesn't actually matter," Past admitted. "But Present, Future, and I are booked until Labor Day."

I raised a brow. "That far out?"

Past threw back her shoulders defiantly. "We're commodities. We stay busy."

"Oh," I said simply.

"Is that all that you require?"

I scanned the paper she had given me one more time. "Yes. Thanks again, Past."

"Cheerio, then!" she said brightly, fading into nothing.

I studied the timeline that she had given me. There wasn't too much on here, but clearly each event was significant. I scribbled out the words Past wanted me to say and jotted down notes regarding my own thoughts on each memory. I stopped, tapping the pencil eraser against my chin thoughtfully. How was I going to make Abby think that she was still dreaming when I woke her? I should have asked Past, but I doubted she would have answered honestly. I had heard the Ghosts liked to keep their techniques a secret so that they would remain valuable.

"You look like you could use some help," Siobhan said, suddenly appearing in front of my desk. She took the same chair that Past had hovered over, sinking into it heavily.

"You look like you've had a tough day yourself."

Siobhan warily wiped her eyes. "I had to break it off with Percy. It just wasn't working with the distance. I'm not able to tell him the truth, so I can't just visit whenever I want. Distance puts a real strain on a budding relationship."

"I'm sorry to hear that."

"It's okay. It wasn't meant to be. I didn't get that glowing pit in my stomach when I saw him."

"Glowing pit?"

"You know what I'm talking about. The glowing pit you feel whenever you're around someone you adore. That person makes you so happy that you feel like you're going to burst. Didn't you feel like that when you were around Matthew?"

"No."

"Then how did you know that he was the one you wanted to marry?"

"I was young and dumb. I didn't know what real love was."

"It sounds like you still don't," Siobhan said, frowning. "Have you even tried to date anyone since the divorce?"

"No, I have other things that are more important in my life that need my attention."

"You really should put yourself out there again."

"Why are you here? Did you want to pig out on some ice cream? Ice cream always makes a breakup feel better."

She shook her head. "No, I'm really not that upset, actually. I am here on an official capacity, though. I'm a Muse. You need me."

"I was trying to think of a way to ensure Abby thinks she's still dreaming when we do our memory trip."

"That's easy. Go big."

"Big?"

Siobhan leaned forward in her chair, excited. "You can't be subtle. If she wakes up and the room is hazy, she'll just think that her eyes are dry and she needs eye drops. If she wakes up and, say, there is a raceway in her bedroom, she will definitely think she's still fast asleep."

"I was leaning toward hazy," I said.

"No. That's not going to work."

We were both quiet as I thought. Finally, I said, "A circus! Abby will wake up in the middle of a circus."

"With lions?" Siobhan was skeptical.

"No, I'll make them stuffed lions."

"A circus has a lot of parts to it."

"I'll focus on one section, then."

She sighed. "I did tell you to go big." She smiled broadly. "A circus it is! I'll even help you create it."

The tent was a classic red-and-white vertical-striped dome with several circular sections roped off with matching velvet rope. In the center ring, I had created a few stuffed lions and they were in various positions pretending to perform tricks. Siobhan had created the lion tamer, though I did notice that it bore a strong resemblance to Percy. She was more upset than she was letting on, though I knew not to say anything. She would deal with her breakup in her own way, at her own pace.

The outer rings contained kittens performing the same tricks as the lions. Instead of being stuffed toys, I had made them look like animated characters that seemed to have recently jumped out of a cartoon.

The rest of the details remained blurry on purpose, the main focus being the trapeze I had made. It was high in the air and looked like it was made from mint candies. The safety net underneath was invisible. Siobhan had already vanished, leaving me alone to do the final checks on my creation. Satisfied, I snapped my fingers and was suddenly wearing long, black robes. I ran my hands over my hair, turning it bright pink.

I popped into Abby's bedroom. She stirred slightly as I touched her hand and, without a sound, transported us to the circus. She woke up on the balcony, the trapeze tied off to its side.

"God bless America!" she screamed.

"Calm down, Abby," I said soothingly.

"What in the hell is going on?" she demanded. She looked at my outfit and hair. "What are you doing? What is that you're wearing? Is that *pink* hair? It's one thing for the students to go nuts, but you're an adult, Carmen. Come on."

"You're dreaming," I said simply.

She pinched her forearm. "That hurts! I am definitely not dreaming."

"It's a very real feeling dream," I insisted.

She looked around, noticing the rest of the circus. She squinted at the lion tamer. "Is that my realtor?"

"It looks like him, doesn't it?"

"Those lions aren't real," she said, ignoring my question. She sat on the balcony's floor, crossing her legs. "This isn't real. This cannot be happening."

"It's just a dream."

"It feels awfully real to be a dream," she argued.

"Why would I have pink hair and wear black robes in real life? I like *Harry Potter*, but I'm not dressing up unless there's some kind of convention. Why would you be in a circus with Percy and fake lions and animated kittens? Why would you be on top of a balcony where a trapeze is waiting to be used?"

Abby took in her surroundings once again. She stood up and poked the trapeze. "If this is a dream, it won't matter if I fall, will it?"

I peered down where the invisible safety net loomed. "It won't."

She leaped off the balcony and I nearly yelped from shock. The safety net caught her easily, though she did bounce high into the air a few times before settling on her back. She screamed the entire time.

I appeared on the ground next to the safety net, which I had now turned pink to match my hair and so that it could be seen. She rolled off it and looked at it with wonder. "What a dream," she murmured.

"Glad you like it. Give me your hand." Without waiting for a response, I grabbed her hand and I transported us to the first memory.

Abby was in kindergarten. Her mouth widened into a yawn as she awoke from nap time. She dutifully rolled her red-and-blue mat and put it inside her assigned cubby hole.

"What's this?" the adult Abby asked.

"I don't know. This is your dream."

"I miss nap time."

"Me, too."

"I used to hate them when I was a child." She laughed softly. "I'd love to have one every day now. I would if it didn't interfere with my bedtime later."

We watched as the younger Abby began pulling off toy bricks from the shelves. A group of girls waved her over to their play group and Abby ignored them. She stacked the bricks in a way that she made a wall surrounding her. With a loud roar, she crashed through the bricks. "I'm Godzilla!" she yelled.

"Look at how happy I am," Abby said wistfully. "I loved those toy bricks. Those girls would make fun of me for playing with them because they were 'toys for boys,' but I didn't care. I loved them."

"Why didn't you care what they thought?"

Abby tilted her head thoughtfully. "I guess because I was young and inhibited. Their opinions didn't matter to me."

"Would it matter now?"

"Do you mean do the opinions' of five-year-olds matter now that I'm an adult?"

"I'm suggesting that if there was a scenario where you could play with toys as an adult, would you still choose the bricks or would you go play with the other adult women?"

"That's a weird question."

"Fine." I touched Abby's hand and we were transported to another time. Abby was in a classroom with large, bright fluffy letters across the entrance that spelled, "Welcome to Second Grade!" At the back of the room, I spotted eight-year-old Abby at a small piano.

"Not the piano." Abby groaned.

Her younger self sat ramrod straight on the bench, her fingers lightly hovering over the keys. "Every good boy does fine," she whispered to herself.

Her instructor filled the rest of the bench with her girth and was pointing at the musical notes in the songbook in front of her. "Stop saying the phrase each time you play. Abby, you really should have learned these notes by now."

"I'm sorry," Abby apologized. "I just can't remember them. It doesn't make sense to me."

"It should. You've been playing for six months now. You're falling behind the rest of my students."

"I'm trying. I really am."

"I don't see how," the instructor argued. "If you were really practicing, you would know your notes by now and wouldn't have to think about it each time I ask you to play. You can either stop wasting my time or you can start studying like a good girl and make use of your parents' money."

Abby started to cry and the instructor looked at her earnestly. "That's enough, Abby," she said sternly.

"I practiced for hours each week," the adult Abby snarled. "I really couldn't grasp the concept of music. If she had been more patient with me, I might have. Not everyone progresses as quickly as others."

"Is this why you decided to become a special needs teacher? To be patient and kind to those who don't learn as quickly because someone wasn't that way with you?"

Abby looked at me, her expression sad. "I never thought about this moment when I wanted to become a teacher. It just felt like a calling."

"Sometimes we bury bad memories because they're too painful, but they etch who we are later. I think this is part of what swayed you to achieve the profession you have today."

"Maybe," she murmured thoughtfully. Younger Abby was still crying as she tried to match her instructor's graceful movements across the keys.

"I don't want to see this anymore." Abby's jaw was tense, her eyes flashing.

"You're the boss." I sent us to another scene, one that took place a year later. Abby had learned the notes and she was playing very well for someone so young, but her face was sullen and withdrawn.

"Abby, you need to show more heart!" the instructor snapped. "It's like watching a chicken get its head cut off listening to you play. It's just pathetic."

Abby immediately stopped playing. She yanked down the key cover, nearly slamming the instructor's fingers in the process.

"You nearly broke my fingers, young lady! You just wait until I tell your parents about your little outburst."

"I don't want to do this anymore," Abby said, her voice small.

"You don't want to do what?"

"I don't want to play the piano anymore."

The instructor huffed. "Absolutely not. You will continue to practice."

Abby turned her whole body to face her instructor. "Why? You don't like me. I don't play well. I hate this. It doesn't make me happy. Why do you play? Is it because you like the extra money you earn outside of teaching?"

The instructor stared at her, flabbergasted. "I play because I enjoy it."

"Do you play basketball?"

"No."

"Why not?" Abby prodded.

"I don't like it."

"Don't you see, ma'am?" Abby asked, her voice stronger. "My playing the piano is like you playing basketball. I don't like it. I dread every lesson we have." She took a deep breath, and exhaled slowly. "I quit." Abby stood up and marched to the door, never looking back.

Present Abby and I stood silently as we watched the instructor gather her songbooks and place them on a bookshelf. "I hated that woman," Abby said quietly. "Did you know that she died about a year later? I wasn't even sad when Mom told me. I refused to attend her funeral."

Another transport led us to Abby in middle school. She had styled her hair in braided pigtails and wore bright, shiny braces. She had chosen black and orange bands over her brackets in the spirit of Halloween that was only a few weeks away.

"I can't believe I wore pigtails in middle school," the adult Abby said, moaning.

"Braids are never out of style," I said, trying to be helpful.

We were in the cafeteria and Abby was moving slowly through line, smiling and asking each employee if they had a good weekend. "See you tomorrow, Wendy!" Abby said, leaving the cashier. She joined her friends at a table and noticed they were already laughing. "What's so funny?" she asked.

"Look at Lucy Donovan. She chopped all her hair off for a ballroom dancing competition! She looks so stupid! She looks like a boy!" one of her friends said.

"I think she looks nice," Abby replied.

Another friend scowled. "Abby, no one has hair that short if they're a girl."

"Maybe she doesn't want to be a girl. Or maybe she's a big ol' lesbian!"

The others giggled. "She can go to the thrift store and buy a bunch of flannel shirts! She'd be lumberjack lesbian." A pause. "Or would she be a lumber*jill*?" Another outburst of laughter followed.

"Lucy is as graceful as they come. Have you ever seen her dance? She's wonderful," Abby said defensively. "She's been competing for years. If her teacher told her she had to cut off her hair, then she didn't have a choice."

"Hey, everyone, Abby has a crush on Lucy!"

"I do not!"

"Then why do you keep talking about Lucy like that?" the leader of the group sneered.

"She lives in my neighborhood. I've been over to her house and her mom is the one who owns that ballroom dance studio downtown. They've tried to teach me a few dances, but I've got two left feet."

"God, Abby, why are you so weird?" the leader snapped.

Abby looked down at her food, then guiltily toward Lucy. She turned to her friends and whispered, "Her house is really weird, you know."

"Shut *up*! Tell us all about it!" another friend said excitedly. Suddenly, all of the girls were looking at Abby in awe as she gushed about the strangeness of Lucy's home.

"Most of that wasn't even true," Abby said.

"It wasn't?" I asked.

"No." She was looking at Lucy going through the food line. "I just said those things because I didn't want them to think I was weird anymore."

"Did they give you a hard time after that?"

"No. Not really. I just wanted to fit in, you know?"

"At the cost of someone else's dignity."

"I was a preteen!"

"Preteens are jerks," I said simply. "Were you happier then?"

Abby answered slowly. "I was happy that they weren't mean to me and I felt like a part of a group. But, no, I wasn't happy about putting others down. I just didn't want to be lonely."

"You could have chosen different friends," I pointed out.

She snickered. "That's not done so easily and you know that."

"Let's see something else."

"This is a really weird dream," Abby murmured.

"Sure is," I said hastily. We appeared in a hallway crowded with students. They were gathering different books for their next class and it was easy to spot sixteen-year-old Abby reaching into her own locker.

"Abby, did you know that Jeff Grinder asked me out?" a friend asked. Before Abby could respond, she began to giggle uncontrollably.

"What's wrong with him?" Abby asked.

"He's just odd. Like, *really* odd."

"I don't think he is."

Her friend rolled her eyes. "Whatever. He's not my type."

"How is being a nice guy who wants to take you out somewhere not your type?" Abby pressed, annoyed.

"He's just not my type." Her friend shrugged.

Abby's eyes narrowed. "You know what, Linda? He's a nice guy. He works hard after school at his dad's mechanic shop and he makes good grades. Your problem with him is that he isn't part of the popular crowd."

"You know our people and his kind of people don't mix."

"I'm going to pretend you didn't just say that," Abby snapped. She started to walk away, then paused. She turned around and added, "Get over yourself, Linda!"

"Way to go, Abby!" I cheered.

Present day Abby nodded. "I was so desperate to be a part of the 'in crowd' and I didn't like who I had become. That was the straw that broke the camel's back I guess. I didn't like being mean and so I just went along with what other people said. I thought it was better than actually saying mean things myself."

"What happened to this Jeff fellow?"

"Wait and see," Abby said. She followed her younger self to her Spanish class and watched as she took a seat next to a young man. He had short, spiky black hair and stubble that wouldn't be fashionable on men for another fifteen years. He wore a red shirt that said, "Feed the Ferrets. Save a Superhero."

"Is that him?" I asked, pointing.

"It is," Abby answered.

The teacher hadn't arrived in the room yet and Jeff leaned over, whispering to Abby. "I heard what you said."

"What did I say?" the younger Abby asked.

"Just now. In the hallway."

"Oh." Abby blushed. "I didn't realize you were standing nearby. I'm sorry about Linda. She can be such a bitch."

Jeff vigorously nodded his head. "That she is! Listen, you don't have to apologize for her. You're not her keeper." He paused, gathering his courage. "I do want to thank you for sticking up for me. People just don't do that, it seems, but you did. And to the Queen Bee no less."

Abby blushed even deeper. "You're welcome," she said shyly.

"Did you ever date him?" I asked.

A smile tugged at Abby's lips. "For a couple of months," she said. "He graduated and went off to college. He lives in St. Louis now, I hear."

"Abby, didn't it make you feel good to stand up for someone?"

"It did," she admitted. "But that's not why I did it. I did it because it was the right thing to do."

"Then why can't you stand up for yourself against that awful Lennox woman?"

She looked at her feet. "I dislike conflict."

"What about the other teachers? Don't they say anything to her?"

"I wouldn't know. I eat lunch in my classroom instead of the teacher's lounge."

"Abby," I said sternly. "You're not a teenager anymore. You don't have to accept that kind of behavior."

"You don't understand."

"What don't I understand?"

"This is my dream, right?" Abby suddenly grabbed my hand and the next memory we saw was her high school graduation. No one except for her family clapped as she walked across the stage to retrieve her diploma.

"After I told Linda to get over herself, I was an outcast. I was always an outcast of the popular clique, really, but they wouldn't even let me hang out with them after that. I was expendable. I never fell into another group of friends. I had people I talked to during class, but the friendships never went beyond school grounds."

Another time hop and we were at the University of North Carolina's library. Abby was twenty-one and sitting with a small group of people in a study group.

"See? You made friends once you got away from high school."

"Sort of. We lost touch after graduation when we went our separate ways. I went on to graduate school and was too busy to make friends."

"You're not too busy now, though. You get out and go to yoga, you go to kickboxing, and you go to church. You're putting yourself out there."

"You still don't get it."

"Then explain it to me," I said softly.

Abby went to pull out a chair, but her hand passed through it. "I can't even sit down in my own dream?"

"Sorry, but we don't technically exist right now."

She groaned. "Wonderful."

"Abby," I said, steering her back to our conversation.

"I only know how to get along with people one way, and that's through gossip."

"Gossip can be fun. Studies show that smart people gossip."

"Really? They'll waste money to study anything, won't they?"

"Apparently."

"I don't mean innocent gossip. I mean talking about people behind their backs, telling others things that you weren't supposed to tell. I feel like the way to fit in is to agree with others, regardless of how awful they are. The only way to be accepted is to conform."

"That's asinine," I chided.

"Is it, though? The teachers I work with seem to have forgotten that they're not in school themselves anymore and they have these cliques. It's just like high school. You have your popular clique, cool clique, stoners, band geeks, the smart kids, et cetera."

"You have stoners?"

Abby rolled her eyes. "The county threatens random drug testing, but they don't actually do it unless there's reasonable cause. The stoners go home, smoke, and are fine by the time they come to school."

"Abby, I have to ask, if you're so unhappy, then why don't you leave?"

Abby burst into tears. "I couldn't leave those kids!"

I sent us back to the circus. Out of her memories now, we were able to touch objects and I snapped my fingers for a chair to appear. One didn't appear out of nowhere; instead, one walked across the three rings and joined us, then spread its arms as if inviting an occupant.

"How nice of you to join us finally," I said.

"What a weird freaking dream," Abby repeated, sitting heavily in the chair.

I thought about what the snowman had said. "Have you ever thought about building something?" I asked timidly.

"What? Like a new school?"

"Not necessarily a school, but something that would include the kids."

Abby quietly stared at the ground, lost in her thoughts.

I checked my watch and sighed. The night was almost over. "Come on, Abby. We need to go to one more place."

We popped into a fifties-style diner where the smell of greasy, delicious hamburgers was almost intoxicating. A young waitress sauntered over, her ponytail high on her head and tied off neatly with a bright yellow ribbon. "What will you have, honey?" she said.

Abby glanced at the waitress, startled. The woman sounded like she had been smoking cigarettes for the last twenty years.

"Two slices of pie, please."

"Any preference?"

I thought for a moment. "Apple," I answered.

Chapter Ten

Abby finished her pie and I gently touched her hand one last time. She was growing sluggish and I ushered her into her bed, yanking off her shoes and tossing them haphazardly into her closet.

"Am I still dreaming?" she asked, her voice thick.

"Of course," I replied.

Abby closed her eyes, her breathing already slow and even. Positive that she was fast asleep, I transported myself back to my own bedroom.

Wearily, I sat on the edge of my bed and tugged off my own shoes. Too tired to put them away, I fell back onto my soft mattress.

"You didn't do too badly," Simon said.

"You can't just show up in my room," I protested grumpily.

"I'm not in your room. I'm talking to you through your phone speaker. Meet me in my office."

"In the morning," I replied, stifling a yawn.

"It *is* the morning," Simon pointed out.

"Son of a—"

"Don't say bad things about my mother," Simon interrupted.

Grumbling, I snapped my fingers and found myself standing in Simon's office. Another snap and a chaise lounge appeared.

"None of that," Simon said, waving his hand. My chaise lounge disappeared. "You can sit in a regular chair like everyone else."

"Can't you just pat me on the back and tell me I did a good job? I'm not like Abby. Abby is going to wake up feeling refreshed as if she received a full eight hours."

"Sorry," Simon apologized insincerely. "There was a glitch last night that we need to discuss."

"A glitch? She cried, but I expect everyone cries during a memory trip. Scrooge cried like a baby when he had to relive his first love leave him."

"Scrooge was an asshole."

"Did you know him?"

"Not personally, but he had to be bad enough that Dickens wrote about him."

"Funny that people think it's a work of fiction."

"If you think that's funny, then you need to get out more," Simon chided. He steepled his hands together and leaned forward on his desk. "You went to an unauthorized memory. That *she* led you to, no less."

"I thought people could channel whichever memory they wanted."

Simon frowned. "Carmen, that's why we send guides instead of sending people out on their own. The guide knows which memories need to be relived."

"That's not true," I argued. "Past had to give me a list. I wouldn't have known otherwise. That's why we have the Ghosts as specialists. They can pick out of a person's brain exactly what needs to be seen."

"So can a Cupid."

"I hate fucking Cupids."

"One shows up at your divorce and suddenly you hate all of them."

"That was just a bad time to get the paperwork messed up."

"I won't disagree with that, but they're nice. My neighbor is a Cupid. She's going to let me surprise Cindy with a trip down memory lane to see the first time we met for our anniversary." Simon's eyes twinkled mischievously. "I should be thanked for that *really* well at the end of the night."

I grimaced. "How bad is this?" I asked, redirecting the conversation.

"It's bad, Carmen."

"How much trouble am I in?"

"You're not in trouble."

"Are *you* in trouble for sending me instead of one of the Ghosts?"

Simon shook his head, his jowls quivering with the motion. "I got a little slap on the wrist. The problem is that Fate has a plan and the plan wasn't followed accordingly."

"Fate knows that there are outside factors that change plans." I yawned, this time not bothering to try and stop myself.

"Fate is very strict when it comes to memory trips."

Annoyance was stirring at the pit of my stomach. "Simon, what's the real problem here?"

"Abby channeled your magic."

I snickered. "Impossible."

"Possible. We didn't think so either until it happened last night."

I sat up in my chair, suddenly wide awake. "This was just during the memory trip, right?"

Simon shifted uncomfortably in his chair. "We don't know."

"You're going to have to give me more than that."

"I can't tell you what we don't know. We don't know if she was able to channel the magic simply because you had taken her on a memory trip. We don't know if she could do it another time. We don't even know if this is isolated to one individual. It could be that anyone who isn't a witch or wizard can touch one who is and do whatever they want."

"What about the secrecy? Only spouses know and those people aren't willing to take advantage of their loved ones."

"You are so naïve sometimes," Simon said sadly. "While a person may not be willing to take advantage of his or her spouse, that doesn't stop that person from taking advantage of someone else."

Nervously, I began to wring my hands. "This is an isolated issue. Abby thought she was dreaming. We'll just create some kind of special gloves so that only our magic is accessible by us when we take someone on a memory trip. In the meantime, Fate can have a team research all of the stuff you just said and, if necessary, create some sort of spell to prevent magic transference from happening."

"We've thought about that and we will do that. However, there has already been a ripple effect."

"Simon, I am deeply sorry. I had no idea what kind of trouble that would cause." I hung my head, ashamed.

"There is one thing that can fix it."

"What?"

"You need to go back in time and ensure it doesn't happen."

"What? People don't just travel back in time whenever they want."

"You're forgetting what your pal, Enid, does for a living."

"But they don't affect anything! They've taken precautions," I protested.

"It's just for that one moment. When you get done seeing Jeff Grinder talk to Abby, don't ask her about his future. Just take her on to the next memory at the college."

Feeling overwhelmed, I said, "I can't do that on my own. It's one thing to have Past give me memories to show Abby, but it's an entirely different ordeal to travel back in time."

Simon laughed, loud and heartily.

"I don't know what you find to be so funny," I scolded him. "I've created a big problem here that I need to resolve."

"I'm sorry," Simon said, still chuckling. He wiped the corners of his eyes. "Carmen, that's why I think you're a great employee and friend. You want to handle things on your own so that you don't trouble anyone else. *Of course* you're not going to time travel on your own! You're going to have Marcy help you."

"Marcy Bloomberg?" I could feel my pulse quicken with excitement.

"The one and only."

Marcy Bloomberg was legendary. She was able to freely travel into the past *and* the future. While she wasn't allowed to change what had already happened, she would tweak certain events that went unnoticed overall, but had a major impact on the future. I had heard that she had suggested to a man that cats were amazing, which sparked him into opening one of the first cat cafés. Apparently, twenty years into the future, he was going to do something unspeakably horrible, but Marcy assured us that his cat café would still be a huge success and he was content for now.

"Wow," was all that I could say.

"Don't get starstruck. She's just a person, like you and me."

"Oh, please. She's incredible!"

Simon shrugged. "No one is perfect."

"I am," my android suddenly said, standing in the doorway. She looked at me curiously, then turned her gaze to Simon. "Am I supposed to start looking that disheveled?" She wrinkled her nose. "I don't like it."

"What?" I looked down at my rumpled clothes and ran a hand over my hair that could have used a hairbrush. "No, you're not supposed to look like this," I said hastily, embarrassed.

"What about the attitude?" the Carmen android asked.

"Carmen, you're meeting with Marcy tonight." He looked at the android. "She doesn't mean to be rude. She's just had a long night."

"Oh." My android looked at me again. "Go home and take a shower. Use concealer for those circles underneath your eyes." She tilted her head. "Maybe use a lot."

"Goodbye, Simon," I said.

"It's always nice to see you, Carmen!" the android said, smiling. She was still waving when I disappeared.

"You look downright giddy," Finn said through a mouthful of pasta.

"There's someone from work visiting that I'm excited to meet." I reached across my wooden dining table to grab the bowl of spaghetti and meatballs Finn had made. Giving myself a generous second helping, I said, "This is pretty good, Finn. You're learning."

He winked. "I told you I could be good at something else other than just the guitar."

"Being the guinea pig for your cooking experiments hasn't always been this good."

"The tilapia I made wasn't so bad," Finn protested.

"Finn, it was burnt so badly that I had to buy a dozen air fresheners just to get rid of the smell!"

"Fish might not be my specialty," Finn admitted. "It's the heads that get me. I don't like preparing them with them staring at me like that."

"Then why not go to the store and buy them already beheaded?"

"And cheat by not preparing the entire meal by myself?"

"You eat cereal for breakfast. If you're going to prepare the entire meal, doesn't that mean that you need to mix the ingredients for your own cereal?"

"That's just taking it a bit to the extreme."

"I'm just making a point."

"A ridiculous point." Finn laughed. "Who makes their own cereal? Overnight oats are not a thing. They're mushy and gross. Give me a box of little wheat concoctions that have a nice crunch and I'm good to go."

I laughed, too. "Either way, I'm just happy that you're learning."

Finn paused, his fork midway between his mouth and his plate. "Did you say you're excited to meet someone from work?"

"I did." I took another bite of pasta.

"That's kind of sad. You should be excited to go to a concert, not meet someone from the office. Or maybe you're lonely working in the office at home all day and any human contact is something you relish. You're living vicariously through me, aren't you?" He raised one eyebrow quizzically.

I groaned. "It's not like that. Her name is Marcy and she's great. I've heard lots of wonderful things about her."

"Is she some kind of building permit queen?"

"Something like that."

"A concert would be more fun."

"The concert is your deal, Finn. Roach invited you, not me. Besides, I don't think I'd really enjoy a band called *Dragon Fly Spitters*. What does that name even mean?"

"It's a metal band."

"Do dragonflies even spit?" I wondered, clearing the table. I walked through the swinging door between the kitchen and dining room and placed the dirty plates in the sink.

"Does it matter? It's a cool name for a cool band. They're going to be in Raleigh. You could always come up with us for the drive and do other stuff instead of the concert." Finn followed me and grabbed a paper towel and kitchen cleaner. He re-entered the dining room and began to spray the table, scrubbing away the splashes of pasta sauce that had accumulated around where his plate had been. He leaned too far forward and gently banged his head against the chandelier that hung over the middle of the table, causing it to sway. "Ouch!"

"Don't mess up my chandelier," I shouted from the kitchen, ignoring his pain.

Finn joined me next to the sink, still rubbing the side of his head.

Rinsing marinara out of a bowl, I said, "I don't think I can go, but if things change, I'll let you know."

The doorbell rang and I jumped. Marcy was early.

"I'll get that," Finn offered. He walked out of the kitchen, leaving me to finish the dishes.

I hurriedly waved my hands and the dishes cleaned themselves. I was placing the last plate in the drying rack when Finn reappeared with Marcy in tow.

"That was fast," Finn observed.

"That's because I don't procrastinate when it's my turn to clean," I said easily. I dried my hands on a dish towel and turned around, stunned at what I saw.

Marcy Bloomberg was tall, slender, and one of the most beautiful women I'd ever seen. She dressed in 1940s style clothing, even down to her horn-rimmed glasses. Her hair, on the other hand, was a thick, frizzy, dark mass haphazardly French-braided in an effort to tame it.

"Hello!" I greeted, holding out my hand. "I'm Carmen Devereaux. It's so wonderful to meet you."

Marcy shook my hand limply. "Yes, thank you," she said quickly. "Shall we get started? I've got a lot going on."

I cleared my throat. "Of course. Finn, I'll see you in the morning."

"Okay," Finn said suspiciously. He watched Marcy follow me down the hallway and into my office, his head shaking slightly in disapproval.

Once the office door was closed, Marcy said, "You live with your stepbrother? Aren't you a little old to have a roommate?"

"It's for my job that he's here," I answered, feeling defensive.

She rolled her eyes, which were an almost unnerving shade of violet. "Whatever. It's odd. And maybe just a little bit stupid considering he's mortal and you're not." She walked behind my desk and sat in my chair, leaving me to take a seat in my own guest chair.

I could feel my awe for this woman ebbing away. Before I could say anything, a loud ring came from her pocket. She removed her cell phone and began to read her incoming text.

"Ever been married, Carmen?" Marcy asked, scrolling through her phone.

"Once."

"I've been tracking my piece of crap husband. He doesn't think I know he's cheating."

"I'm sorry to hear that. Mine was also unfaithful. He—"

"Ha! He's not cheating in *that* way. Not on *me*." Marcy looked insulted. "He's cheating on our diet." She was exasperated. "You know, I work and I work and I go home and still have to cook these meals that suit our diet. Mind you, it wasn't me with the problem. It was him. He was eating junk and I thought, without shopping for it, it wouldn't be in the house, and he wouldn't eat it. But, no, he just conjures it right up! Or he goes straight to the source, which is why I installed an invisible tracking app on his phone. He's at the gas station right now. I know he's going to buy those little powdered doughnuts. He can never seem to create them himself with the right taste, so he buys them. Those and the chocolate-covered frosting ones." She shook her head furiously. "I see you, you dirty scoundrel!" she yelled at her phone.

I shifted my legs, uncomfortable. "I've heard that indulging once in a while makes it easier to stay on a diet overall. It keeps you from binging later," I offered.

Marcy scoffed. "My husband weighs three hundred pounds. I've been telling him over and over that if he doesn't do something about it, I was putting him on a restricted diet. He used to play football, you know."

"Aren't those guys naturally bigger people?"

"That's not the point, is it?" Marcy snapped. "He's not training like an athlete anymore and so he can't eat like he's burning eight thousand calories a day."

"Shouldn't we get to the time traveling?" I asked, trying to change the subject. My idea of Marcy had been crushed. She wasn't a wonderful lady who did wonderful things. She was an entitled lady with an overinflated ego who did wonderful things.

"We've got time." Marcy waited, then laughed and repeated herself. "Isn't that funny? I made a pun!"

"Yes, I got the joke," I said warily.

She looked at her phone. "He's leaving. He didn't purchase anything! Hallelujah! He might be adjusting better than I thought after all!"

"Marcy?" I pushed.

"Yeah, yeah, yeah. Here, give me your hand." She stood and briskly walked around the desk until she was in front of me. She reached for my hand and grabbed it roughly, yanking me up from my seat.

Her phone rang again as the world swirled around us. We stopped immediately and she started scrolling through her phone once more. "I can't believe it! He went back inside! That son of a bitch!"

"Marcy," I said calmly.

"I can't believe I was so proud of him for having willpower!"

"Marcy," I said again, warning in my tone.

"That won't happen again, I can tell you that."

"Marcy, you fucked up," I said bluntly.

The time traveler finally tore her gaze from her phone and met mine. "What did you just say to me?"

I pointed to our surroundings. We were in a classroom with children no older than eight who were quietly working on their cursive exercises. Marcy and I were facing the room and, in the reflection of the windows, I could see that I, too, was no older than eight.

"You took me to *my* past *and* made me a third grader again," I sneered.

"I didn't mean to go so far," she apologized, grabbing my hand once again. "By the way, you just look like a child to everyone else here. I can see the real you, but that's just something special to my type of witchcraft. Not all of us are born with this traveling ability."

"How wonderful," I said sarcastically before we were swept away. I wondered if Abby had felt as queasy as I did being the one transported from time to time instead of being the guide.

When we stopped again, Marcy was already looking at her phone.

There was loud music thumping nearby and I turned to see several teenagers giggling.

"I can't believe I'm at the prom with Jeremy Picket!"

My heart began to beat quickly. "Oh, no." I moaned.

"Carmen, I just love your dress!" one of the girls cooed.

I glanced down at the bright green gown I was suddenly wearing. "No, no, no," I muttered. "Marcy, you're wrong again."

"Carmen, if you haven't noticed, I have a bit of a situation here. I'm going to pop back home and then I'll be right back."

"What? No! You can't leave me here!" I panicked.

Marcy looked around. "It's not so bad. You're at your own prom. Smile and be happy! Most people would love to go to prom again. I promise I'll be back in a jiffy! Don't change anything!"

Before I could respond, Marcy was gone.

Chapter Eleven

I stared at myself in the bathroom mirror. I was eighteen again and wearing bright, green eyeshadow that matched my dress. My hair was in curls piled on top of my head and I wrinkled my nose in displeasure. This was not supposed to be happening. I should not be here reliving this night.

"Your date is waiting for you," someone said behind me. I turned and frowned, trying to remember the girl's name.

"Thank you," I said. I went back to the gym and scanned the room for Xander Powell. His eyes locked with mine across the room and my heart jumped in my chest. I had dated him for almost two years and broke up with him right before college. In this case, it would be in about three months. He had been so angry with me that he refused to speak to me again.

"Hello, beautiful," he said, kissing my cheek.

I turned away, embarrassed. Even knowing that we were both the same age, the fact that I was here as a thirty-two-year-old woman inside an eighteen-year-old's body with a real eighteen-year-old felt very inappropriate. "At least you're legal," I muttered.

"Legal? We both are," he said, smiling mischievously. "Which is why there won't be any problem at the hotel later," he whispered in my ear.

I shuddered. I had slept with Xander on prom night, happily embracing the cliché even though neither of us were still virgins at that point. There was no way I could go through with it again, what Marcy said be damned. It just wasn't right. Surely our not sleeping together wouldn't change anything. We only had a short time left together as a couple.

"Maybe we should just go to the club afterward," I suggested.

"Baby, we talked about this. I want to spend the whole night with you."

"You'll get to," I promised. "But think of the club as if it's an after-party."

"All right," he grumbled.

"Shall we dance, then?" I asked awkwardly.

As Xander hooked his arm around mine to lead me to the dance floor, another person gently tapped my shoulder.

"Julio said he doesn't want to stay here with me anymore!" cried Maeve Wu.

"Maeve?" I said, stunned. I let go of Xander's arm and embraced the woman who had been my best friend in high school. "It's so good to see you!"

"We got ready together three hours ago," Maeve said, sniffling.

"It feels like a lot longer," I said, reluctant to release her. Maeve had disappeared on a dig in Egypt five years ago. Rumors flew about her whereabouts and I was told not to intervene by Simon. He had told me that mortals take care of mortal business.

"I think Julio meant he didn't want to hang out at the prom anymore," Xander clarified.

Maeve tilted her head thoughtfully. "You think so?"

"I do," Xander replied gently.

I looked away, trying to hide my expression. Teenagers were incredibly dramatic.

"What do you think he wants to do instead? We didn't make plans for after the prom."

"You should go bowling," I said.

"Bowling?" Maeve swept a strand of silky black hair off her forehead. "Wow, Carmen. We get dressed up and you want to go bowling."

"Bowling is fun! That's what all of the kids are doing these days!" I said defensively.

"Baby, you sound like an old fogey."

I bit my lip to stop myself from yelling. *Baby.* I hate being called that. "I am just being a sensible adult who wants to have clean, wholesome fun."

Maeve rolled her eyes. "Okay, Mrs. Robinson, we get it. You want to go bowling. We'll go bowling. In a prom dress." She exchanged glances with Xander. "Do you want to check out nursing homes afterward?"

Xander guffawed. "Nice! High five!" he shouted, holding his hand in the air. Maeve swiftly hit his palm with her own.

An hour later, we were trading out high heels for bowling shoes. Maeve held up her blue-and-red-striped shoes next to her sunset orange gown. "These don't really complement my dress," she pouted.

"But you do," Julio said sweetly, kissing her cheek. She blushed.

I groaned and frantically searched for Marcy, pleading silently for her return.

To my dismay, she was nowhere to be seen.

"Rise and shine! It's a new day! It's Monday!"

"No," I muttered, throwing a pillow over my head.

Mom yanked it out of my hands and sent it flying into the hallway. She waved her hands and the blankets were yanked down to my ankles. "Monday is a new day! A new beginning of a new week!" she sang.

I did not miss my mother singing to me in the mornings. Despite my alarm clock, she always waltzed into my bedroom singing and making sure that I never even attempted to hit the snooze button. Before my very first class at Notre Dame, she had appeared in my dorm singing and my roommate had almost succeeded in tackling her to the ground, assuming she was an intruder. Mom had graciously stepped aside, or so my roommate had thought. She had actually transported herself to the other side of my bed, wished me good luck on my first day, and waltzed out the door. My roommate had promptly put in a transfer request to get away from "the girl whose mom won't leave her alone." The transfer had been denied and it had been painfully awkward living with her for an entire semester.

"I'm up, I'm up," I grumbled. My feet padded against the cold wooden floor and I thought about the beautiful floral runner my mother would use to cover it in several years. I thought about the weekend's events as I went through my morning routine. After bowling, no one had wanted to go to the club. We had returned to the hotel where I insisted we upgrade our room and everyone stay in one place. I had explained that we would soon be going our separate directions and it would be the last time we'd all be in one place at the same time. The others excitedly agreed while Xander had fumed silently.

I made myself a quick breakfast of bacon and eggs, forgetting that Lewis would leave for work at the same time I left for school.

"That smells good," he said. "You don't happen to have any extra, do you?"

I pointed to the microwave and blinked a couple of times so that a piping hot plate was waiting for him when he opened the door.

"Perfect!" he said happily. "You even made me toast and buttered it!" His toast was midway to his mouth when he paused. "What do you want?" he asked suspiciously.

"Nothing," I said, munching on a piece of bacon. "I just made breakfast, that's all."

"Uh-huh," he replied. "This is blackmail breakfast, isn't it?"

I grinned, realizing he was joking. "Of course. One day you'll have to take my mom somewhere in Europe on a second honeymoon."

"You're in cahoots together!"

"If that were the case, I would have told you that you should take me with you, too." I finished my breakfast and washed my dishes before shouting goodbye over my shoulder. I walked to the bus stop, wondering what I was going to do at school. I hadn't been to high school in fourteen years. I was worried about Finn and Abby's progress in my absence, if the future was even still occurring at the same time as my past. I rubbed my temples as my head began to ache. There was a reason I wasn't a time traveler, though I now had a good reason to kill one when I saw her again.

I couldn't deny a certain nostalgia in riding the bus once more. The smell of the old seats, the feel of the textured fabric against my hands, the sound of the engine rumbling as it trudged from stop to stop picking up more students.

Surprisingly, I still remembered the location of my old locker, though I had to use my magic to remove the combination lock. It had been long-forgotten along with my senior class schedule. Opening the thin door, I saw that I had taped the schedule to the inside and smiled. I yanked it off and stuffed it into a folder I pulled from the top shelf. Homeroom and first period was math and I sauntered off to class, dreading it. It had been a long time since I had done any calculus.

"What in the hell are you doing? That's Tanya's seat," a shrill voice from behind me snapped.

I slowly turned around to face a petite girl with blonde hair and brown roots at least three inches long. "Jessica Parker," I said.

"Carmen Devereaux," she retorted, her voice mocking mine.

"I apologize for taking Tanya's seat. I didn't remember it belonged to her."

"Yeah, so you better move your ass."

"I'm seated. If Tanya wanted this spot, she should have been responsible and shown up to class on time."

Jessica started kicking the back of my chair.

"Jessica, I suggest you grow up. Where Tanya sits today does not determine neither her nor your futures."

"What in the hell are you talking about? Just move already." She started kicking the back of my chair again. I created an invisible wall between the two of us so that I could no longer feel her foot.

"Just move, you damn vampire! You telling me you're growing a backbone now in the last week of school? Bitch, I rule this place."

"You don't rule anything, Jessica. You're going to run the cash register at the minimart and that's about as far as you're going to go."

"What?" Jessica asked, surprised. "What are you talking about, bitch? I ain't going to run a minimart!"

"I didn't say that. I said you were going to run the cash register," I corrected.

"I'm going to be a model! Did you hear me? I'm going to be a model!" Jessica shouted. Her breathing grew heavy and she began to pout. "I'll walk the runways in France, then maybe Paris."

I opened my mouth to correct her again, but decided against it.

The math teacher finally entered, apologizing for his tardiness. Tanya was still nowhere to be seen and I stifled a laugh. Mr. Wheeler was only in his twenties and it had been rumored that he had flings with the eighteen-year-old students. If I remembered correctly, Tanya was one of the alleged students. A few minutes later, she joined the class, absently wiping the sides of her mouth. She frowned when she saw me in her chair and took the empty seat behind Jessica. She leaned forward and whispered to Jessica, asking her if she had any lip balm.

To my relief, the rest of my classes were fairly easy. There were only a few days until graduation and most teachers, having already administered the standardized tests and given the results, were allowing their senior students relative freedom in the last week they had before they "entered the real world."

My last class of the day was English, and I smiled at the thought of Dr. Tanning. While he had often been a bit too harsh, I remembered him fondly for his blunt mannerisms. It wasn't every teacher out there that had the nerve to write, "This makes no sense!" in bright red ink on papers his students had worked so hard to complete to his standards.

"Ah, Carmen, you seem to be in a good mood," Dr. Tanning observed as I took a seat in front of his podium. "And sitting in front of the class instead of trying to hide in the back. You've got a backbone today, don't you?"

"That seems to be the consensus," I replied casually.

"Good for you. Good *for* you. Today you'll be the lucky first one to deliver her speech."

I cleared my throat. "Speech?"

"Yes, a speech. Did you think I didn't mean it when I gave you an assignment on Friday to have a speech ready today? I don't care that you had your prom. The world out there does not care about the frivolity in which you engage during your weekends. If you have a presentation for work due on Monday, they frankly don't give a damn that you were out gallivanting on Saturday," Dr. Tanning said, his voice rising. "Now get up here and give us your how-to speech."

"Any how-to?" I asked timidly. I remembered why I preferred to sit in the back row.

"Are you unprepared? I will give you a zero and drag down that A average so fast that your head will spin, young lady!"

I nervously glanced around the room and spotted Maeve slouching low in her seat. "Of course I'm prepared," I said easily as an idea popped into my head. "I just need to get a prop and a volunteer." I reached into my backpack where I had created a pink mat that, as I unfolded it, was mysteriously longer and wider than it looked as it was laid out on the floor. "Please push your desks to form a semicircle on one side of me," I instructed.

The desks screeched against the floor as my classmates moved them and they gathered around me, sitting cross-legged on the floor. They watched me curiously and I glimpsed at Dr. Tanning who was frowning at me from his seat behind the podium.

"Maeve, will you please be my volunteer?" I patted the spot on the mat next to me.

"What am I volunteering for?"

"Maeve," I said, my teeth clenched. "I need your help."

"You owe me," she muttered under her breath.

I smiled brightly. "As you know, Maeve is my best friend. I'm about to hurt her."

"You're what, now?" Dr. Tanning demanded. He leaned one part of his head nearer to me, as if the closer ear might hear my words more easily.

I waved my hand absently. "Oh, I'm not serious. That's what the tapping is for." I looked at Maeve. "When something starts to hurt, tap me. Don't tap the mat because I might not hear you."

"Would you please get to your topic, Miss Devereaux?"

"I would love to if you'd stop interrupting me," I said. I cringed inwardly, waiting for Dr. Tanning's retort. He said nothing. "A lot of you don't know that I've been taking Brazilian jiu-jitsu for the last several years." I'd actually taken it in South Bend and had stopped after returning to New Bern. I had meant to pick it up again, but yoga and kickboxing classes drained my time and, at thirty-two, my body didn't rebound as quickly as it had when I was younger. Kickboxing would have to go if I was going to resume my jiu-jitsu training.

"You have?" Maeve asked, surprised. "I didn't know this."

"It was just kind of my thing I did on my own," I replied quickly. "Okay, let's go over the basic positions." When I got to the position of mount, a chorus of giggles erupted. "Yes, let's all laugh at the name of the position." Maeve was flat on her back and I straddled her hips. "Yes, it's funny that I'm sitting on top of her. Oh, ha ha," I said, my tone dry. I began to punch Maeve, stopping my fists just before they hit her face. "This is why mount is great. If you're fighting, and you have this top position, you can rain punches. It's also a dominant position for submissions."

Immediately the class went silent.

"Is mount still funny?" I asked quietly.

They shook their heads no.

"Okay, let's continue. Let me show you how to escape from mount. Maeve, please hook your left arm over my right arm like this," I said, instructing her movements. "Now step your left leg over my right leg and bridge your hips upward and over." Maeve rolled me onto my back. "Now she's got side control." I looked at Maeve and grinned. "Thanks," I said, sitting up. She sat next to me, watching me carefully. "Guard, side control, and mount are your basic positions. I've shown you some very basic movements to escape them. Are there any questions?"

"How long did you say you've been training?"

"Where do they offer classes?"

"Can you kick my ass?"

"Are you done, Miss Devereaux?" Dr. Tanning asked.

"Yes, sir," I said.

"It was only meant to be a five-minute speech. It was not meant to become a thirty-minute demonstration."

"I was excited to share my knowledge, sir," I said.

"I bet," he said skeptically. He jotted down a note. "A minus," he said. "You went over your time limit. Imagine if you were in advertising and you only had five minutes to pitch an idea. The client wouldn't be happy if you made them listen for an extra twenty-five minutes."

Rolling up the mat, I said, "But I'm not going to go into advertising."

"You get my point anyway!"

He was such a hard ass. I smiled slightly. "Yes, sir," I replied.

The day of my high school graduation, I sat in my bedroom. I hadn't seen or heard from Marcy in a week and I was furious. I had been going to my classes and interacting with my mother and Lewis as though nothing were different, though they and my friends could tell that something was off-kilter about me. Mom had briefly commented on my more adult-like behavior and I had held my breath, nervously waiting for her to pry. Relief flooded through me when she did not, though she paid closer attention to me than she normally would have.

I was terrified that Marcy had lost me in time somehow and I would have to relive my life. I knew I was not supposed to change anything, but I had already decided that I could not—*would not*—date and marry Matthew Ferrara again. I didn't want to lose my calling as an Influencer, but I could only hope that Fate would allow me this privilege even without him in my life.

"Please tell me that's not how you're going to wear your hair," Mom said, frowning as she stood in my doorway.

I ran my hands over my hair. It had been almost to the middle of my back when I was a teenager. "What's wrong with wearing it straight? No one is going to remember it anyway."

She snapped a photo with a camera that she had created. "I'll remember." She walked across my room and sat next to me. "Is there something wrong?"

"No," I lied.

"There is," Mom said flatly. "Honey, are you upset about graduation? Don't be! You'll go to college and meet new friends. You'll have a great time and earn your degree. Then your life will *really* begin and I just know you're going to do great things."

"Thank you," I said, my voice thick with emotion.

"I don't think that is what's really bothering you."

"No, it's not."

"I didn't think so. I never thought of you to be the one afraid of change." She caught my gaze. "But you're not going to tell me, are you?"

"No."

She sighed. "All right. You know I'm here with open ears when you want to talk. Until then, let's do something with this hair. It's just hanging there." She ran her fingers through my hair, soft waves forming in their wake. "That is so much better," she said, pleased with herself. "How do you like it?"

I went to the mirror that hung on the back of my door. "It looks nice," I answered.

"Change your clothes and fix your makeup." She took another photo. "And stop looking so sad!"

She left me alone as I stood in my closet, trying to decide what to wear. I couldn't remember what I had originally chosen and wound up putting on a black dress. Before I even made it to the landing, my mother vetoed it. "You're not going to a funeral!" I changed once again, choosing a peacock blue dress that was sleeveless with a deep V-neck and cinched at my waist, then flared outward slightly.

Standing at the landing once more, my mother looked over my dress, nodding in approval. "Make it go to your knees."

I tugged at the bottom and the fabric lengthened until it grazed the top of my knees. "Better?"

"You look beautiful, honey," she replied.

"I don't even want to know how much that dress cost," Lewis said as I walked down the stairs and joined them in the living room.

"I paid for it out of my allowance," I said.

He pretended to wipe sweat from his brow. "Dodged a bullet with that, didn't I?" he joked.

For the second time in my life, I begrudgingly stood for photo after photo that Mom insisted on taking. Even if she had known that I was stuck in the past and was really thirty-two, she still would have made me suffer through her photo session.

The car ride to the school was long and silent. I was thinking about each action I had taken in the last fourteen years. Fourteen years. I could not live through that again. I was very happy in the present. I missed my life. I even missed Lenny the Snowman. Angrily, I wiped away a tear that had fallen down my cheek. Mom noticed and blinked softly, fixing the makeup that had smeared in the process.

"Calm down," she said quietly. "We're having a party after this and all of your friends are coming. Today is an exciting day!"

"I know," I said, struggling to keep my voice even. "These are happy tears."

"How about no more tears? You'll make me cry."

Forty minutes later, every student, parent, and other various family members and friends of families had taken a seat in the gymnasium. It had been decorated in the school colors of orange and black, along with congratulatory banners from local businesses for the graduating class. I groaned as the speeches began. They had been uninspiring then and I gently shook my head in dismay as I realized that, even as an adult, the words of wisdom being given to us were still just as lackluster.

Finally, they began to call our names and one by one, we stood to receive our diplomas and cross the stage. At the end of the ceremony, we threw our hats into the air and cheered happily.

More photos were taken as friends hugged, cried, and hugged again. Mom captured every moment with her camera, which other parents had commented on its uniqueness. "I guess Lewis must've got a raise at work since you've got that new fancy camera!"

Mom smiled sweetly, snapped another photo, and moved on.

Back at home, my graduation party was in full swing. The backyard was adorned with balloons, graduation-themed confetti, and a large banner that said in giant pink letters, "CONGRATULA-TIONS, CARMEN!" My mother had boasted that she could reuse it at my college graduation, which is exactly what she had done.

Several family members had shown up from out of state and they swarmed around me, asking me about what I wanted to major in and where was I going to go to school. I answered politely and, finally, feeling overwhelmed, snuck away to my bedroom. Peering at my reflection in my mirror, I began talking softly to myself. "You're an adult. You can figure out a way to get back to the present. Go back out there and face those people. You were the life of the party the first time you did this, so go do it again!"

"You act like reliving your past is the end of your life," my mirror chided.

"What in the hell?" I asked, flabbergasted.

"Oh, yes, a talking mirror. How original. Is that what you're thinking?" the mirror asked.

"That is definitely not what I'm thinking."

"You've been moping all week. I knew something was wrong the moment you showed up from prom."

It was surreal and very strange watching myself talking, even though the lips on my face weren't moving. "How could you tell?"

"You stand differently. You move differently. You talking to yourself sealed my conclusion."

"Oh," I said, not sure how else I should respond.

"You fooled everyone else, if you were worried about that. Your mother is clueless. She just thinks you're upset about moving to Indiana."

"I *had* been nervous about it then," I admitted.

"You're a smart girl. Or I guess I should say you're a smart woman. You'll figure this out."

"Any ideas?"

"I'm just a mirror. What more do you expect from me?" My image shrugged.

"Why are you just talking to me now?" I asked.

"I didn't really need to until now."

"What changed?"

My image rolled its eyes. "Come on, that's obvious. I can't have you going out there and turn into some crazy person who talks to herself. Next thing you know, you'll be rehearsing arguments you want to have with people, but in a nice manner so you don't come off seeming like you're too saucy."

"Saucy?" I raised a brow.

"That's right. Saucy."

"I've never rehearsed an argument I wanted to have."

The mirror smiled sardonically. "But you have rehearsed a job interview."

"I might have done that. Okay, don't look at me like that. Yes, I have done that."

"Looney."

"That's not 'looney,'" I said, quoting the mirror. "That's perfectly normal. I didn't want to sound like a blabbering idiot."

"You do realize you're still talking to yourself, don't you?" my image asked smugly.

"It's not really to myself, though," I pointed out.

"It would look weird if someone just walked in and saw us." The mirror smirked as I tried to respond.

"All right, that's enough of this conversation. You're not even being helpful."

"Sure I am," the mirror argued.

"You most certainly are not," I said, annoyed. "You offer no solutions. You just teased me instead."

My image laughed. "I did do that, yes. Hey, are you taking me to college? I could stand to see some new scenery."

"Absolutely not," I answered. I started to leave my bedroom.

"You're such a spoiled sport," the mirror complained.

It was still complaining long after I left it.

"There you are!" Maeve grabbed my hand and dragged me back down the stairs and toward the party. "Your mother has been looking all over for you."

"I'm sure," I murmured.

Maeve stopped. "Are you okay? You've been acting strangely all week."

I nodded. "I'm all right."

"You're such a liar," Maeve replied. She looked around and whispered, "Is something wrong? Really?"

I took a deep breathe. "Maeve, you want to be an archaeologist, right?"

"You know I do. What, you're not going to lecture me like my dad did for not going into law school and following in his footsteps? I just don't want to be in a stuffy office all day. I want to learn about our past, maybe even make a discovery of my own!" she said passionately.

"Stay away from Egypt."

"What? Why?" she demanded. "You know that's one of the places I've wanted to go see."

"Please," I begged. "Trust me on this."

Her eyes narrowed. "No."

"Maeve, I have a really bad feeling that something is going to happen to you if you go. Please promise me that you won't go."

"Damn, Carmen, you're shaking! Do you really feel this way or did my dad put you up to this?" She sighed. "Of course not. I'm sorry. You know how I get paranoid when I talk about my dad. All right. I promise. I won't go to Egypt. There are plenty of other options, I suppose."

I wrapped my arms around my friend to hug her. "Thank you," I said, relieved.

"If someone makes a cool discovery in my absence, though, I'm never going to forgive you."

"I wouldn't expect anything less from you," I replied.

"Now can we get back to your party? Evelyn is so nice for throwing this. Dad is so mad at me that I'm surprised my parents even came to my graduation."

"He'll come around," I told her. The truth was that her father never fully accepted what she did until she'd disappeared. It was then that he realized how proud he had been of her for making her own tracks instead of following his.

Outside, a game of corn hole had been set up and several people were gathered around it. "They've set up a competition," Mom said, standing next to me.

"I'm surprised you didn't conjure up more boards."

"It made sense for us to have two hidden in the attic, not six," she said. She looked around at the guests laughing, drinking, and eating. "Are you having fun, sweetie? Look at your friends in the pool. Don't you like that swan floatie I made?" Little did my mother know that she would spark a hipster trend for social media with that particular creation.

"I am. Thank you so much for having this."

"You're welcome." She put her arm around me and squeezed. "You're my favorite daughter."

"By default."

"It's still nice to be the favorite, isn't it?" she said affectionately. I chuckled. "It is."

"Oh, my. I can't believe it!" my mother suddenly whispered angrily.

"What's wrong?"

She pointed a long, red fingernail toward the corner of the backyard. "Do you see that?"

In the corner stood three pale, shimmering figures. Two of the people quietly watched the activities and I followed their gaze. Across the yard was a young couple holding hands, giggling as they talked to each other. The guy leaned forward and gently brushed a lock of hair across the girl's forehead and tucked it behind her ear.

The third figure watched the couple intently. She was dressed in an outlandish costume of a bright pink tutu with red tights and a cropped top that bore a giant heart in the middle. She held a miniature harp.

"It's a Cupid!" I whispered excitedly.

"They are so obnoxious," Mom said, still watching them. "When your father and I were going through our divorce, one just showed up for no reason. Now they only answer to formal requests."

"They're still working out the kinks on that," I said, thinking of the Cupid that had shown up after my own divorce.

"Hopefully this couple will get things worked out," my mother said softly. "But I don't want them hovering and trying to crash the party. I know we're the only two that can see them, but I don't want any funny business."

"There won't be." I thought for a moment. "Mom, I really appreciate everything that you've done for me."

"You're welcome, sweetie."

"I'll go talk to the Cupid and see how long they're staying."

"Okay, but don't take too long. I made a cake!"

"Sounds delicious," I said warmly. I strolled across the yard until I was next to the shimmering figures. "Hello," I said, careful to keep my back facing the partygoers. I didn't want them to see me talking to a blank space.

The Cupid looked at me, annoyed. "I'm sorry, but I'm with clients right now. If you need anything, you can contact our office. Do you need that information?"

"No, thank you. I do need your help, though."

"I told you I'm with clients," the Cupid said, her tone terse.

"I heard you, but I'm desperate. I was left here by accident in the wrong time. I'm thirty-two, not eighteen. I've already been to college, gotten married, got divorced, moved back to my hometown, and procured a new job. I am not going to relive that. I *can't* relive that."

The Cupid grimaced. "I'm not supposed to take hitchhikers."

"I am begging you to help me," I pleaded.

The couple, who had been ignoring me, turned and stared at me. "Go ahead and take her back with us. We don't mind," the guy said.

"This is exactly what pisses me off about you, Gerard. I cannot stand that you speak for the both of us!" shrieked the woman.

"I'm sorry, Greta, but she looks like she needs help. Do you actually mind if we take her back with us or are you just bitching to bitch?"

"Hey!" shouted the Cupid. "What did we discuss?" she said, sweetening her voice. "We should speak to each other in a loving, positive, and supportive manner."

"Fine, take back the beggar," Greta mumbled. "I'm tired of her whining anyway."

"That's the spirit! Kindness is always wonderful!" the Cupid said cheerfully. "Now," she said, speaking to me, "I'm going to have to do something to separate your current body and your former body." She produced a crossbow from a sling behind her back.

"I thought Cupids used bows and arrows," I said nervously.

"Most of us do, but the crossbow really pops, don't you think? It makes me look fierce."

"Cupids aren't supposed to look fierce," I pointed out.

"No," she said, shaking her head vigorously. "Not fierce as in scary. Fierce as in *runway* fierce." She gestured toward her outfit. "Like I *slay* this outfit. I don't mean slay as in murder it. I mean slay as in I kill it, I pull it off."

"Uh-huh," I replied.

"Are you sure you're from the present?"

"I am, but I'm older than you, and I don't use those slang terms."

"Oh," the Cupid said thoughtfully. "I guess you wouldn't. Well, let's raise the roof, shall we?"

"Too young for that one, at least."

"Whatever. Let's do this." She raised the crossbow and shot me in the chest.

Chapter Twelve

White-hot pain coursed through my body and I screamed. I fell to the ground, pain washing over me in waves. As I writhed in agony, I saw my younger self saunter back to the party, completely unaware of what had just happened.

"Stop being such a baby!" Greta yelled.

I clutched my chest, expecting to feel a bolt. Instead, I felt nothing but the fabric of my shirt and warily rose to my feet.

"Are you all right? That looked like it really hurt," Gerard asked worriedly.

"What is this? Are you trying to be her knight in shining armor?"

"No," he replied, his teeth clenched. "Someone has just been shot with a crossbow. That someone has been hurt. I was concerned for that someone's well-being."

Greta flung her hair over her shoulder. "I don't see what the big deal is. It was a magical bolt, not a real one."

The Cupid pouted.

"Thank you," I said, my voice hoarse. I looked over my body and discovered that I, too, had become pale and shimmered.

"We'll just wait here for a few more minutes," the Cupid whispered to me. To the couple, she said happily, "Don't you see how your romance was budding? Greta, don't you see yourself as carefree, open to the world, and to love?"

"This feels a little one-sided," Greta said defensively. "I feel like I'm being attacked. I'm *not* heartless. I *care* about people."

I doubted that greatly. Greta and my stepbrother's wife would get along famously.

"Then why don't you show it more?" Gerard asked cautiously. "You certainly don't seem to care about me."

While Greta and Gerard argued, the Cupid and I moved away. "Do you ever see a couple and just know that they're doomed?"

"I'm always supposed to believe in the power of love," the Cupid said breezily.

"So you do, but you just can't say it out loud."

She smiled and lowered her voice. "She's a real pill. He could do better," she admitted. "Love will bring him someone who is worthy of his devotion and admiration."

"What about her?" I asked. Greta's hands were flailing in the air as her voice grew higher and higher with anger.

"Love might help her learn to love herself before sending her someone else," the Cupid answered smoothly.

"You're good."

She laughed lightly. "Thank you. I am, after all, almost like a politician. I represent the state of Love."

"I'm ready to go back. Take us back," Greta demanded.

Gerard shoved his hands into his pockets. I caught his eye and tried to smile, but he merely frowned and looked away. I recognized that expression. He was giving up on Greta and was already mourning the end of their time together. Greta wasn't even aware of how much she had wounded him. She probably never would and would feel blindsided when he parted ways with her.

"There's so much more to see," the Cupid said, though her enthusiasm was waning.

"I don't care!" snapped Greta.

In a flash of bright red and pink smoke, we were gone.

Smoke was still swirling around us after we stopped moving. We were in a bustling office that looked like it came straight out of a midcentury newsroom. "Are we back?" Gerard asked.

"Yes. You'll have to sign the exit paperwork. Last desk on your left. The person's name is Grover. He'll help you with any questions you might have. Oh, and, if you don't mind, there's a survey at the end that I'd love for you to take. It helps us be better, which also helps you!"

Greta practically stomped away. Gerard looked at the Cupid sadly. "Thanks for trying," he said.

Whispering in his ear, she said, "It will be tough to leave her, but you need to. You will find love again. It will be powerful and true. I promise you this."

He brightened slightly. "Thank you."

Watching him walk away, I asked, "Can you see the future?"

The Cupid shook her head. "No, but you get to learn to trust your gut feeling when it comes to this job."

I held out my hand to shake hers. "Thank you so much for your help."

She returned the handshake. "You're welcome, but you can't leave yet. I have to make a report about why I brought back an extra passenger and I'm going to need you to sign it. You'll also need to log a complaint against whomever left you in the past."

"It was Marcy Bloomberg."

The Cupid inhaled sharply. "Seriously? I am so happy I am not you right now. She is going to want to throttle you. Her record is spotless."

"You're going to have go to back and try it again."

"The hell I am!" I seethed.

Simon nervously straightened the already-neat stack of papers on his desk. "Yes. That's final."

I slammed my hands down on top of his desk. "No, it's not. I am not going anywhere with that woman. I don't care how great she's supposed to be, I don't care that Abby channeling my magic caused a *ripple*, and I don't care what Fate thinks. I refuse. No more memory trips. No more time traveling. I'm done. I just want to get back to my work and put this whole experience behind me."

"I'm afraid it's not that easy, Carmen," Simon said gently.

"I swear that if I see Marcy again, you'll regret it."

"I understand why you're upset," Simon began.

"Oh, do you? Really?" I could feel my temperature rising as anger boiled beneath the surface.

"Calm down. People will hear you and no one knows you're here. They all think you're downstairs working on that Vegas mess."

"Marcy left me in the past, Simon. She never even came looking for me," I said, not bothering to lower my voice.

"She was going through a tough time," my boss replied simply.

"A tough time?" I laughed mirthlessly. "Did she even tell you what happened?"

"Her husband was having an affair."

"No, he wasn't."

"You of all people should be understanding. You went through the same thing."

"My ex-husband cheated on me with other women. Her husband is cheating on her with *food*."

Simon stared at me, flabbergasted. "Food?"

"Yes. She put them on a diet and he's not been following it. She was distracted because she was tracking his movements and caught him buying doughnuts and that's how we wound up with me in the third grade again. She apologized and transported us to my senior year of high school, right before she became furious and promised to be right back and that's the last time I saw her. She was so focused on him eating a fucking doughnut that she couldn't do her job and she almost royally screwed me over."

"Really, you'd only have screwed yourself over if you had changed the past."

"But I didn't," I lied. I didn't think that not sleeping with Xander would change the present, and I had been right. Telling Maeve about not going to Egypt, however, had the outcome I wanted. She had switched her studies from archaeology to paleontology and was working at the Museum of Natural History in New York City. In the brief amount of time I was able to research her, I discovered that, while she and I remained on good terms, we had drifted apart as we'd gotten older. I was okay with that. She wasn't missing and that gave me comfort.

"I'm sure you didn't," Simon said, skeptical. "I'm sorry, but you'll have to do this again. I also need to tell you that you should drop the complaint because it will make working with Marcy much easier."

"Hell will freeze over first, Simon."

"You really don't care about the repercussions of someone else channeling your magic?"

"I do care," I answered. "But I don't believe that one person doing that one time is going to suddenly alert the rest of the mortals that witches and wizards are real and that, should they touch us during a memory trip, they can do whatever they want with our magic. Just make people wear special gloves so there is no transference of power."

Simon leaned back in his chair and propped his feet up on his desk. "Okay."

"Okay? Is that it?"

"That's it."

"I'm not in trouble?"

"This incident will show up on your record as a slight insubordination, but you recommended a solution, so I am sure that it will be expunged by next year." He chuckled. "I told them you wouldn't be interested in going back with Marcy."

"Then why did you push me so hard?"

"It's my job." He shrugged.

"What happened while I was gone? How was my absence explained to Abby and Finn?"

Simon looked at his feet guiltily.

"Simon, what happened?" I demanded.

He held out his hand and a bottle of water appeared. He took several sips before responding. "The tech took the android to New Bern to be you. Here, people thought you took an impromptu vacation."

"Samuel and Carmen were in my house for a week?" I sunk into his guest chair and rubbed my eyes. "Finn."

"Now, Carmen, Finn never realized there was a difference."

"Because the Eraser came by," I said, groaning. "You couldn't have just written a letter as if it was from me stating I had to take a quick business trip? Finn recognizes magic, Simon! He's probably wondering why he feels a little fuzzy after the delivery man stops by."

"Oh. Huh." Simon pursed his lips and tilted his head. "I suppose that would have been a better idea. If it makes you feel any better, Samuel and Carmen never actually spent the night in your house. They were just there whenever we assumed Finn would see you."

"No, Simon, it doesn't, but I suppose I don't have a choice. I can't change it."

"You know, if you went back and changed what Abby did, I'm sure Marcy would fix her mistake," Simon urged.

My jaw clenched. "If I ever see Marcy again, it's going to be because I'm watching her eat the food that I secretly poisoned. She won't die from it, but she'll have plenty of time sitting on a toilet, hopefully thinking about how sorry she is for screwing up and not doing her damn job properly."

Simon flinched. "That's a bit harsh, isn't it?"

"It's not harsh enough."

"Abby never even noticed you were gone. The android called her to tell her something with work came up and you had to postpone your plans," Simon said, trying to steer the subject back on track.

"That's a relief. Listen, Simon, I'm tired. I want to go home and I want to check on my charges."

Without waiting for his reply, I disappeared.

My house was quiet when I arrived. Slowly, I sauntered from room to room, grateful to be back in my own home. I paused in the doorway to Finn's room, reluctant to go inside for fear of invading his privacy. In the corner, his guitar was proudly displayed in its stand. The amp was in the family room, set up next to the bar so that he and Roach could enjoy a shot at the end of their lessons each week. Finn had joked that, if Roach let them take a shot before the lessons, he might sound better. I had laughed, though I had privately thought that Finn was starting to sound even better than his instructor.

Back upstairs, I began to cook dinner. The ingredients floated out of the dark wood cabinets and joined me at the counter. As I chopped, Lenny suddenly appeared. He was leaning against the pantry, trying to get as far away from the gas stove as possible. He was frowning, his stick arms folded.

"I see you've finally returned."

"I have."

"It took you long enough."

"It wasn't my fault."

"So you weren't deliberately off living it up as a teenager again?" he asked, skeptical.

I stopped chopping, holding the knife in the air. "Of course not. I didn't want to be there in the first place."

The snowman uncrossed his arms and flashed a smile. "I've got to hand it to you, Carmen. You really showed some backbone today when you stood up to Fate!"

"I wasn't taking a stance against Fate. I was refusing to ever be around Marcy Bloomberg again."

"She's so hot except for that hair. You'd think that, as a witch, she'd do something about it. Or at least go to the store and buy some frizz cream."

"That's not very nice," I murmured. I had set down the knife and was now scraping seeds from a cucumber.

"I never thought she was all that great. She kind of has an attitude."

"*Other* than when she's upset about something stupid her husband has done?"

Lenny waved his arms, exasperated. "She's a big deal and she knows it. So, she has that attitude."

"Oh. I see what you mean." I laughed. "I used to really admire her."

"And you'll continue to because she does good work."

"You're such a saint, Lenny," I said. "Did you stop by just to check on me?"

"That's not the only reason why." Lenny sniffed. "Fate isn't upset with you. I know you were worried about that."

"I was concerned about the consequences," I admitted.

"Other than your slight insubordination, there won't be any," he promised. "Fate is more understanding about human nature than people realize. That's why there are options, to accommodate humans."

"What about snowmen?"

He rolled his eyes. "I should know better than to talk in specifics with you. They're understanding with *all* creatures." He looked at the blue-and-white-tiled floor. "Keep on doing what you're doing. I need to go. I'm starting to puddle here."

"You're what?" I asked, but I was talking to no one.

The back door opened and Finn kicked his shoes off and tossed them down the stairs. "Good to see you," he said. He took a few steps and scowled. "What the hell? Why is there water over here?"

Ah, so that's what Lenny had meant by puddling. "I dropped some ice earlier. I guess I didn't get all of the cubes."

Finn grabbed a dish towel and soaked up the mess. "Making Greek food?"

"I had a craving. Care to join me?"

"Sure," he said, wringing out the towel and tossing it down the laundry chute in the hallway.

He helped me prepare the rest of the meal and even set the table while I plated the food. He poured a generous helping of the tzatziki sauce over his chicken. He took a bite, smiled, and scooped another helping into his mouth. "This is so good!"

"Thank you."

"I missed you, you know."

"Missed me? I never went anywhere," I said, feeling guilty for lying.

"It was like you weren't here last week. I'd see you and you'd barely talk to me."

"I'm sorry about that," I apologized, unable to meet my stepbrother's gaze. "It was a stressful week."

"I was afraid you were wanting some permanent alone time and I was going to have to start looking for an apartment."

"What?" My eyes widened. "Oh, no! I love having you as a roommate. You're family."

"You do?"

"Of course. If you piss me off, I can just complain to Lewis that his son is being a jerk," I said, my tone light.

Finn exhaled, relieved.

"What do you say we all go to Atlantic Beach in a couple of weeks? It will be June, Morehead City won't be overcrowded just yet with tourists, and we can rent a boat and a jet ski."

"When you say 'we,' does that mean *all* of us?"

"We can't ask our parents to go and not invite Randy and his family."

"Cecily is about to pop. Maybe she won't want to come," Finn said hopefully.

"I'm hoping the pregnancy hormones will overwhelm her system and make her a nicer person."

"You're such an optimist."

"Some might say a dreamer when it comes to Cecily, but I think we all are."

"Right on," Finn replied. "Your treat for this, right?"

I smiled. "I suppose."

Atlantic Beach was bustling. Locals and tourists strolled down the soft, white sand, their skin glistening with a mixture of sweat and sunscreen, smiles on their faces.

Cecily was scowling. She raked her hands through her hair and tied it into a loose, messy bun on top of her head. Rubbing her extended belly, her scowl deepened. "This baby needs to come out already!"

Her husband gently rubbed her lower back. "It's not so bad, honey. When the baby arrives, we'll have a new, beautiful bundle of joy and Apple will have a little brother or sister."

"Tell me again why you didn't want to know the sex of the baby?" I asked, taking a sip of water.

"What does it matter to you if we know or not?" Cecily snapped.

I shrugged. "I just thought it would be easier so you would know which kind of clothes to buy." I took another sip and returned my water to the cup holder. I had rented a pontoon boat for the day and my family, for the most part, had been enjoying themselves. Mom and Lewis sat near the front of the boat, Lewis's arm draped around my mother, feet lazily dangling in the water as I slowly drove us out toward Harker's Island. Finn had taken the seat next to me, claiming himself as the co-captain. He had already downed three beers and was slouching in his white chair, his hat pulled over his eyes.

Apple ran up and down the deck of the boat, her giggles piercing the air. Her bright red curls bounced as she flung her arms out and screamed, "I'm an airplane!" Randy was grinning as he watched his child play.

"Not so loud, Apple!" Cecily chided, raising her voice to be heard over the wind as I picked up speed.

Apple stopped, her arms folding to her sides. She dropped to her stomach and began to slither. "I'm a boat! Look, I'm going through the water!"

I laughed and Cecily glared at me. "Don't encourage her," she said. "Apple, get up and sit next to Mommy."

Defiantly, Apple sat next to her father. I ducked my head to hide my smile as Randy picked her up and placed her in his lap. "Daddy, we're going to play in the ocean, aren't we?"

"Yes, honey."

Her brow furrowed with worry. "You won't let me get eaten by sharks, will you?"

Randy squeezed her tightly. "No, sweetheart. I won't let anything hurt you."

She squealed with delight. "My daddy is the strongest, bestest man in the whole wide world!"

"It's 'best,'" Cecily corrected.

"Nuh-uh, Mommy," Apple argued.

Cecily sighed, too tired to disagree. I felt a pang of guilt for judging her so harshly. She was a week overdue and the sun was blazing overhead. She had to be extremely uncomfortable.

"Don't you do that," Finn said, his lips barely moving.

"Do what?"

"Feel sorry for her."

"She *is* past her due date and that would make anyone crabby."

"No," Finn muttered.

"If you had a kid rolling around on top of your bladder for forty weeks, you'd be upset, too."

"That's why I have a penis so that I can just do what Randy's doing. Offering back rubs and soothing words. That's the life."

I rolled my eyes. "You're such a gentleman."

"I am!" Finn said, tugging his hat further down. "I can't help it if she's rebuffing his kind gestures."

"How can you even tell what he's doing with your eyes covered? I thought you were napping."

"I was trying to, but those two keep shouting at each other. Keeps a man awake."

"You just didn't want to look at my mom and your dad canoodling."

He grunted. "Yeah, that's gross."

"I think it's sweet."

"You would, you sucker. I'm surprised I haven't caught you watching that television for women channel." He pointed at me. "Your day is coming and when it does, I will never stop making fun of you."

"You already make fun of me," I countered.

"This will add another layer of depth to my jokes."

"That's funny, I thought your idea of a joke was your attempt at cooking."

Finn shoved his hat back into its proper place and looked at me out the corner of his eye. "You said I was getting better."

I laughed. "You're so defensive!" The truth was that Finn *was* getting better, though not just at cooking. I felt like he was really making his way to his new path.

"We should have invited Roach to this shindig. He's like family."

"You know someone whose name is Roach?" Randy asked, sliding into the bench seat behind the captain's chair.

"It's my guitar teacher," Finn explained.

"Oh. I didn't realize that was his name," Randy replied. "Cecily wants to know if we're almost to the island."

I looked ahead where the island was clearly visible. "It's right there. It's not too far from Shackleford Banks."

"She didn't know that was it," Randy said quietly.

"Is she not having a good time?" I asked.

My stepbrother shook his head. "It's not that. She just needs to pee." He got up and returned to his family.

I smirked at Finn. "I told you she was just uncomfortable."

Finn looked away, frowning.

Finally approaching the island, I slowed as I pulled next to one of the docks. Finn and Randy hopped out to tie us off while Mom and Lewis disentangled themselves from each other. They grabbed the food cooler while Finn and I took the cooler full of beverages. Randy held Apple's hand and, with the other, juggled the giant umbrella and beach towels. Cecily stuffed her swollen feet into her flip flops and carried nothing as she waddled behind us.

Cape Lookout loomed over us and Mom shielded her eyes against the sun as she looked upward. "It's always such a neat sight," she said, pointing to the lighthouse. "Have you ever been up it?"

"I'm not walking up there," Cecily said, breathing heavily.

Mom shook her head slightly, a smile on her lips. "No, dear, I don't mean that we do that today. It's normally closed to visitors and I think the attendant's house is closed as well. I was just asking if anyone had been there. It's quite the view from the top!"

"Huh," Cecily replied. "No, we haven't, but that might be something we do down the road." She cradled her round belly. "Anything to help get rid of the pregnancy weight. I think I put on at least sixty pounds this time around."

My mother patted her shoulder. "All babies are different. You'll lose the weight chasing a toddler and baby around the house."

For the first time that day, Cecily laughed. "I hope so! This one is almost impossible to keep up with!" She looked at Apple and Apple grinned mischievously. She paused suddenly, then grimaced. "The baby is kicking."

I hesitated, then rested my hand against her belly. I willed her to feel lighter, for her back to hurt less, and she winced uncomfortably. "Your hand is awfully warm, Carmen."

"I'm sorry," I apologized. "I just wanted to feel the baby kick."

"You'll get to one day if you ever find a man and get started. You're not getting any younger, you know." She stretched and took a deep breath. "This ocean air makes me feel almost light as a feather! Honey, we need to try and make it to the beach more often."

I painted a smile on my face. "I guess I'm not, Cecily," I said, my voice tight.

She remained oblivious.

"Our work is always unnoticed or unappreciated. Sometimes both at the same time," Mom said, sidling next to me. We watched as Cecily spread the towels while Randy struggled against the soft breeze to set up the umbrella. Lewis and Finn placed the coolers around the base to help keep it in place.

"I feel badly for her," I admitted.

"I know you do. It's okay. She *is* family. Hopefully she'll have an attitude adjustment after the baby comes."

"You're such an optimist, Mom."

Mom smiled broadly. "It's a hell of a lot more fun than being a pessimist!"

Apple ran into the water, Randy chasing after her. We were on the sound side of the island where there were virtually no waves. I thought about what Apple had said on the boat and, as a precaution, created an impenetrable net so that nothing could reach our little spot on the beach. There was a ripple effect as the net settled. Mom, the only one who noticed, mouthed, "Thank you," and joined her granddaughter.

Hours passed as we played in the surf. Finally we took a break and ate the sandwiches we had brought. Apple enviously watched Finn pluck out a soda from the cooler. Her father handed her a juice packet and she tried unsuccessfully to stab the straw into it. Frustrated, she handed it to Lewis and hugged him tightly when he returned the packet to her, straw ready to use. Everyone was her hero today.

Full from lunch, we sat underneath the umbrella, its shade covering us all and I silently thanked my mother. She merely smiled and leaned back against her towel, her toes dug deeply into the sand.

"I'm ready for the waves," Finn declared, rising to his feet. "Would anyone like to join me on the other side of the island?"

We all grunted in response.

"Fine, I'll go by myself." He put on his shoes and left, his footsteps echoing on the boardwalk as he walked away.

"Someone should have gone with him," Lewis said.

"Dad, he's not a child. If he wants to play in the real waves, let him. The rest of us are just enjoying our day in the sun. Being lazy. Look, even Apple's about to fall asleep."

"Am not," she argued, her eyes closed as she leaned her head against her mother's lap.

"Today's a family day," Lewis pointed out.

"We don't have to do stuff together all of the time," Randy replied.

"I'll go," I said. I begrudgingly got up and shoved my feet into my water shoes. I found the entrance to the boardwalk and followed the winding path. Several plants and bushes surrounded me and, along the way, were plaques to explain the vegetation and what types of animals lived on the small island. Having been to the island several times growing up, I had already read the plaques and today I ignored them as I walked to the other side to join Finn.

I spotted his shoes first when I arrived at the other beach. He had kicked them off as he ran down to the surf and I picked them up, carrying them in my hand as I searched the water for him.

At last, I caught a glimpse of him as he dove into a wave. He came up as soon as the wave crashed over him and began to swim out toward the sea. He always loved going out farther than the rest of us, despite Lewis's protests.

Several other people were on this side, laughing and splashing as they played in the sun. I couldn't help but smile as I observed them and my stepbrother being carefree.

"Do you think anyone else noticed that over there?" a stranger asked, appearing next to me.

"Notice what?" I looked at the stranger. He had a bucket hat pulled down low on his head and a long, straggly beard he had dyed purple.

The stranger pointed. "Out there. When you see a bunch of fish together like that, you'll probably see some predators."

I followed the direction in which he was pointing and gasped. A fin rose slightly out of the water, disappearing so quickly that I doubted seeing it.

"There it is," the stranger said proudly. "Told you there'd be one."

"Hey!" I screamed, waving my arms. "Hey, get out of the water!" The people ignored me.

I amplified my voice. "Get out of the water! Shark! Shark in the water!" Hearing me clearly, the people scattered, scrambling up to the beach.

The fin rose again and I scanned the water, my eyes locking on Finn. He was lazily floating on his back, oblivious.

"Finn!" Even with my voice still amplified, he couldn't hear me.

"Fish food, indeed," the stranger said.

I dropped his shoes and ran down to the surf. I dove into the water, terrified. Finn was my stepbrother and my charge. This was *not* his path. It couldn't be. I used magic to help me swim faster and hoped no one would noticed my speed as I raced to him. "Finn!" I yelled. Closer, he was able to hear me. "Finn, move! Come toward me!"

"Can't I just get some alone time? I love you all, but I just need time to myself." He stopped floating on his back and made himself upright.

Reaching him, I grabbed his hand. "We have to go. There's a shark out here."

He froze as we both felt it.

Bump.

"Holy shit," he said, exhaling.

There was no time. I transported us away and onto the beach, near the boardwalk. Finn blinked several times as he took in his new surroundings.

"I need some Erasers out here!" I shouted. "Now!"

"What did you just do?" Finn demanded. "How did we get here? Carmen, answer me!"

The people who had seen us from the beach were running toward us.

"Oh, great, just take your time! It's not like a beach full of people just saw that!"

"You're such a drama queen. Keep your voice down."

"About damn time. I thought you were always nearby."

The Eraser's cheeks reddened. "I am, but there was this really hot lady. She really was wearing an itsy bitsy teeny weeny yellow polka dot bikini." He paused. "You know what? Never mind." He gently touched Finn's shoulder. "Are you all right, sir?" he asked. Finn's eyes glazed over. "You got out of that water awfully fast!"

"I'm a fast swimmer," he murmured.

The Eraser turned toward the crowd that had gathered around us. "I know you all have questions." He clapped his hands and a neon yellow wave of light erupted from them, washing over the people. "You saw an amazing feat today, folks. This young man dodged a bullet today with his swiftness from the shark. This is certainly a tale to tell your friends!" He smiled warmly. "Anything else?"

The crowd dispersed, suddenly uninterested.

"I didn't know you all could do that," I said.

He scratched the back of his head sheepishly. "It's a gift, really."

"Thank you," I said sincerely. "I didn't have a choice."

"I know you didn't. I would have done the same thing."

I hesitated.

"They won't remember this. *He* especially won't remember it. He's going to think that he saw a dark shape coming toward him from far away and he swam back to the shore," the Eraser assured me. "Trust me, I'm good at my job. You just worry too much."

I laughed nervously. "I suppose I do. Thank you again."

"Any time, Carmen," the Eraser said.

Finn groaned, rubbed his eyes. "Dude, are you hitting on my stepsister in front of me?"

"I would never do that."

"It sounds like you are," Finn argued groggily.

"See you around," I said.

"I'll keep my eyes off the ladies just in case you decide to be heroic again." The Eraser winked and walked away.

I helped Finn to his feet and started to lead him back to our family before pausing suddenly. I searched for the stranger that had warned me.

He was already gone.

Chapter Thirteen

F inn was quiet the rest of the day. He shuffled his feet aimlessly as he walked out of the garage and toward the back door, his eyes seeing nothing.

"Finn, do you want to talk about what happened today?" I asked gently once we were inside the house.

He folded his arms and leaned against the wall. Still not looking at anything in particular, he replied, "What more is there to say? I saw a shark coming toward me and I somehow outswam it. Everyone's relieved that I'm safe and there's not much else to say about that incident."

"I think 'incident' isn't a strong enough word."

He shrugged. "It's the best I've got. It's just..." his voice trailed off. "Never mind."

"Finn, what is it? You can talk to me. It's just us."

He sighed. "It doesn't seem like it's real. I think something else happened, but I can't really figure out what it was." He cleared his throat. "I think you saved me today, but you were nowhere near me, were you?" He met my gaze and I quickly looked away.

I swallowed the lump that had formed in my throat. "Some weird guy with a purple beard saw a group of fish and said there would probably be something bad nearby. I saw the shark and yelled. That's probably what you heard and it caught your attention, so you saw it, and you swam away."

"I don't remember you yelling."

"You did just go through a traumatic experience."

Finn uncrossed his arms and threw his hat on the counter. "I even kept my hat on somehow. Isn't that strange?"

"I think you need to take a shower, have some of the pizza I'm about to order, and then you need to rest. It's been a long day."

He nodded. "That doesn't sound like a bad idea. Listen, Carmen, I appreciate what you did for me today. Even if I don't remember everything clearly." He turned and headed down the stairs. A few minutes later, I could hear the shower running.

I ordered the pizza and went outside to the garage where I quickly vanished to Enid's living room.

She shot off the couch, startled. She was wearing a black negligée and I turned away, embarrassed. "Holy shit, Enid, I'm so sorry. I had no idea."

She grabbed the blanket that hung off the back of her couch and wrapped it around herself. "I could have sworn that there was still a door with a doorbell on my house."

"I know, I'm sorry," I repeated. "Obviously you're waiting for someone, so I'll leave."

"I'm not waiting on anyone."

I turned toward her, my eyes trained on the floor. "So you're just wearing someone's very sexy secret around your house on a Saturday evening?"

"You can look at me, Carmen." She sniffed. "Yes, yes I am. I made myself steak and shrimp for dinner and had a few glasses of wine. I took a bubble bath. Now I'm about to watch one of my favorite chick flicks wearing my favorite lingerie."

"You took yourself on a date tonight," I said, understanding.

She flashed a perfect, white smile. "I did."

"I like that," I replied.

Enid pointed to the other side of her couch and motioned for me to sit. I declined. "You're not staying for very long, then. What did you want?"

"Enid, your great-grandmother was one of the people who fought for spouses to be able to know about magic. How did she do that?"

"She got a lot of signatures from witches and warlocks and presented her case to the Council."

"Was it that simple?"

Enid scoffed. "Of course not. She had to do it without them knowing about it."

"Why?"

"Because they're set in their ways when it comes right down to it, Carmen. We were persecuted for years and they didn't want anyone who had no magic to know about us. That's something that's very hard to keep from your spouse, though people could take a few notes from your mother on how it's done."

"I want to make it so that anyone can know as long as that person goes through a proper vetting process."

Her jaw dropped. "No. Absolutely not."

"Why not? I'm tired of lying to people, Enid."

"You're going to need a better reason than that if you're going to try and change the law."

I frowned. "Finn recognizes magic. It's not fair to him and others like him who wouldn't do anything against our kind if they knew. The Eraser assigned to him is a nice guy, but I hate seeing Finn so fuzzy and unsure of reality. He's not stupid. He knows something is off."

"You'll need an avatar to work for you on your behalf." Enid's blanket slipped as she gestured for another wine bottle to fly toward her from the kitchen. She didn't bother to readjust the blanket as she poured herself another glass. "Something inconspicuous." A pen and piece of paper appeared and she scribbled a few notes on it. She handed it to me and said, "Use this for your lingo. It's similar to what my great-grandmother used and it will stick when you pass out the petition and send it on to the Council."

"Thank you."

She waved her hand, shooing me away. "You're welcome. Now go away. I'm on a date."

I reappeared just as the doorbell rang. The pizza was warm and smelled incredible, its scent wafting downstairs and alerting Finn to its presence. Joining me in the kitchen, he stuffed a slice into his mouth before I could take out two plates for us to use.

"You even got enough so that I could have cold pizza for lunch tomorrow."

"That's gross, Finn."

He raised his eyebrows in mock horror. "You don't like cold pizza? What kind of American are you?"

"I think it's a guy thing."

He grinned. "It might be."

"I see you're feeling a little better," I said, feeling relieved.

"I am," he replied, wiping marinara sauce off his chin. "Today might be a little foggy, but I did some thinking and I decided that this is going to refresh my focus. I'm going to start looking for another job. I'm not going to quit construction yet, but I just want to see what else is out there and see if anything sounds interesting."

"That was an awful lot of thinking in the last forty-five minutes."

"That's another difference between men and women. You women take forever to make up your mind. Us men? We don't need to weigh the pros and cons. We make a goal and execute."

"He said that men 'make a goal and execute,'" I said, repeating Finn.

Abby laughed. "Women make goals, too, but I guess we do take longer to actually decide on a goal and how we're going to reach it."

"That's what I thought!" I leaned forward, grunting as I touched my toes. Abby and I had just finished kickboxing and were stretching.

She had lost several pounds and I beamed inside as she leaned forward and hugged her legs.

"Show off."

"I'm not the one who's been slacking on her stretches she's supposed to be doing at home."

"I guess I get a failing grade for not doing my homework."

Abby put the bottoms of her feet together and leaned forward, her forehead touching the gray mat. "Homework is very helpful and you're only hurting yourself when you don't do it."

"Thanks, Ms. Windsor, for making me feel badly about myself." I brought my own feet together, but my head came nowhere near the mat.

"I'm just being a good leader," Abby said cheerfully. "Leading by example is one of the best ways to show others how to do things the right way."

"Are you trying to tell me you're my role model now?"

"I am if you're trying to be as flexible as I am."

"You're going to yoga again!" I said with mock accusation. "I thought we quit that months ago."

"I am not!"

"Abby, you're a tree!" I rose to my feet.

She got up and struck a pose, her arms bent outward, away from her body. "It's all about the lightning bolt now."

"You've got to be kidding."

She laughed heartily. "I am, but that place is ridiculous enough that they'd probably try to get that trending."

"You really are stretching at home, then."

"I do it first thing in the morning. It's so relaxing, Carmen. I listen to soft music and it helps me clear my mind before I go to school."

"How is summer school going?" We had grabbed our gym bags and were sitting outside on the grass underneath a small tree. There was a slight breeze that felt wonderful against my damp skin.

"It's going. The whole environment is different from the normal school year. Some kids are more relaxed because there aren't as many students around while others are more anxious because they'd rather be outside playing."

"Don't you mean inside playing video games?"

Abby scowled. "I still have hope for this generation. The art teacher had them draw a bicycle and the students had to ask her to put up a reference. She asked them to draw their own bicycles and over half of the class said they didn't have one because they'd never ride it anyway. I had a great bike when I was their age. I loved riding around the neighborhood all day."

"The street lights coming on were the curfew," I added. "The good old days."

"How old do we sound right now?" She laughed. She took a swig from her water bottle and, after glancing around her, squirted a little down her shirt. "I love the South, but these summers can be brutal."

"I wouldn't have it any other way." I closed my eyes and enjoyed the breeze that had picked up speed. "Speaking of brutal, how is your nemesis?"

"She's not teaching this summer."

"Oh." I opened my eyes and looked at my friend. She was dreamily looking away, her vision unfocused.

"It's been nice going to work and not dealing with her." Her expression darkened. "I get sick to my stomach when I think about August because she'll be there when regular session begins."

"You can't switch schools, can you?"

Abby shook her head sadly. "I am a special education teacher. I go wherever they need me."

"Is there something else you'd rather do?" I asked slowly.

She bit her bottom lip. "Have you ever heard of a gym specifically for children with special needs?"

"No."

"There are a few throughout the country and, from what I can tell, they're great. They're like a giant playground designed with special needs children in mind."

"What do you mean?"

She began to speak excitedly, her hands becoming more animated as she described the gym to me. "They have trampolines that are fun, but they're meant to build leg and core strength. They offer sensory-based toys to help with fine motor skills and auditory processing. Some of the equipment is suspended, like swings, which help with balance. Some have a craft station to help improve hand-eye coordination. There's so much more to them, but you get the idea."

Lenny's words flashed in my mind. Already knowing the answer, I asked, "Do you want to move so that you can work at a gym like that? Would that be more fulfilling?"

Abby was quiet for a long time before she finally answered. "No. I think I want to... I think I want to build a place like that." She firmly nodded her head. "Yes. I want to build a gym for special needs children. I could be in control of the equipment and activities. I could hire a few more teachers so that the kids could have more attention within a smaller group." Her eyes were shining. "That's what I want to do."

"Then do it, Abby."

She blinked several times as if returning to reality. "What? Oh, no." She shook her head. "I couldn't just leave my job like that and where would I get the money for that kind of thing? I just bought a house. I can't afford another loan."

"How much money would you need?"

"I *have* done some research," she said sheepishly. "If I could find a space that was suitable, it would cost a minimum of two hundred thousand dollars for the equipment. Not to mention the salaries for the other teachers I'd like to hire. I would hope that, after the first year, we would have enough participants so that their fees would pay for everyone's salary and I could earn enough to pay back the loan."

"You've done more than just a little bit of research."

"I was curious," she said simply.

The breeze had stopped and the sun was beginning to set. "I think you should go for it, Abby," I encouraged.

"What, do you have that kind of money just lying around? A friendly finance plan for me?"

"No."

"Then it's going to school for me. Maybe Lauren will transfer one day." She smiled. "A girl can dream."

"Always," I answered. We said goodbye and parted ways. As I slid into my Volvo, Lenny's voice was filling the silence.

"You can't just create a gym for her. That's not what an Influencer does. She has to build this on her own."

I turned my key in the ignition and blasted the air conditioning.

"How thoughtful of you. Listen, you can't do that. I know you want to."

"Why not?"

The passenger seat squeaked as Lenny adjusted himself. It looked like he was brushing something off his stomach. "It's against the rules. She has to do this on her own. This is her destiny she has to make for herself."

"If it's her destiny that she makes for herself, then why am I here?"

Lenny rolled his black button eyes. "I don't understand the wording. I'm just the messenger. Yes, this is the path that Fate wanted you to encourage her to take. But she has to do it her own way. How was that? Now do you understand me or do you want me to get out some crayons and draw it for you on double-lined paper?"

"I'll take away your features. Remember, I'm the one who gave you those buttons," I warned sharply. "There's no need to be such a rude snowman after I've accommodated you. By the way, you better not leave another puddle. Especially not in my car."

Lenny was already fading away. "Too late." He cackled.

"Son of a bitch."

At home, I listened to Roach and Finn as I roamed aimlessly around the house, thinking about how to get a petition signed without the Council knowing. I had already typed the document that I wanted others to read, but I needed a way for it to be transported without being obvious.

An idea popped into my head and I sat down in my office, closing the door behind me and locking it. I picked up a plain, number two pencil and rolled it between my fingers. Yes, this would do. I created a slit inside that withheld the document like a scroll that could be discreetly pulled out and read as well as, hopefully, signed. I tapped the pink eraser and the pencil sprouted tiny arms and legs. Its face pushed itself out of the wood, unveiling squinty eyes and a mustache that was so bushy and long, it looped around the pencil's ears.

"This isn't exactly as inconspicuous as I would have liked," I murmured.

"Is it the mustache? I've been thinking of trimming it back a little," it said, a hint of a French accent in its voice. The pencil looked down at itself. "Am I not to receive proper clothing?"

"What would you like?"

"A tuxedo would be magnificent, if you don't mind."

A tiny tuxedo appeared and the pencil frowned. "You're staring at my naked body. I would ask that you turn away until I dress myself."

"My apologies," I said, looking away.

"You may gaze upon me again," the pencil said after a few moments. "You may also call me Egbert." He nodded. "Yes, that will be splendid."

"You're going to blend in a little better than this when I send you out into the world, aren't you?"

Egbert bowed deeply. "Of course, Madame."

"Start with my friends. Then work your way out from there. Any witch or wizard that you think would sign the petition."

His mustache quivered. "Do you believe this to be a good idea? Truly? We can't allow just any Tom, Dick, or Harry to know about magic!" Egbert laughed at his own joke.

"I agree with you, but this would enable others to know who are trustworthy. It would be easier to not have to keep lying to those that we love. There would be a vetting process," I insisted.

"Ah, I understand, Madame. I shall be back within a fortnight!"

"A fortnight?"

The pencil looked annoyed. "I would suggest that you utilize my time away in the most efficient way, starting with reading a dictionary. It is but a polite suggestion for I would never want to embarrass you."

"Of course you wouldn't," I said sarcastically.

"Goodbye!" In a puff of sparkling black smoke, he was gone.

Hearing voices, I followed the sound to the living room where I found Roach and Finn. My stepbrother's eyes held a hint of sadness as Roach spoke to him.

"Hello, Roach," I said warmly. "How was today's lesson?"

"It was totally a good one," Roach replied, a little too enthusiastically.

Finn cleared his throat. "Today was Roach's last day."

"Oh." My eyes widened. "It has been six months, hasn't it? Listen, Roach, why don't you stay on?"

"It's not like that," Finn said, embarrassed.

"Finn, I told you that I want to see you happy and this makes you happy. I don't mind paying for the lessons."

"It's not about the money. I've joined a band and we're going to start touring!" Roach looped his thumb around his middle and ring fingers, leaving out his index finger and pinky as he pumped his fist into the air. "It's going to rock this world!"

"Wow," I said blandly. "Where are you going to start the tour?"

"We're going to play live at Sea Food Festival in Missouri and work our way into the country from there."

"Congratulations, Roach," I said. I glanced at Finn whose eyes were downcast. "I wish you the best of luck."

"Luck doesn't have anything to do with it. It's about my skills!" He stuck out his tongue and shook his head vigorously. "Rock out!"

Roach let himself out, Finn watching him through a window. "I guess that's the end of that."

"Why?"

"There are no more instructors in town."

"New Bern is small. What about Havelock or Morehead City?" I knew that he was disappointed, but I was determined to remain positive.

"There are a couple, but they're booked. Roach checked for me."

"That was nice of him, but Finn, let's be honest here. He'll be back soon enough."

"I doubt it."

"You don't have to stop playing, Finn. You sound just as good, if not better, than he does." I nodded as if in agreement with myself. It was the truth. He *was* better than Roach.

Finn's cheeks flushed. "I don't."

"Yes, you do," I insisted. "There were times that I heard you playing and I couldn't tell the difference between student and teacher. These last couple of months, you really have sounded better than Roach. You should keep playing. I'm sure there are other people you can play with."

He snickered. "I think the term you're looking for is 'jam.' Musicians jam together." A smile tugged at the corners of his mouth.

"Why can't you do that?"

"I don't really know anyone else that plays and, before you say anything, I do not want to hang out with you while you struggle to learn the keyboard." He plopped down on the sofa and put his feet on top of the coffee table. Seeing the look on my face, he quickly kicked off his boots. They landed in a pile next to the table where I suspected he'd forget about them and turn the house upside down looking for them the next morning. "I don't think that just playing will be enough."

"Why not?" I sat down in the chair that Siobhan had created for me and drew my knees to my chest.

"I enjoyed learning," Finn answered. "After what happened this past weekend, I realized that I want more meaning in my life. I thought playing the guitar was enough. Maybe I should go back to school."

"You hated school."

"Your mother had a bad way of waking us up in the morning. It was like she refused to believe we had alarm clocks."

"You slept through your alarm. Even with Mom's singing, you still had to be shaken awake."

"Oh, yeah," he said, remembering. "It was easier when Randy was still at home because he threatened to piss on me."

"That's disgusting. I don't think he would actually do that."

"You never had to share a room with Randy. He pissed in my shoes one day because he was awake and I wouldn't turn off the alarm."

I wrinkled my nose. "I didn't know that."

"Yeah. Didn't you notice the last three months of my junior year that I was up before you were?"

"I just thought you were masturbating really early in the morning. I'd go in the bathroom after you and wiped down everything before I started to get ready."

"You were just a freshman then. What did you know about masturbating?"

"Sexual education is taught in the eighth grade."

Finn flashed a smile. "I should've remembered that. Stacy Hacker got pregnant that year. That slut had three kids by the time we graduated. I guess you could say she's lucky because she's my age and her kids are almost grown already."

"She lost her youth to teen pregnancy," I replied, frowning.

"I try to see the silver lining of things."

"What would you study at school?" I asked, steering us back to the original subject.

He shrugged. "I don't know. Mechanics?"

"You work on cars on the side. Would a degree help?"

"Not really," he admitted. "That's something where they prefer experience over education."

"What about another trade?"

"I'm a great welder already, so I don't need that. I'm a great plumber, but I could earn more money if I got certified in things like medical gas."

"Is getting your certification the same as going back to school?"

"Not exactly."

I narrowed my eyes. "Finn," I began, my tone low and serious. "Would you really go to class? Or would you say you were too tired from work and blow it off?"

"I would go." He was unconvincing.

"What if you were the teacher?"

"What do you mean? Are you saying I should try and teach shop at one of the high schools?"

"You still need a teaching certification to do that."

"Oh." He slumped further down into the couch. "I'll think about it."

"Finn, you can teach the guitar. I'm sure there are others like you who want to learn. Why don't you just take Roach's place?"

My stepbrother's eyes brightened. "Do you think I could do that?"

I reached out and patted his knee. "I do, yes. I think you're great and you'd be a wonderful instructor."

"Should I go to their houses or should the students come to me?"

"What did Roach do?"

"A little of both." He scanned my living room. "Your place isn't creepy. It's nice and inviting. I suppose parents wouldn't mind dropping their kids off here."

"Gee, thanks, Finn. That's awfully nice of you to say," I said sarcastically.

Ignoring me, he continued. "I could make some fliers and hand them out. I'm sure Roach wouldn't mind giving me his contacts so that I'd have a head start on this. This is great!" He leaped off the sofa. "I'm going to use your computer to start making the fliers."

Our cell phones began to ring simultaneously.

"Hello?" we answered.

Hanging up, Finn looked like a deflated balloon.

"Looks like the fliers will have to wait until tomorrow."

"I know," he said, disappointed. "It figures Cecily would choose now of all times to have that baby."

Chapter Fourteen

"How did you get stuck with the baby again?" Abby asked, opening the door to her home. "Whoa, that baby is only two weeks old?"

"Cecily *was* overdue," I said. "I offered to help. Randy's at work and Apple is a toddler, which means she's a handful."

"So you took the kid who doesn't really move yet? How nice of you." Abby flashed a grin. Looking at the baby, she cooed, "Well, we don't mind that you're here, do we?" She gently squished the baby's arms. "It looks like she's got rubber bands on her arms."

"Isn't she adorable?" I said, resisting the urge to pinch the baby's cheeks.

"She is." Directing her attention back to the baby, she asked, "What's your name, sweetie? What do I call you?"

"Kiwi."

"No, I meant her real name."

I sighed. "It *is* Kiwi."

Abby's eyes squinted. "She didn't earn a nickname in two weeks?"

"Cecily has a child whose name is Apple. What more did you expect?"

"I would have thought that your stepbrother would have told his wife that she was being ridiculous and they were going to give their kids normal names. I'm a teacher. Do you have any idea how much crap she's going to receive from her classmates on the playground?"

"I think Cecily believes that the world is filled with rainbows and sunshine and that it only revolves around her and her family."

I followed Abby through the house and to her backyard. "Daddy got so excited when I asked him if he still had this." She was looking at a large jogging stroller. "He was very disappointed when I told him that I wanted to use it for a friend."

I laughed. "Your dad thought that you were pregnant?"

"I don't know which is more upsetting. The fact that he thought I was pregnant or the fact that he didn't care that I'm not married. I know times have changed, but Mom and Dad have always had strong, traditional values. I guess once your child hits her thirties, they just want grandchildren and they don't care how it happens."

Carefully, I placed Kiwi in the stroller. She yawned and closed her eyes. "I can't believe they kept this."

"They've kept just about everything. They wanted to hand everything down to me eventually, but until then, this stuff stays in their attic."

"It must be a nice attic. This stroller looks brand new."

"It's really the third floor of their house. They have a lot of antiques leftover from my grandparents' houses on both sides that they don't have room to display, but don't want to get rid of."

"Your parents have a third floor?"

"It used to be my playroom," Abby said sheepishly.

With Kiwi secured, we began to walk around Abby's block. It was uncomfortably hot and I discreetly swirled my finger to create a pocket of air conditioning. At ten degrees cooler in our pocket, it was simply gorgeous outside.

"It doesn't really feel like it's eighty degrees, does it?" Abby asked. "Maybe my thermometer is broken." She frowned. "Great, one more thing to fix in the old house."

"What else is broken?"

"I had the floors refinished. After I paid for that, the water heater decided it wanted to stop working and I had to buy a new water heater. It was cheaper to buy a new one than have the old one repaired."

"It could always be worse."

"My air conditioning could go out on me next. That happened at the school once and a rat died behind the cement block wall." She frowned. "That was a nasty week. I felt so badly for the science teacher. His room was next to mine. They couldn't get the rat and, for a few weeks, it stank. He had air refreshers everywhere."

"Was it worse than junior year when schools made students dissect cats? My teacher had us bring in scented candles. I think it made it worse. Formaldehyde, dead cat, and scented candles was not the combination I'm sure Mrs. Bridgestone was hoping for."

Abby paused mid-step. "You all dissected cats? We just dissected perch and a worm for biology. Budget issues, I guess."

"We did for anatomy. It was a great class. I don't know if I could do something like that today, though. I'd probably cry too much."

"Funny how we change opinions as we grow older."

"Hey," I chided. "We're not old yet."

"I feel so much older every time school starts again," Abby said, sighing. "I once heard a student in the hallway say that the show *Are You Afraid of the Dark?* was ancient. I used to love watching that show on Saturday nights."

"I loved that show! Do you remember renting the orange VHS tapes and feeling awesome for watching those Saturday night shows on a Tuesday?"

Abby burst into laughter. "I felt so smug. I would be watching those shows and thinking about how everyone else had to wait until Saturday, even though Saturdays showed new episodes."

I checked Kiwi to make sure that she wasn't getting too much sun. She was sleeping, her chest rising and falling rhythmically. We rounded a corner, walking back to Abby's house. "Have you thought anymore about the gym?"

"No," Abby replied lightly. "There's no way I can get a loan. I wouldn't be able to put in the time, anyway. I'd have to keep my job at the school and have lesson plans to do, which take a lot more time than they should."

"Abby, I think you should go for it."

"You're a lot more optimistic than I am."

"You don't even want to go back to school."

"That's not true," Abby protested. "I wouldn't mind it if Lauren Lennox wasn't there. She's not going anywhere anytime soon, though. It is what it is."

We reached her backyard and she fished her key out of her pocket. I felt badly for my friend; she was only holding herself back.

"Do you want to take the stroller with you in case you babysit Kiwi again?" she asked.

"I'm afraid that, if I do, Cecily will see it and want it for herself."

"Would she really do that?"

"Definitely."

"Your sister-in-law sounds like a real gem," Abby said, opening the door. "You can borrow it anytime. I'll keep it in my spare room for you."

"Thank you," I said. I removed Kiwi from the stroller. Her face mushed together as if she was about to cry. "I know, it's awful. I woke you up. It's okay, you'll be in your car seat soon enough."

"You don't baby talk to infants?" Abby asked, watching us.

Kiwi grunted in response and a pungent smell filled the living room.

"Maybe you should start." Abby laughed and handed me the diaper bag.

I laid Kiwi down on Abby's oversized chair. "I think you really need to think about the gym. I think you're selling yourself short," I said as I changed Kiwi's diaper.

"I'll throw that into the trash outside." Abby reluctantly held out her hand to take the soiled diaper as I redressed the baby.

"Stinky baby," I said, nuzzling Kiwi's nose. She turned her head away from me and yawned, unimpressed.

"Do you honestly think that I have a chance of doing this?" Abby asked when she returned.

"I do. I'll help you as much as I can," I promised.

She reached into her kitchen drawer and pulled out a small piece of paper. "I'll think about it some more." She held up the paper, revealing it to be the fortune she had kept when we were painting her home. "Remember this?"

"Yes, I remember you got lucky and actually had a fortune in your cookie."

She turned over the paper. "This is farfetched, but I'm going to play the lottery with these numbers."

I opened my mouth to tell her no, but stopped myself.

Instead, I said, "Good luck."

Abby winked at Kiwi. "This is what we call being foolish. You'll learn it soon enough, kid."

Summer was fading as September began. Abby was purely focused on her students and activities outside of the school, trying her best to ignore Lauren Lennox. Unfortunately, it was more difficult each day to avoid the other teacher. Lauren had formed a clique of her peers that, while they didn't treat Abby badly, they didn't actually treat her like anything else. She felt like she had become invisible.

"Why is she so fixated on you?" I asked. We were seated outside on my patio, the soft sounds of Finn and one of his new students drifting through the door.

"I have no idea." Abby sipped her lemonade thoughtfully. "Some people don't always get along and I understand that, but I don't know what I did to set her off in the first place."

"Maybe she's jealous."

Abby snickered. "Jealous? I'm single with no prospects and she has a boyfriend."

"You're also a successful teacher who doesn't rely on anyone to take care of her. You bought a house that's all yours and it's beautiful. So what if you're single? The right guy will come along."

"I wonder how it would have worked out if Eric hadn't just been looking for some sort of booty call."

"Thankfully, you'll never know."

"He's dating a fifth-grade teacher now. Actually dating, not just flirting."

"Why do you care?"

Abby's brows raised and her voice came out squeaky. "I don't."

"It's okay. People don't tend to like seeing others they dislike be happy."

She laughed and ran her hand over the side French braid she had woven to keep her bangs off her face. "Maybe that's Lauren's problem. I'm doing well at the school, the kids like me, I have my own home, and it's clear that I don't need a man."

The back door opened and Finn stepped outside to join us. "Are you bashing men?" He raised his voice a few octaves and put his hand on his hip. "I'm a strong woman. I don't need a man to make me happy because I make myself happy!"

"That's exactly how all of us are," I said, chuckling.

"Where are the rest of the women? Don't you all have meetings for this kind of topic?" Finn asked, looking around excitedly as if more women were suddenly going to appear.

"Abby and I are the co-chairmen of the man-hating group. We meet once a month to discuss the next meeting's bullet points."

"It's a short meeting," Abby chimed in. "The topic is usually 'Why We Don't Need a Man' and then we just go out drinking."

"Is that a hard lemonade?"

Abby picked up her glass and took a long drink. "It might be," she said slyly.

"Is it really hard lemonade? I could go for some," Finn asked.

"No, it's not," I answered.

"You're such a let-down," Finn said to Abby, shaking his head. He ran inside and poured himself a glass. He smacked his lips in satisfaction when he returned. "This is pretty good, Carmen."

"Thanks. I'll be sure to add some vodka to it next time."

"That sounded like a new student you have, Finn. Was he?" Abby asked.

Finn propped his feet up on the patio table. "He is, but he has potential."

"You have a lot of students so far. You must be a great teacher."

He reddened so slightly that I barely noticed it. "I'm just filling a void that Roach left."

"Initially, yes, but it's been a few months now. People don't stay just because there's someone to do the job. They stay because that someone is *good* at that job."

"You should hear some of the people he's been working with since July. They're catching on as quickly as he did." I smiled proudly at my stepbrother.

"Don't you work with Joel Sula?"

"Yeah, he's one of mine."

"He signed up to join the jazz band at school."

"Your school has a jazz band?" I asked.

"It's one of the after-school programs. He said he's only been playing for a couple of months, but I found that hard to believe. Knowing that he's your student, I can see that now."

Finn tugged at the brim of his hat. "He's just talented."

"I didn't even know there was a guitar in jazz music," I admitted.

Abby nodded as Finn groaned. "You need to brush up on your music," Finn said. "That statement was almost embarrassing."

I stuck my tongue out at him. "You didn't know that hippopotamus milk is pink."

Finn held out his arms. "Who would know that?" he asked, exasperated.

"That *is* kind of an odd thing to know," Abby agreed.

"I know, right?" Finn said.

"I might have a thing for hippopotami. They're interesting creatures."

"They eat people." Finn looked at Abby curiously. "They do!" she insisted.

"Only if you're dumb enough to get into a river with them and it doesn't happen that often."

"Is this what women talk about? Random things? Carmen, you might need to spike my drink *now* if we're going to keep talking about this stuff."

I laughed. "Actually, we were talking about a woman that Abby works with at the school."

"Is she hot?" Finn grinned. "Sorry, reflexive question."

"She's not a very nice person."

"She's a bitch to Abby," I added.

"Why don't you just put her in her place?"

"How would I do that?" Abby put her elbows on the wicker table and leaned forward.

"Kick her ass," Finn answered simply.

Abby laughed so hard that she snorted. "A grown woman assaulting another woman? That's not how problems should be handled."

"I told her she needed to complain to the principal."

It was Finn's turn to laugh. "Have someone else fight her battles for her? No way. Listen, Abby, if I were you, I'd have a talk with this broad."

"Broad?" I asked, eyebrow raised.

"Yeah, she's a broad," Finn said quickly. "I'd have a talk with her and tell her she's being an asshole and that she needs to stop. Otherwise, you'll file a complaint against her."

I looked away quickly, thinking of Marcy. She had sent a very nasty letter after I had turned in my complaint against her. I had politely told her to shove the letter down her throat, assuring her that the paper didn't have that many calories.

"She could start her own business like she's been wanting to."

"There you go. Why don't you do that?"

"It's a long story," Abby grumbled. She wrapped her hands around her glass and frowned.

"What is it?" Finn pressed.

"It's a money issue." She laughed nervously. "Oh. I guess it isn't that long of a story after all."

"Play the lottery."

"I was going to do that, but decided it was kind of absurd. I don't want to bet my hopes and dreams on a lottery ticket."

"What's it going to hurt?"

"I would be poorer than I was before I even started because I wasted money on a lottery ticket."

"I'd go for it," Finn encouraged. "I was a little lost at one point. I wanted to do something else with my life, but wasn't sure what it was. I like construction, I like building things, but that wasn't enough. I mean, I still work in construction, but since I started up with the guitar, I feel so much more…" Finn stopped, struggling to find the right word.

"Fulfilled?" Abby finished.

"That's right. Fulfilled."

"It doesn't cost you anything, though. You're actually making money on the side," Abby pointed out.

"It cost money up front. I had to buy a guitar and amp, then the lessons."

"Hey!" I said.

"Okay, Evelyn and Carmen paid for those things as a Christmas gift, but the fact is that an investment still had to be made."

"Just a little credit. That's all I ask," I said, shaking my head.

Finn put his hand up to the side of his mouth, blocking it from my view. "She's so needy," he said in a stage whisper.

"I am not."

"And she's nosy. Look at her. She's eavesdropping on our conversation."

Abby and I laughed. She pulled a piece of paper out of her pocket that I recognized as the fortune she had kept. "I've been wanting to play these numbers," she conceded.

"Then play them. You should at least try. If you don't win, then you're going to need to tell that broad to piss off. If you do win, then tell that broad to piss off and start something that you'll love."

"You make it sound so easy," Abby said.

"That's because it is," Finn replied simply.

"You're willing to make a deal with me?" Marcy asked, incredulous.

"That's right, and you're going to take it."

"Why in the hell would I do that? I don't like you," Marcy deadpanned.

"I don't like you either, but I have a good reason. You left me in the past and forgot about me. You don't like me because I filed a complaint against you and that ruined your perfect record."

Marcy shifted her weight, then scowled. "Could you have chosen a worse place to meet than this damn field?"

"This is a meadow."

"It's the same thing and there are mud puddles everywhere. Do you know how hard it is to find this style of shoes?"

"You don't buy those. You create them."

"Same difference. I take the time to accrue them."

"No one can see this place and I wanted to meet with you privately."

"Get on with it, then." Her cell phone beeped. "I think my husband is going to that diner with the patty melt."

"Diet still not working, huh?"

"No."

"If you let him cheat on it once a week, the diet might be easier to follow," I offered.

Marcy's lips pursed and her eyes narrowed. Her forehead relaxing, she said, "You know, that might actually work."

"I want you to go to the future and make sure the lottery numbers are these." I handed her a copy of the fortune Abby had kept.

"Did you think that offering me marital advice was enough for me to do this for you?" she asked, incredulous.

"No, that one was for free. I'll remove the complaint I made against you." I knew she'd be interested in reinstating her spotless record and reputation.

She tapped her chin with her finger, thinking. "Will you explain that it's because I'm the best time traveler and you actually enjoyed your jaunt in the past?"

"Too far, Marcy," I warned.

She flashed an insincere smile. "I'm just kidding. Fine, I'll do it. Wait, it's not for you, is it?" She looked at me, her gaze accusatory.

"Of course it's not for me," I replied, insulted.

"I had to check. Ethics and all that."

"I'm sure your ethics are on the straight and narrow." I was disingenuous but she beamed anyway.

"They really are!" She reached out to shake my hand. "We're good after this, aren't we?"

"I still don't like you."

"I don't like you either, but we can at least be professional about it." In a flash, she was gone.

I transported myself back to my office. Sparkling black smoke was still in the air. "Egbert?" I whispered.

"It is I," he announced, bowing deeply.

"Where have you been? It's been months!"

"When you call on my services, Madame, I ask for more than a signature. I can be very *persuasive*."

"What do you mean by that?"

The pencil leaned casually against the side of my computer monitor. "I'm good at reasoning with people."

"I thought that the petition spoke for itself."

He scoffed. "It needed flourishing."

"Flourishing?"

"Did you not read the dictionary like I suggested?"

"I know what that means, Egbert. Why did my petition need flourishing?"

He absently stroked his mustache before he spoke. "Not everyone quite understood why you wanted to pass a new ordinance. I, being very eloquent, was able to explain it to them."

"How many signatures?"

"Over one million."

I was so shocked that I nearly fell back in my chair.

Egbert grinned. "I know. I told you I was persuasive."

Chapter Fifteen

P etition in hand, I marched through the double doors leading to the vast chambers where the Council met each month. The ceilings were at least twenty feet high and painted a bright gold with a hint of cyan. A winding staircase rotated next to the bench where councilmen and councilwomen sat ten feet higher than everyone else. As a bailiff walked by, the staircase spun so quickly that it became a blur and those closest to it could feel the wind it generated. The rest of the room was a soft beige with matching brown-and-cyan-striped chairs.

As a councilman entered, the staircase stopped spinning, allowing him to climb to the bench. He took a seat at the end and tugged at the shoulders of his zebra-printed gown. It had been argued that traditional robes of the Council were merely black and white, but they still reminded everyone of a zebra and they had added a budget line for next year to redesign and produce new robes.

The chamber was crowded today. I took a seat next to a leprechaun and he nodded toward me, though I couldn't help but notice he tightened his grip on his pot of gold. I glanced down at my navy blue suit and black heels. I ran my fingers over my silver necklace that held a small charm in the shape of a guitar that Finn had bought for me as a thank you gift. Shrugging, I crossed one leg over the other and waited for my turn.

"Gilligan Nguyen."

The leprechaun jumped out of his seat and practically ran to the podium with his gold. He placed a gold piece on the ground and a stepstool appeared, allowing him to step onto it to reach the microphone.

"You're Gilligan Nguyen?" asked one of the council members, a hint of surprise in his voice.

Gilligan sneered. "Am I supposed to be named Seamus O'Brien and have red hair?" He shook his head. "Honestly, what year is it?"

The councilman cleared his throat. "I was just, uh, clarifying for the record."

"I bet you were," the leprechaun said in a stage whisper. A few chuckles rose from the crowd. "I bet you want me to do a little jig for you right now and know where I keep my rainbow! It's the only way anyone who isn't a leprechaun can touch my gold! I'll never tell you!"

"Mr. Nguyen!" the councilman bellowed. "You're trying my patience. What is it that you wanted to be accomplished today?"

"I want permission to move my rainbow."

"To where?"

"I can't tell you where! It's a secret!"

"Then why do you want to move it?" The councilman was exasperated.

"Because I think someone knows where it is now. Duh!"

"Do you want to spend the night in our jail? It's no picnic like the mortal jail, I can assure you."

The leprechaun shook his tiny fists at the councilman. "You're not making this easy for me, *sir*." He practically spat out the word. "I tried to talk to you in private because this is a private discussion. But no, you refused."

"You should have submitted a request with my secretary."

"I did that."

The councilman put his head in his hands as he struggled to maintain his temper. "Meet me in my office in four hours and we can discuss this."

"Will you sign a nondisclosure agreement so that no one knows where my rainbow is?" The leprechaun was suspicious.

"Yes, I will. Just, please, are we done with you now?"

"We'll determine that in four hours!" He jumped off his stepstool and smooshed it down with his hand so that it resembled a gold coin again.

"Who do we have next?"

"The Council calls Carmen Devereaux."

The leprechaun purposefully bumped into my knee on his way out of the chambers. He laughed gleefully as he scurried out the door and I limped slightly as I walked to the podium. Some leprechauns could be jerks. I reached into my suit pocket and pulled at the petition. I blew on it and several copies floated across the room and landed in front of each council member.

"My name is Councilwoman Dolores. I see that you want to extend the knowledge of our existence to individuals beyond spouses."

"That's right, Councilwoman Dolores."

"Why?"

My eyes flickered to my pocket where my notes were kept. I had practiced my speech several times in front of my mirror, slightly relieved that this mirror didn't respond and yet a little disappointed because the feedback would have been appreciated. "There are mortals in this world who recognize magic. When that happens, an Eraser shifts the person's memory to recall a more plausible, mortal explanation for events that were witnessed. What most of our kind do not understand is the complete confusion the mortals are left in because of this process. I have seen first-hand a mortal becoming hazy, unsure of himself, and angry that he feels like he cannot trust his own mind. I have also seen a mortal lashing out toward myself because he felt like reality was off and, while he would never harm me, he was clearly upset with not knowing—no, not *understanding*—the truth. This isn't fair for our kind to do this to mortals. It was this exact kind of treatment that drew enough suspicion that led to the Salem Witch Trials.

"I'm not asking that we enable all mortals to know about witches and wizards. I'm asking us to allow others, even beyond family members, to know about us after a careful vetting process. This is done for anyone working at a mortal job and it has been successful. I believe this same process will be successful for us. There will be no more lying to those that we love and trying to cover up our magic. We won't have to hide ourselves anymore to people that we trust."

"How do you propose we stop these mortals from telling other mortals who haven't been vetted about us?" the councilwoman asked.

"Add a charm to the tattoo," I answered easily. "It would disable them from even bringing up the topic to mortals who don't already know."

The council members whispered eagerly to each other. I took a deep breath to calm my nerves and glimpsed at the crowd behind me. I spotted Simon sitting where I had been and he gave me two thumbs up in encouragement.

"You're doing great!" he mouthed.

"I see that you have several signatures here," the councilman who had spoken earlier said.

"Yes, sir. There are one million, two hundred ninety-three thousand, and four signatures."

"I have to ask you how you were able to obtain so many followers of this petition without our knowledge."

"I don't believe that you can ask me that," I said. My heart pounded inside my chest.

He chuckled. "No, I suppose I can't. I'll just assume that you're a very clever woman."

"Roland, quit badgering her," Councilwoman Dolores chided. "Let us discuss this in more depth. Do you mind waiting, Ms. Devereaux?"

"No, Councilwoman. Please, take all of the time that you need."

She nodded and waved her hand. A soundproof wall appeared as the Council debated.

The chambers were filled with whispers as the crowd spoke amongst itself. There was a mixture of agreements and disagreements with my proposal, and I found myself disappointed. I had hoped the people wouldn't be so divided.

At last, the soundproof wall vanished and a hush fell over the room. Grim faces looked back at me and I tried to swallow my mounting anxiety.

"The Council has decided that we will allow your proposal to be an amendment after a trial period of one year and one day. We will add the gag order charm to the tattoo along with a detector to alert us should the mortal attempt to speak with others who haven't been approved to know about us. If this trial period is successful, this will become a full amendment."

"Hell yeah!" someone cheered from the back of the chambers. An applause erupted.

"There will be order!" Councilman Roland roared. The room fell silent again. "Ms. Devereaux, is there anything else that the Council can help you with today?"

"No, sir. Thank you for your time."

Unable to hide the smile on my face, I turned to leave the chambers. Simon followed closely behind, congratulating me on my victory.

"I am so proud of you, Carmen. You really are an Influencer."

"I couldn't have done it without Egbert," I admitted.

"And yet you haven't thanked me properly," he said, appearing on the windowsill next to Simon and me. "Good to see you, Simon. Will that lovely wife of yours be cooking another French cuisine? The chocolate mousse she made last weekend was utterly delightful."

"Cindy made chocolate mousse and you didn't invite me?" I asked.

"You were busy."

"You didn't know that."

"Pardon our dear Carmen. She forgets her manners from time to time. Allow me." Egbert turned to face me directly. "Sometimes you don't get invited to dinners. It's sad. I would suggest that you do something that makes you happy, or, if I may, do something that would improve your position in life so that you get invited to such dinners in the future."

"Isn't he just the nicest pencil you've ever met?" I said, my teeth gritted.

Simon frowned. "Egbert, you were rude. I believe Carmen is owed an apology."

Egbert's mustache quivered. "But, sir, I was only suggesting a way to improve her station."

"Her station is just fine. You, on the other hand, could stand to be a little more humble."

His mustache quivered even more.

"Simon, you made him cry," I whispered.

"You're still a good pencil, Egbert. We are all grateful for everything that you do," Simon added hastily.

Egbert straightened and threw back his shoulders, proud.

"We would love to have you back for dinner. I believe Cindy is going to prepare Japanese food this weekend if you would like to join us."

Egbert bowed deeply. "It would be my honor." To me, he added, "I'm sorry for insinuating that you were lower than the filth on the bottom of my shoe and that you have no manners."

"Thanks," I replied, unsure of how to respond.

"I have been called upon for other lobbying tasks. I *am* quite good at this, aren't I?" He smiled. "Thank you for allowing me the opportunity to showcase my real talent, Carmen. Without me, you wouldn't be where you are today!" He smirked and added, "Simon, I will join you and Cindy on Friday. Goodbye!" He disappeared in a puff of sparkling black smoke.

"I can't believe he was actually sincere to me just now."

"I can't believe he's still using the black smoke that has glitter in it. I told him he needed something more business appropriate." Simon shook his head. "He's a pencil, though. He marches to the beat of his own sharpener."

"Did you know that another one of my students got a gig with a band?" Finn was beaming ear to ear.

I had just returned home after convincing Abby to play the lottery. Finn was right. It wouldn't hurt her to try. I even drove her to the gas station myself so that she could buy her ticket and had let Marcy know she needed to fulfill her end of the bargain. I had already dropped the complaint against her in good faith.

"Another school band?" I murmured, distracted by my thoughts about Abby and her great future fortune.

"No, a real band!" he said excitedly.

"School bands *are* real bands," I pointed out.

"I'm talking about *Justice Flowers All*."

My attention snapped to Finn completely. "Wait, are you serious?"

"Yes!" He was pulsing with energy, ready to burst. "Their guitarist decided to leave because they didn't like his girlfriend. Stupid of him, but great for Phoebe!"

"Holy shit, Finn, that's incredible!"

"She's doing a press conference with the band to announce the switch. It's coming on soon. You have to watch it with me!" He was already dragging me toward the door.

"We're not going to watch it here?"

"No, I want everyone to see her, so we're going to Dad and Evelyn's house."

"You want to rub it into Cecily that you're not a 'nobody.'"

"That's right."

"I don't think she's ever called you that."

He slammed the door to his truck. "Not in so many words, but I know she thinks that about me."

Finn excitedly drummed his fingers against his steering wheel as we drove to our parents' home.

When we arrived, Mom set out several trays of finger food. "What if they haven't had dinner yet?" she asked Lewis.

"I'm sure they've eaten. We don't need this much food," Lewis said gently.

"I might," Randy said, stuffing his face with small cucumber sandwiches. "Aren't these meant to go with tea?"

"Would you like some tea?" Mom asked.

"No, but a soda would be great. Cecily, why don't you get me one, honey?"

There was the briefest of pauses as everyone waited for Cecily's reply. "Sure, dear," she said cheerfully, disappearing into the kitchen and returning with beverages for her husband and herself. She handed a juice box to Apple. "So this is a big moment for you, isn't it, Finn?" she asked, settling on the couch with Kiwi on her lap. "Uncle

Finn is a big guitar teacher now!" she cooed toward her baby. Kiwi squealed happily.

"Let's all take a seat. The press conference is about to start!" Mom ushered everyone into a seat and turned on the television.

Dolls hanging from fishhooks with flowers for their eyes loomed in the background of several empty chairs. Slowly, band members began to appear on the screen, sitting down heavily as if the world's weight was on their shoulders.

Phoebe, with her bright pink hair and magenta streaks, bounced on the screen like a child on a trampoline. She was practically giddy as she sat next to the bass player.

"We've decided to air some awesome news today," one of the band members said, his voice monotone.

"That's Leo," Finn explained. "He's the lead vocalist."

Only Mom and Lewis were unaware of who he was. "He needs a haircut. It keeps getting into his eyes," my mother said.

"That's the style," Lewis replied.

Leo continued on the screen, his voice still without inflection. "Our former guitar player who shall not be named has decided to part ways with us." There were several boos from the audience. He held up his hands. "The band comes first. Always. *Always.*"

The other bandmates nodded solemnly while Phoebe beamed.

"We have found a great guitarist. She's everything this band embodies and more. Give it up for Phoebe Witherwasher!"

The crowd cheered enthusiastically as the camera focused on only Phoebe.

"Hi, everyone!" she said, still grinning. "I am beyond excited about being a part of this wonderful band and I want to thank Leo for reaching out and asking me to join! He saw me playing just for fun at a coffeehouse and look at me now! I hope that I can live up to your expectations and then some as the new guitarist!" She paused. "I'd also like to add that this would never have happened if it hadn't been for my guitar teacher, Finn Cleary. If you want an amazing teacher who gets you mega-band worthy in just a few months, go see him!"

The band finished their press conference with questions about their upcoming tour, though no one was listening anymore. All eyes were on Finn.

His own eyes were misty, his jaw working as he tried to form words.

Lewis got up and hugged his son. "I'm so proud of you, son!"

"Finn, did you bang her?" Randy asked, thinking no one could hear him.

"No," Finn answered. "She's a student."

"Honey," Cecily began after an hour of indulging on finger foods, "I'm ready to go home. Aren't you? Or would you rather stay for a little while longer while I take the kids home and put them down for the night?"

"Why don't you go ahead and take the girls outside and put them in their car seats? I'll be out in just a minute."

Cecily kissed him on his cheek and left with their daughters.

"Is no one going to say anything about this?" Finn asked, breaking the silence.

Randy looked at each of us sheepishly. "I put my foot down," he said softly.

Finn cupped his hand around his ear. "I'm sorry, I couldn't hear you. What was that?"

"I put my foot down," Randy said, louder this time. "We had a conversation about her behavior and treatment toward me. She's better now, isn't she?"

"Or she's patiently plotting your death," I suggested.

"No, it's not like that. We really *connected*. I think she respects me as an equal now in our relationship." He turned to Finn. "Congratulations, brother. Good job." He slapped Finn on his back and joined his wife.

"I can't believe Randy finally let his balls drop," Finn said, incredulous.

"It's about damn time," Mom said. "It's a great day for both of my boys!"

Within days, Finn had received so many calls for new student enrollments that he had to start turning down people. "There's no way that I can do this and my day job." His face was tense with guilt. "I hate telling people no."

"You could always make this your full-time job."

He shook his head. "I can't. What if this is just an influx because of Phoebe?"

"I'm sure that's a huge part of it, but you do have a natural talent for this, Finn."

"What if students start quitting because they either can't afford it, don't like it, or for whatever other reason and I'm left without enough money to pay my bills? I can't live with you for forever, Carmen."

I smiled inwardly, happy that Finn had already thought about this and had reached a conclusion without help. "Then keep doing what you're doing. If you continue to grow, down the road, this could be it for you. You could even rent a studio where you could meet students."

His eyes brightened. "I could call it *The Acoustical Ear.*" When I didn't respond, he added, "The name could use some work."

"Agreed," I said, heading downstairs to the family room.

"Where are you going? Aren't you meeting your friends or something? It's Friday night."

"I kind of wanted a quiet night," I admitted.

"Oh, because the house is going to be filled with students each evening now?"

"Something like that," I murmured. Tonight was the night the lottery numbers were going to be announced and I knew that, once Abby won, it would be a whirlwind for her.

"You hardly ever see your friends anymore," Finn pointed out. "I know it's a far drive for them, but it seems like they haven't been home to see their families in a long time."

"I'll see them soon." I glanced at my feet, guilty. I had seen my friends quite often; we had a daily lunch date lately. I was anxious to tell Finn the truth, but I had to wait until the forms were developed before I could fill them out for his proper vetting to begin. Supposedly that was going to happen before Halloween, but I wasn't holding my breath.

"Do you mind if I watch some TV with you?" he asked, already following me downstairs. "I won't even ask for control of the remote."

"I'm watching *The Golden Girls*," I warned.

Finn stopped halfway down the stairs. "I'll see if Randy wants to go grab a beer. With Cecily's new attitude, maybe she'll allow it." Without saying goodbye, he bounded up the stairs, the door slamming in his wake as he went through the back door.

"I don't know why men don't like that show," I said to myself. I plopped down on my couch and turned on the television. I had a copy of Abby's fortune in my hand to ensure that the numbers were correct and waited patiently for the evening news to finish before the numbers were announced.

A car accident, mystery meat in the cafeteria, and a heart-warming puppy story later, a young, buxom woman with bleached blonde hair and bright red lipstick appeared on the screen. Her dress matched her lipstick and sparkled when she moved. She stood next to five tubes that were empty. A man's voice boomed as it announced the date and, one by one, a ping pong ball with a black number printed on it popped into each tube.

It was a perfect match to Abby's fortune.

I unconsciously held my breath, waiting for Abby's phone call. My phone remained silent and, after another hour passed, I decided to visit Abby in person. I created a clear, glass vase filled with yellow roses and drove to her home where I found her outside putting up Halloween decorations.

She furiously drove a sign into the ground that read TREATS, NO TRICKS on it. A witch that looked like it had ran into her front door was already hanging up and I winced when I saw it. Riding brooms was old-fashioned and I had never known a witch or wizard to have green skin. When she saw me approaching, she waved, though her smile was wary.

"Is this a bad time?" I asked.

"No, I can put you to work helping me," she said. She handed me a lifelike dummy and some rope. "Will you hang this up from my tree? I think you can reach the lowest branch without me having to get out the ladder."

I set down the flowers and did as she asked me. "Abby," I began after I was finished with my task. Before I could continue, she handed me Styrofoam tombstones.

"These will make a cute graveyard, don't you think?" She laughed at herself. "I meant to say spooky! These will make a *spooky* graveyard!"

Side by side, we slid the stakes into the ground so that she had a small, ancient-looking graveyard. Once completed, she looked over at her yard. She had really outdone herself on her decorations. Along with what I had helped her with, she had also installed several fake spiders eerily crawling over her windows, a coffin that looked real that opened and closed when someone got too close, and a zombie that crawled out of the bushes on its belly when someone rang her doorbell.

"How did you set it up to do that?"

"That was the easy part. It's all based on an app that you download for free. It's part of having a Smart Home."

"Halloween decorations are Bluetooth capable now?"

"Yeah, isn't it cool?" She smiled broadly. "Thanks for helping me! I just love this holiday." She noticed the flowers sitting on her front porch. "Are those for me?"

I nodded. "Actually, I came over to deliver some good news since you seem to have missed it."

She picked up the vase and sniffed the roses. "They smell so good and they're yellow for friendship! How thoughtful! I needed these. I was supposed to attend a Halloween party tonight."

"Why didn't you?"

"I found out Lauren was going."

Following Abby inside to her living room, I said, "Abby, I told you that you shouldn't let that woman get in your way. You missed a perfectly good party just because of her."

"I was busy."

"Decorating could have waited until tomorrow."

She placed the vase on her dining room table and joined me in the living room. She sat down in her overstuffed armchair and sighed. "She told me today that some of the games I came up with for the kids were stupid."

"Abby, go to the principal and complain."

"I don't like conflict. It's easier this way, I promise," she said, trying to reassure me.

Her tone made it clear that she was finished discussing Lauren Lennox. I hid my frustration as I informed her, "You missed the lottery number announcement tonight, didn't you?"

"I was busy," she repeated.

"That's too bad."

"It's too bad that I saw that I wasted my money on a lottery ticket? I told you that would happen."

"Abby, you won."

Abby's face was a series of expressions: shock, surprise, anger, happiness, disbelief. "There is no way that I won that jackpot."

"You did," I said.

"Carmen, stop joking with me. What happened? Did I get one number right and so I win twenty dollars?"

"Abby, you won it all!" I pulled out my cell phone to show her.

She began to breathe quickly and, fearing that she was about to hyperventilate, I rushed into the kitchen to retrieve a paper bag. Finding none, I created one and gave it to her. She breathed into it, trying to calm herself. "I can't believe this! This is incredible!"

"Congratulations, Abby!"

Tears of joy streamed down her face and she wiped them away, looking at the flowers once again. "I win the lottery and all you have to give me is a lousy vase of flowers?"

"Hey, you're the millionaire. I could have told you to go buy your own flowers."

We laughed and she replied, "Drinks are on me tonight!"

"I thought you weren't much of a drinker."

"I just became a millionaire. I'm buying the good stuff!"

The next month really did become a whirlwind. By Thanksgiving, Abby had already met with a lawyer and financer to discuss how to handle her newfound wealth. She had told no one other than her parents about her winnings and had promptly paid off her own home. She would have paid off her parents' home as well, but that had already been done years ago. Instead, she paid for an extravagant vacation for them and they were currently in Spain, staying in one of the finest hotels Barcelona had to offer.

She had set up a meeting with an architect to discuss building her gym for children with special needs. For the first time in a long time, she was truly happy.

On the day of Thanksgiving, my family came to my home where I hosted a beautiful meal. Stuffed and sleepy, my family returned to their own homes, leaving Finn and me alone.

"I don't think I could move if I wanted to," Finn said, groaning. "That turkey was the best. No, the English trifle. No, wait, I think I liked the deviled eggs the most." He barely nodded. "Definitely the deviled eggs."

I looked at the swinging door between the kitchen and dining room that hid the mess I had made while cooking. "There's still some work to be done."

"Do you need help?" Finn offered.

"No, it'll be fine." I waved my hand and, within seconds, the kitchen was clean and the dishes and pots returned to their places.

An Eraser knocked on the door and I answered it cheerfully. "There's no need. I'm about to tell him."

The Eraser looked disappointed. "I haven't even gotten to eat anything yet. You know I've been assigned to be near your situation."

"There are leftovers in the refrigerator."

"Thank you," he said, walking past me and going into the kitchen.

As he rustled around in the kitchen and used magic to reheat his dinner, Finn stared at me in disbelief. "What in the fuck is going on?" he demanded. "I told you," he said, shaking a finger at me. "I told you that weird stuff happened in this house!" He was backing away from me as he spoke.

"Finn, listen, I'm really sorry that I couldn't let you know about me. You have no idea how many times I wanted to tell you."

"What is there to tell? You do weird stuff! I can't explain it! I just know that it happens!"

"Finn, I'm a witch," I said slowly. "There are witches and wizards in this world. Until recently, we couldn't tell anyone but a spouse about us."

"No, that's not true. Witchcraft isn't real."

"Sure it is," the Eraser said, entering the living room with a plate hovering in the air in front of him. The knife was slicing his turkey into smaller pieces. "If it wasn't for your stepsister, you still wouldn't know about us."

"What does that mean?" Finn was backed up against the wall now.

"She went to the Council. It's our version of high court. She secretly sent out Egbert to get a petition signed. Yeah, sorry, I know about Egbert. I saw him when I was having to keep an eye on you. Don't worry, I didn't tell the Council that that's who you used to help you out with them."

"Who is Egbert?" Finn demanded. "Why were you watching Carmen?"

"Egbert is a pencil who is also a lobbyist," the Eraser explained.

"Too much too fast," I warned.

"Then put the tattoo on him so that his brain doesn't implode. I know he recognizes magic, but this will prevent the overload."

"Finn, I need to see your forearm."

"Egbert is a *pencil?*" Finn was near hysteria now.

"Finn, please," I insisted, reaching for his arm. "This will make it easier. I promise. You will understand everything."

While Finn remained motionless, I grabbed his arm and he screamed. "Don't touch me!"

Quickly, I shoved up his shirt sleeve and ran my hand over his arm. The tattoo burned bright red for a moment before fading into nothing, hiding undetected just beneath his skin.

"You could have done that without burning him," the Eraser said thickly as he swallowed mashed potatoes.

"I was in a rush," I replied sharply. "Finn." I snapped my fingers in front of his face. "Finn, are you still with me?"

Finn sank to the ground, curling his knees up to his chest. "So witchcraft is real and I'm not crazy. Weird things *were* happening around here." He looked up at the Eraser. "Why were you watching Carmen? I've seen you before, haven't I?"

The Eraser nodded. "My name is Stanley."

"I didn't know that," I said.

"You never asked," Stanley replied. Noticing my guilt, he added, "We don't really give out our names, but I made an exception just now." He looked at Finn and continued. "I'm an Eraser. I Erase the memories of magic for mortals. See, before your stepsister's petition, only spouses were allowed to know. Now witches and wizards can tell people that they trust after filling out the proper forms and the people are vetted."

"You had a background check done on me?"

"It's part of the process," I answered simply.

"She went through a lot to change our rules because of you. You're her stepbrother and she cares about you. She hated that she had to lie to you about magic."

"Is this true?"

"It's true," I said. "I wanted to tell you so many times, but I wasn't allowed."

"Then why did you ask me to move in with you?"

"Because you needed the help. You're family. We help each other. Look at you now, Finn. You're doing what you enjoy. You're happy, right?" I looked hopefully at my stepbrother. Everything that I had done for him so far was to guide him the best way that I knew how to the path that he needed to take. I didn't want Simon's prediction to come true and have him end up sad and alone.

"You couldn't have done that without her help, Finn," Stanley said. "You'd still be struggling and lost without her."

"That's enough, Stanley," I said, my voice low. I was not going to tell Finn about my job as an Influencer.

"I was just trying to be helpful. I suppose you don't need me anymore, do you?"

"Probably not."

"Care if I make myself a doggy bag?" Without waiting for a response, he returned to the kitchen. There was a loud popping noise as he disappeared.

"He's been showing up and taking away my memories?"

"He alters them. It's his job. It is people like him that help keep our secret."

"So you're a witch," Finn said slowly.

"That tattoo won't allow you to tell anyone else."

"I won't tell anyone," he promised. "Is Evelyn one, too?"

"She is, but Lewis doesn't know."

"Why not?"

I leaned over and grasped Finn's hand to help him to his feet. "I don't know," I answered honestly. "I hope she'll tell him one day. Until then, she'll continue hiding her magic from him."

"Will I feel hazy anymore?"

"Without an Eraser to mess with your memories, you'll feel fine."

He paced around the dining room table, thinking. "You can just go anywhere you want, whenever you want?"

"Yes."

"So when I said you haven't seen your friends in a while, that wasn't true, was it?"

"No. I see them often."

"You can create whatever you want? You don't even have to cook, do you?"

"I don't, but I enjoy it sometimes. If I'm recreating something specific, it doesn't always come out as good as the way a trained chef would make it."

There was another bout of silence. "Is my guitar real?"

"Of course it's real."

"No, I mean, is it really a '59 Les Paul?"

"I went to the music store and took photos of one so that I could replicate it exactly," I conceded.

"So it's not actually real?"

"It would pass for one if someone inspected it."

"Oh." He ran his hand over his thinning hair. "I'm okay with this."

"Are you? You can ask whatever you want if it will help you understand this better."

"No, no. My guitar is still awesome. That's what really matters." He flashed a smile. "Thank you for telling me."

"You're welcome."

He pointed to his head. "Do you think you could help me out with this?"

"You want me to give you back your hair?" I asked, a little surprised.

Finn shook his head. "No, that wouldn't look natural. I was hoping you could create some more hats for me to cover it up. That's more my style, anyway. Goes with the guitar."

I disagreed that a North Carolina Panthers hat matched a classic electric guitar, but who was I to judge my stepbrother's wishes?

Chapter Sixteen

G nomes mingled with the guests, joyfully offering beverages and appetizers. Stanley plucked his favorite spinach and artichoke pinwheel from a gnome's tray and stuffed all of it into his mouth. Realizing the gnome had already moved on to another guest, he tracked him down to retrieve more food.

"He's an interesting character, isn't he?" Enid said, poorly attempting to be nonchalant.

"Go talk to him. You're driving me crazy just staring at him like some schoolgirl." Tess shooed away our friend and looked back at me. "What do you think of your New Year's Eve party?"

"You took Mrs. Crouch's gnomes again," I complained.

"They were so great at your housewarming party last year that I thought they would like to help again."

"Tess, you dressed them in shimmering gold and silver metallic outfits," I said flatly.

"I did and they look fabulous! Gold and silver are like neutrals."

"They look like they just came from Vegas's version of *The Wizard of Oz*." Siobhan had sidled next to me. "I see you invited Percy. It's a little awkward." She shifted her weight uncomfortably from one foot to the other.

"You broke up almost a year ago. Besides, you're the one who invited my boss."

"You like your boss," she pointed out.

"I do," I said, smiling. We watched as Simon and Cindy performed robot dance moves on the dance floor. "They're so cute when they try to outdance each other."

"I don't know if that's really dancing," Siobhan said.

"You just stand there and shake your ass when you dance," Tess interjected. "That isn't dancing either."

"At least I know how to move my hips instead of looking like some sort of stiff piece of cardboard."

I laughed and took another sip of my wine. My house was packed with friends and family, all happily chatting or dancing to celebrate the New Year. Finn was deep in conversation with Roach, who had returned to spend the holidays with his family. Roach's band was expanding, but not nearly as much as Finn's business. Another student had been drafted into a new band that was already gaining success and Finn was looking into studios to rent to accommodate his new clientele. They looked at him as some sort of guitar guru who, after working with him, could go onto greater things. He was magical to them and I was extremely proud of my stepbrother.

Abby joined us, her cheeks flushed with excitement. "The architect is finished! Now there will be a bid process and we can get this project off the ground!"

"Are you going to continue to teach?" Tess asked.

"I will until the end of the school year. Then I can really focus on *Play the Spectrum Kid's Gym*." She hesitated. "What do you think of the name?"

"It's wonderful," I said warmly.

"You know," Abby began coyly, "I finally solved my Lauren Lennox issue."

"How did you accomplish that?"

She smiled wickedly. "She approached me before Christmas break and told me that she had heard that I was going to open this gym for children with special needs. She told me how great of a teacher she was and that I would be lucky to have her working for me once I got it opened." Abby paused dramatically. "I told her to go to hell."

My eyes widened with surprise. "Abby!"

"It felt so good to say that! I don't think she'll give me any more problems for the rest of the school year."

I hugged my friend. "I am so happy for you. You've gotten everything you wanted."

"I couldn't have done this without you. Seriously."

"You had it in you already. You just needed someone to pull it out of you."

She smiled. "What about you? What do you want?"

"World peace," I said, my eyes twinkling.

"That's her beauty pageant answer," Siobhan said. "It's because she's not even sure what she wants. She might need a Muse." Mischief glinted in her eyes.

Through the window, I saw snow swirling and I excused myself. Outside, Lenny had already formed. "Thanks for inviting me to your party," he quipped.

"You puddled in my kitchen *and* in my car."

"You could have put a plastic bag around my base," the snowman suggested.

"I've already got my neighbor's gnomes in there and some of the guests assume they're little people. How would I explain a living, breathing snowman?"

"I'm going to have a party and only invite snowmen and snowwomen. No humans allowed." He crossed his stick arms and nodded sharply.

"What if I transform you into a gnome? Temporarily?"

"I like being a snowman. Don't try to change me," he replied stubbornly.

"I was just trying to help. What did you need, Lenny?"

"Fate wants you to know what a great job you did with Abby and Finn. You were right on schedule with them."

"It took a little over a year."

He shrugged. "These things take time. You can't expect to change someone overnight. Guidance takes a while."

I pushed my shoulders back, standing straighter with pride. "Please thank Fate for me for their praise." I couldn't hide the grin on my face.

"The android is going to keep doing your old job, though we're going to tell people what she really is and probably rename her Lucy or something. I think people realized it wasn't actually you."

"Gee, you think?" I asked sardonically. "I don't know why we couldn't have just gone with my cover that I use here, that I work from home for the permit office."

Lenny tilted his head curiously. "How about that," he murmured. "That would have been easier than having Sam build a replica of you. Well, hindsight is twenty-twenty, right?" He chuckled to himself.

"Is there anything else you need, Lenny? I have a party to get back to."

"Fate has a new assignment for you."

"Already?"

He scowled. "Yes, already. This is Fate we're talking about here." He glossed over the details, promising to fill in the rest the next day.

"Why not just finish telling me now?" I asked.

He peered over my shoulder and into the window filled with people having a good time. "I'll take you up on your offer. But I don't want to be a gnome. Those outfits are too damn frilly."

"That was Tess's doing."

He grunted. "You can turn me into a leprechaun."

"You know I can't just give you a pot of gold."

"No? You can't blame a snowman for trying."

I rested my hands on the top of his head and, in a flash, he had morphed into a leprechaun. He hopped around happily, even jumping to click his heels together. "This is nice!"

"I'm glad you're satisfied."

"How long until I turn back into a snowman?"

"I gave you until six o'clock in the morning."

"What if I make a lady friend tonight?"

I groaned. "Lenny," I started.

"I'm just pulling your rainbow. Get it? I said rainbow because I'm a leprechaun!" Lenny laughed gleefully and rushed inside my home.

I lingered behind, thinking about the year's events. My new assignment was to begin immediately and I pondered where I would be one year from today. With a smile, I returned to my party.

About the Author

Stephanie Grey is a graduate of East Tennessee State University with a degree in journalism. Writing has always been her passion, and she enjoys exploring different genres. Her debut novel, *The Immortal Prudence Blackwood* about an immortal hunting serial killers, earned rave reviews from readers and is quickly becoming a cult favorite. When she's not writing, she enjoys spending time with her husband, Brazilian jiu-jitsu, visiting museums, reading, and playing with her cat. One day she may even turn into a crazy cat lady because nothing in life is interesting without a little bit of crazy.

Visit her at:
www.stephaniegreybooks.com
and www.bhcpress.com

CPSIA information can be obtained
at www.ICGtesting.com
Printed in the USA
BVHW031241271020
591920BV00001B/178